D0267962

0043438083

THE LADY MARGARET

This is the love story of Margaret Beaufort and Edmund Tudor, Earl of Richmond — one of history's truly great romances. At a time when King Henry VI was faced with ever increasing opposition from the Yorkist supporters — which was to break out into the Wars of the Roses — both Margaret and Edmund were destined by their birth to prominence on the side of Lancaster. It was inevitable that they should become deeply involved in the ensuing struggle. In vivid contrast to the turbulent background of power-seeking nobles, their gentle passion ran its idyllic course to found the Tudor monarchy.

Books by Betty King
Published by The House of Ulverscroft:

WE ARE TOMORROW'S PAST
THE FRENCH COUNTESS
THE ROSE BOTH RED & WHITE
MARGARET OF ANJOU

BETTY KING

THE
LADY MARGARET

Complete and Unabridged

ULVERSCROFT
Leicester

First published in Great Britain in 1965

First Large Print Edition
published 2000
by arrangement with
Robert Hale Limited
London

British Library CIP Data

King, Betty, *1919 –*
The Lady Margaret.—Large print ed.—
Ulverscroft large print series: romance
1. Love stories
2. Large type books
I. Title
823.9'14 [F]

ISBN 0–7089–4309–8

Published by
F. A. Thorpe (Publishing)
Anstey, Leicestershire

Set by Words & Graphics Ltd.
Anstey, Leicestershire
Printed and bound in Great Britain by
T. J. International Ltd., Padstow, Cornwall

This book is printed on acid-free paper

Acknowledgments

My sincere thanks are due to the following people who kindly supplied much valuable information: Lord Luke of Pavenham; Miss Godber, County Archivist of Bedford; Mr. R. D. Lowless, M.B.E., Town Clerk of Pembroke; Mr. F. P. White, M.A., Keeper of the Records of St. John's College Cambridge and his Librarian Staff who were particularly patient and helpful; Miss D. H. Giffard, Public Records Office; Sir John Cecil-Williams, The Honourable Society of Cymmrodorion; The Staff of the Enfield Public Library; The Staff of the British Museum Reading Room.

I am most grateful, too, to Mrs. F. Archer, Mrs. J. Maunder Taylor, Mrs. M. Burton, Mr. N. Stoddart, Mr. M. A. Yannaghas, B.A. Hons. and my family for their unfailing assistance and encouragement.

Prologue

It was an exceedingly hot and airless day. The sun shone down unremittingly, from a brazen sky, on the Palace of Greenwich. The broad Thames flowed sluggishly by, its surface unruffled for there was no breeze. The trees were still and the well kept lawns sloping down to the river's edge were brown and cracking, for the Controller of the Household had forbidden the gardeners to water while the court was in residence and there was no sign of rain to replenish the supply.

The Lady Margaret, the King's mother, his wife, Elizabeth and three of his children, Harry, Meg and Mary, were sitting under the great oaks, grateful for the deep shade. They were surrounded by a small retinue of ladies, waiting women and nurses, their brightly coloured or sober skirts befitting their station spread around them as they rested on the grass.

The Lady Margaret sat a little aloof from her daughter-in-law and her three grandchildren and watched them with affection. She held herself upright in the straight-backed, cushionless chair, her head poised gracefully on a slender neck. A compact, serene woman who gave the impression of one who had come to terms with life and gained thereby a deep, inward control. This was betrayed now in her quietness and the stillness of her well kept hands as they lay along the arms of the chair. She appeared cool and unruffled in contrast to the other younger women who were constantly fanning moist pink faces and shifting to ease clinging garments. She achieved her calm despite the perpetual irritation of the hair shirt which rubbed against the tender skin of her back and breast. Her tiring women had tears in their eyes when she allowed them to help her put it on, for they vowed that she had no more need of atonement than an angel, her only possible sin being an almost idolatrous love of her long dead husband and pride in their son.

Her hands were unusually idle because she had lately given up working on the tapestries for which she was famous. She found that at sixty-one years of age the close stitches jeopardised her sight and she could think of no worse ordeal than blindness, for then she would be unable to follow her studies and scholarly activities. She never ceased to bless her mother's progressive outlook that prompted her to have her daughters, as well as her sons, taught to read and write and to think for themselves. She was engaged at the moment in the translation from the French of *The Mirror of Gold for a Sinful Soul* and she had other works in hand to send to Master Caxton for printing on his miraculous presses. It was her early interest in learning which prompted her, when she was able, to found two colleges at Cambridge, one which she hoped to name Christ's and the other St. John's. She was giving thought, also to the promotion of two chairs of divinity, but had not decided at which university they should be. Much of her time was devoted to the supplications of the needy and the rest she spent in devotion, finding her ardent and simple faith more of a comfort now than at any time since that terrible November, over forty years ago.

Despite the dignified assurance her eyes were luminous and interested in the pale, oval face and her generous mouth softened with pleasure as she watched her grandchildren, suddenly tiring of the inactivity, jump to their feet and begin chasing each other in and out of the low slung branches that swept majestically down to the ground. In the fashion of the day, and regardless of the stuffy heat, they were dressed in exact copies of their elders' padded, elaborate clothes and they made splashes of brilliant colour as the sun caught velvet and silk.

After only a short time, Meg protested that she was exhausted and they returned to the women and fell down, panting. They took proffered kerchiefs and mopped, laughingly, at damp brows. Harry, however, was unable to sit still for long and he wanted to show off to this convenient audience his newly acquired skill at the Galliard. He dragged his protesting younger sister, Mary, to her feet, and making a deep, mocking bow, pulled her into the dance. The girl's nurse tried to restrain them, claiming that his lordship would overtire her charge, but Harry ignored the interruption.

The Lady Margaret, while silently agreeing with the woman that it was much too hot for violent exercise, knew that they would only dance as long as they were able.

They made a handsome pair, their Plantagenet colouring of golden skins and tawny hair perfectly enhanced by the canary doublet of the boy and the rose velvet kirtle of Mary's. Their eyes flashed with excitement as they leapt, turned and momentarily touched hands in the intricate movements of the dance. Quite suddenly Mary said she had had enough and sank down, gracefully, on to a stool. Harry, undaunted, threw off the heavy doublet and continued alone. Elizabeth of

York, his mother, called out half-heartedly for him to stop but he only laughed off her weak request and leapt the higher, clapping his hands above his head and steering some imaginary partner beside him. Opposition always stiffened his determination and he brought out every reserve of strength until, as if completely bored with the performance, he too threw himself, sprawling into a seat. He was immediately surrounded by a bevy of twittering, adoring, solicitous women, who forgetful of the heat, were all anxious to help him into his doublet while at the same time were full of extravagant praise for his prowess at the dance. He accepted their concern with a rueful smile and their praise with a disparaging grimace, thoroughly enjoying his power over them. At ten years of age he had already discovered women could deny him nothing. Something about the child disquieted the Lady Margaret and she was constantly reminded of his maternal grandfather, the profligate King Edward: they were alike in so many ways. Harry had inherited, with the attractive colouring, great charm. His frame, too, promised the massive animal perfection that had been Edward's and had proved the King's downfall. The Lady Margaret hoped fervently that the marriage negotiations which were in hand for the boy would provide him with a suitably passionate girl who would give him an outlet for the desires that she was convinced were not far from the surface already and which would, if not channelled aright, in time prove troublesome to them all.

She thought, as she had many times before, that the Queen was too lenient with this child, as indeed she was with all her children. It was no secret that the royal nurses were grateful to the Lady Margaret's wisdom and guiding hand in the upbringing of their charges. Quietly and without intruding on the authority of her daughter-in-law, she had given advice which had resulted in sensible feeding, sound training and later, good education for her grandchildren. If Elizabeth were aware of her influence she accepted it without comment, glad to be relieved of some of the responsibility and if she perhaps, considered the Lady Margaret's standards too high, she did not exert herself to say so. This latitude and disinterestedness in her daughter-in-law the Lady Margaret attributed to a complete reversion from the Queen's own overshadowed child and girlhood, when Elizabeth had been subjected to strains far beyond her comprehension and power to combat. It was as if she wanted a peaceful, unharried youth for her family, and believed that the way to give it to them was to allow them to do very much as they pleased. She did not realise, as the Lady Margaret did, that self discipline could help them to override their difficulties and troubles and lay the foundations of real happiness.

Elizabeth had had in her father, the late King, a shining hero, who had received adulation from his earliest years. He had been looked to as the Yorkist hope, and never having a wish ungranted, wanting her mother, had married her secretly; this, when Warwick was already making overtures at the French court for the hand of a French princess. What should have been an idyllic match was further doomed, before long, by the countless infidelities of the tawny giant who found it impossible to remain faithful to any one woman. His shortcomings proved a source of great distress to his wife, who was considerably older than he, and was reflected to his young children, who were prepared to worship him for his kingly bearing and his easy, lazy charm.

After his death had come an anxious period of uncertainty about the succession, when all manner of rumours and alarms were bruited abroad. Elizabeth and her mother were advised to seek Sanctuary, which they did in the Abbey of Westminster. From here they watched, helplessly, as Elizabeth's two young brothers Edward and Richard, were taken, ostensibly for their protection, to the Tower. They had waited, hopefully at first, for the proclamation of the elder as the new King and for their release, but with every day the questioning doubt became dread certainty that they would never see them again. Elizabeth had been faced with her own grief for her much loved brothers and her mother's broken-hearted despair.

It then became apparent that her Uncle Richard had seized the crown for himself. This was a great shock but worse was to follow, for his wife Anne sickened and died suddenly. In no time the new King scandalised his Court and Council by seeking the hand of his niece, Elizabeth. He hoped by this move to strengthen his tenuous hold on the Throne as she, without her brothers, was the last Plantagenet heir. Elizabeth, weakened by grief and horror stricken at the proposal had enough resistance in the face of graceless importuning to refuse him again and again. It was certain that from this time he lost all support in the south and only commanded loyalty in his Yorkshire domains. This was not sufficient, when the time came to meet the challenge of the Lady Margaret's own son, Henry of Lancaster. Richard was defeated on the field of Bosworth and dragged with ignominy from the place while the crown was snatched from where it had rolled from his head and placed, with universal rejoicing on that of Henry.

Now watching Elizabeth, Henry's Queen for nearly fifteen years, the Lady Margaret noticed the drawn look on the delicate fair face and the heavy shadows under her eyes. Her whole demeanour was impassive and listless as if she found life overwhelming and called off the unequal contest to become a spectator. The older woman considered that her daughter-in-law was far too young for this sad withdrawal which showed more than a lack of tenacity and courage and might point to some deep lying illness.

It could be that she found marriage with Henry VII an overwhelming strain, for although as his mother, with her strong affection for him tempered with years of separation, with an astute appreciation of how his character had been moulded, she knew that this union, which she had done much to bring about, could not be a very happy or satisfying one for her son's wife.

Henry's passion was for England and the stability of his island kingdom. To become her sovereign he had endured privation and imprisonment for the greater part of his life.

There had been one interminable period of fifteen years when he and his mother had not met for even a brief hour, during which it would have meant instant death for him to set foot on English soil. Now that he had attained his goal his life's work was the restoration of the country's economy after the disastrous wars of the Roses.

He spent hours, accompanied by his elder son and heir, Arthur, closetted with Morton and his other advisors working out schemes to improve the financial state of the realm. It was not unlikely, therefore, that this marriage, which had served to put an end to the alienated Houses of Lancaster and York by wedding the surviving heirs, was suffering by neglect. It was almost as if he had used his wife as an instrument in the provision of royal heirs as part of the plan and had never thought of her as a woman with feelings and emotions of her own. To the Lady Margaret it was almost unbelievable that Edmund's son should be so unlike him in this. To her husband, of such beloved memory, Margaret had always been of foremost importance. Closing her eyes her throat tightened as she looked back on the long and dreary years since Edmund had held her in his arms and she had been so completely happy. She relived for a moment the day when she had become the Countess of Richmond and had stood at his side, the happiest, proudest girl of the age. She could see as if it were yesterday, the chapel at Bletsoe, where they were wed and the gentle smile with which he had greeted her at the porch door, enfolding her in mutual unassailable joy.

Drawing his memory to her comfort, she sighed and opening her eyes returned to the problem of their son and his wife. Henry had been robbed of pettiness during his fifteen years of privation and banishment, but his sense of humour had evaporated as well, and the Lady Margaret had to confess to her priest, Bishop Fisher, that she sometimes found her son intolerably dull. She had no complaints about his filial affection and duties and indeed, sometimes had to try and steer him to his Queen for her advice and counsel.

As a father he had found the appealing ways of small children attractive, but now that his family were fast growing to young man-and-womanhood, he thought of them mainly as pawns in the chequer-board of European politics. After protracted and difficult negotiations he had contracted an alliance for Arthur with Katherine, daughter of the powerful Isabella and her husband, the King and Queen of Castille and Aragon. This had been a triumph for his diplomacy and great preparations were being made for the nuptials which were to take place later this year. This marriage would establish England as a European power rather than a rain swept island, which losing its glory in France, sacrificed its nobles in a death struggle between the Houses of the Red and White Rose.

Arrangements, as she knew, were also on hand for the betrothal of Harry and for the little Mary, who, at the moment was promised to the Emperor Maxmillian's son, Charles. It was the marriage of her eldest grandchild, namesake and god-daughter that the Lady Margaret felt most keenly. Harry and Mary could take care of themselves but unless Meg altered considerably, she was not going to find life easy.

She moved slightly so that she could look at the girl. She was lovely in a fine, delicate way, resembling more her mother and brother Arthur than her glowing sister and Harry. Her grandmother loved her for the warmth of her affectionate nature and the cleft in her chin which reminded her of Edmund. Although in her early teens only, she was promised in marriage to James, King of Scotland and was to wed him next year. At the thought of this and the perilous journey, even the Lady Margaret's resolute heart faltered somewhat. It was no use comforting herself with the remembrance that she had been the same age when she had married, for James, with any virtues he might possess, was not Edmund. It was rumoured too, that he had a strong liking for women, flaunting his mistresses quite openly. It would take more than the appeal of a young and inexperienced girl to turn him away from these heady delights. She made a mental note to speak with the child and provide her with many books and pieces of canvas to work. She murmured a prayer and was glad when she heard the girl laugh at a sally of Harry's and call out to him that she would plait him a crown of daisies and make him the King of the May.

Always ready to be the centre of someone's attention Harry, surprisingly obedient knelt in front of her while she threaded the small white flowers and pushed them into the golden curls. Meg held him at arms length, her whole face soft with love, as she surveyed her handiwork. The Lady Margaret was vividly reminded of the day, when as a three year old child, she had sat in the meadow at Kingston Lacey while her nurse had made a ring of daisies for her.

Daisies. Her own emblem, woven in the

tangles of the red rose, the lilies of France, the Beaufort portcullis and the dragon of Wales.

Daisies. Daisies in the meadow at Kingston Lacey. She remembered the stillness and a lark twittering high overhead. She felt again nurse's solid reassuring presence and her soft hands as she fitted the coronet. It had all seemed so peaceful, so quiet and so secure that she felt an almost physical shock as she recalled the clatter of the horses' hooves as they entered the nearby courtyard bringing a messenger with news that shattered that security for her family until her son came to the throne.

1

Margaret Beaufort, with her mother the Duchess of Somerset and her stepsisters, Elizabeth and Margery were staying for the spring and early summer of 1444 at the manor of Kingston Lacey.

This was a secluded, comfortable unfortified house, which had belonged to the House of Lancaster, for many years. Beyond the deep, lawless New Forest, close to Wimborne in Dorset it had been a favourite home of John of Gaunt, Duke of Lancaster and his third wife Katherine Swynford, Margaret's great grandfather and mother.

Her father John, had inherited it from his father when the Beaufort family's claim to legitimacy was proved, and he found it a good place to leave his wife and their three-year-old daughter when he was absent in France and London on affairs of state. He also thought it distant enough from the trouble centres of the North and the Marcher Borders where the Percys and the Mortimers were constantly at odds, and from London where the delicate balance of power was constantly threatened.

The wars in France, which had been draining the resources of the English for almost a hundred years, had turned from the victories that had been secured under Henry V, into disaster, since the Maid of Orleans had seen her visions and rallied the Dauphin and his supporters. To add to this England's ally, Burgundy, had thrown in her lot with France. Paris had long since been lost and Normandy and Gascony imperilled.

A sense of impending national disaster spread among the people and a scapegoat was sought. The Lancastrian power behind the throne of the gentle and peace-loving son of Henry V, was the obvious choice, and while Cardinal Beaufort and Gloucester, uncle to the King were capable of taking criticism it was rumoured that John, Duke of Somerset, was finding it too much of a strain.

This had been forcibly brought home to his wife a week since when she had received two of his squires who brought news that their lord would be coming to Kingston Lacey in the near future for a period of rest and recuperation. This was unusual and somehow to the Duchess boded no good, for her husband, while cursed with the male Lancastrian urge for power, had also inherited the tremendous self-searching conscience which came up every now and then.

16

She knew the sensitive nature and the indecision which occasionally assailed him.

Quiet preparations for his stay were going forward and the day of his homecoming was perhaps the first that Margaret remembered.

It began as every day did with her nurse drawing the heavy curtains back from the window. She stirred and opened her eyes to the bright light that streamed into the room.

Her nurse helped her dress, putting on a periwinkle blue cote-hardie with a matching sideless surcoat. She brushed her hair, bringing glints into the short shoulder-length tresses and put on a starched cap, and bade her sit on the stool by the oaken table for her bowl of bread and milk, fresh from the dairy. This finished they both knelt and said their morning prayer.

Margaret looked questioningly at the woman as they stood up.

'May I go to my mother, now?'

'We shall both go along to her presently and see if she is not too busy to have you with her for a little. It all depends if your father is expected today or not. There'll be so much for her to look to that however much you want to be with her, perhaps you'll have to wait.'

It was the custom that each morning and evening Margaret spent an hour with her mother and it was most unusual that this routine should be interrupted. It was obvious that nurse considered the coming of the Duke as a momentous occasion and her charge was not going to be allowed to forget it.

Margaret knew very little of her father, except that he represented to her the shining, fairy-like hero of the stories that she had heard. He had inherited, with the Lancastrian pride and sensitivity, the superb good looks and physique of his grandsire. The ruddy gold of his hair was echoed in the coppery lights that glinted beneath Margaret's own starched cap. For most of her short life which had been spent here, or at Bletsoe her mother's own Manor, she had seen little of John Beaufort. As far as she could remember it had been winter, with snow lying crisp and sharp on the ground when he had last been at home. She recalled a vague impression of strong arms lifting her up above his head and the spontaneous warmth of his affection.

Nurse bustled round the chamber, straightening the bed clothes and putting away fresh-washed linen shifts in the coffers that stood against the wall. She set Margaret to play with the small ivory figures that had been a present for her Saint's day. Nurse was an ample kindly woman, dressed in sober grey wool and she had been with the Duchess since before the first St. John had been born. She had had the care of them until the boys, as was the custom at the early age of seven or eight, had gone to the Earl of Warwick's household, and the girls to the charge of a younger woman who saw to their needs and took them to the chaplain for their daily lessons. Of all the five children that nurse had helped to rear she regarded this girl-child with special devotion. It was not simply that she was the daughter of a Duke or an eventual heiress to two great Houses, but from the first, as she lay in the wooden cradle of the Beauchamp family, she had possessed a charm which melted the heart of the most sophisticated. She had not even been especially good, for all the Duchess' children had from the earliest age been taught that discipline was essential. In this the nurse and her mistress were in complete agreement.

Her charm lay in the quick, responsive smile and the happiness that radiated from the small person. She was fast developing a lively interest and a questioning mind. Nurse confessed to her gossips that she was often at a loss to satisfy the child's eager thirst for knowledge, and that she would be glad when she accompanied her sisters, Elizabeth and Margery for their daily lessons. Lady

19

Somerset was often ridiculed by her contemporaries for her belief in the education of girls, but she wisely ignored the criticism and continued sending them to the chaplain of whichever manor they were inhabiting, for several hours daily of French and Latin and the writing of their own language.

The woman, having finished the ordering of the room sent a page scurrying for warmed water and washed Margaret's hands and face in preparation for the visit to her mother. Leading her they crossed the panelled landing and knocked on the heavy oaken door of the solar.

Hearing her mother's voice bidding them enter the child rushed to where she sat on a leather seated chair and was gathered on to a velvet clad lap where she threw her arms round Lady Somerset's neck and snuggled close. Over her head the mother smilingly dismissed nurse and promised to send her small daughter to play with the others before she took up too much of her time.

Margaret, wife of John, was a handsome, warm-hearted woman with an air of authority. She had been widowed while still young and left with four children by her first husband, Sir Oliver St. John. He had made it his dying wish that she should marry again as soon as her mourning days were over and a suitable match presented itself. He had not considered it wise or safe for a wealthy heiress to remain a widow and unprotected when raids on manors and abductions of women had become daily occurrences. He had advised her to choose someone of whom her family had sound knowledge and she had not found it too difficult to succumb to the wooing of the then Earl of Somerset. It was welcomed on all sides as a matching of equals. The Lancastrians considered the marriage gave added strength to their side in the interminable jealousies and rivalries that had sprung up between the descendants of the sons of Edward III.

That her husband was perforce absent from her more than she cared for the Duchess accepted as normal in these troubled days. He gave her the priceless protection of the all powerful name of Beaufort and the backing of a private army of seasoned and well-appointed retainers. She looked forward to his impending visit and tried to push out of her orderly disciplined mind the misgivings that the couriers with their coming had roused in it.

Now she cuddled their daughter to her and spoke gently of the coming of her father. Margaret listened wide eyed, eagerly asking if he would have his charger or another horse and whether she would be allowed to sit in the saddle in front of him. At her mother's request she knelt beside her and repeated the daily prayer which nurse had taught her, then went to the long table which stood under the window and brought the dish of comfits to her. She stood on tiptoe, hands behind her while she made the choice for the day. The cook fashioned the delicately flavoured, perfumed marchpane in different shapes for her and it was a highlight of the visit to see what he had prepared. Today, in honour of her father's homecoming he had made roses and tinted them lightly with red. She took one and popped it into her mouth, biting into it with her small, white teeth and sighing with pleasure.

Her mother gave her a brief kiss on the top of her head and sent her out to the walled garden to find her sisters. As Margaret looked back as the page held open the door for her, she saw Lady Somerset recall her steward and go on again with the day's preparations; the lady of the manor wanted everything to run smoothly while her husband was here; for peace and well ordered living was the return that she gave him for his care of her. She knew better than anyone else the price that he had paid for so much soldiering. He had commanded the English in France since the death of Richard Beauchamp, the Earl of Warwick her kinsman and with his brother, Edmund Beaufort had been instrumental in the capture of Harfleur. The furthering of England's interest across the narrow channel had been his dedication, made more pressing by his capture and retention in France for some years. She alone had understood his bitterness at being by-passed as Regent of France in favour of Richard, Duke of York, another of the King's cousins. Of late his letters had been melancholic and contained a hint of the hopelessness of keeping a wise and stable Government under the weak, too gentle leadership of Henry VI.

This young man had been thrown into kingship when he was barely twelve months old by his father's untimely death and had relied during his reign on other men's guidance. His father's brothers, with Cardinal Beaufort, Warwick and others had acted as Regent during his infancy. They had all had power to sway and command him and now on reaching manhood it was as if he was unable, or unwilling to think or judge for himself. Margaret Somerset realised that John found this almost impossible to bear.

After the steward had left her and she had picked up the tapestry hanging on which she was working she found she was facing again the indeterminable disquiet she had felt. She hoped with all the strength of her determined spirit that her husband was not completely discouraged with the reverses in France and that she would be able to soothe him and send him back refreshed to his duties at court.

Meanwhile her daughter, wrapped in the cocoon of happiness that surrounds and protects the very young had found her half-sisters and they had wandered through the gardens, where the sun's warmth was beginning to draw out the sweet scent of the blossoms, and made their way down to the small stream beyond the low wall that marked the beginning of the meadow.

Here they were indulging in the incomparable and forbidden joy of bathing their feet. Elizabeth, the eldest of the three did give a passing thought to nurse's reactions if she saw Margaret sitting on the bank, dangling her pink, rounded limbs in the clear, running brook, but the delightful splashings and Margaret's gurglings soon convinced her that this was a legitimate way to keep her half-sister occupied and amused.

Margaret's joy was complete when a small shoal of minute fish glided within inches of her feet. Their glistening backs reflected the colours of the rainbow as they darted from one bank to the other.

Regretfully Elizabeth decided that the hour was getting near for their dinner and she bade the others dry their feet as best they could and return to the house. This took longer than expected as Margaret could not resist picking a handful of the celandines that grew in the marshy ground above the stream.

Arriving back at the small door behind the hall which led to their part of the house they were met by nurse who looked with horror on her charge who she had sent out spotlessly clean. She whisked her off, not sparing the others and especially Elizabeth for having so little sense.

Margaret resigned herself to a torrent of rebuke while her feet were dried with a linen towel. Nurse sent for a steaming bowl of broth and when this was finished tucked the little girl into her bed, with dark forebodings of chills and aches.

It was not long before Margaret drifted off into a sleep and as she drowsily watched little fishes swimming across the ceiling remembered that she had forgotten to speak with the girls about her father's expected homecoming.

It was late afternoon before she awoke and this time nurse took her out, walking sedately on the paths around the lawns. It took all her persuasive powers to ask the woman to sit on a grassy bank while she plucked her some daisies as a token of her sorrow for displeasing her this morning. With much grumbling and complaints of damp being bad for old bones she creaked down on the ground and spread her skirt about her. Margaret ran about in the lush grass picking the tiny, starlike flowers which she threw into her lap.

Margaret watched enchanted as nurse made small slits in the stalks and threaded the blossoms into a fillet which she put round her head. Making a great effort, with her tongue pushing against her lips, the child tried to copy her.

It was so quiet, so warm and peaceful that when the stillness was shattered by the urgent beat of a horse being ridden at top speed into the courtyard followed by a woman's startled high-pitched scream it was so astounding that the daisies forgotten, Margaret rushed to nurse and buried her head against her shoulder to shut out the terrifying noise.

In the courtyard all was confusion as the young man, in the silver and azure livery of the Lancasters, threw himself from his horse, which stood wreathed in sweat and breathing heavily. Menials came from kitchen and scullery to assist the dairymaid, who startled at the precipitate arrival of the courier had tripped and sent her heavy pails of water flying across the cobbles.

'My lady,' panted the young man and as the steward appeared. 'Take me to her at once.' The messenger hastily straightened his tunic and struggled for composure as they hurried inside and knocked on the solar door.

The Duchess was standing at the window, for she had heard the disturbance, and with fast-beating heart had looked to see what caused it.

Now hand to throat, she turned quickly and knew at once that her fears were justified.

'What is it?' she asked with a sharp drawn breath.

The young man fell on one knee and hesitated. His fresh, young face was strained and perplexed.

'My lady, it is my lord. He has met with an accident.' Relief flooded her. Only an accident when she had feared worse, and still more that she could not bring herself to put into words.

But the respite was short lived.

The young man, bracing himself, looked up into the still lovely face and blurted out, hating himself for bringing such dreadful news.

'An accident, yes, my lady, but my lord is

dead. His neck is broken.'

The woman sank into a chair, her knees were trembling so violently that she could not still them. Waves of panic swept over her and her teeth chattered.

With a great effort she gasped, 'How?'

So shocked was she that she could hardly make sense of the incoherent jumble of explanations that poured out.

It seemed that the party, encumbered with baggage horses were about a mile from Kingston Lacey, close to the banks of the Stour, when the Duke had sought to alleviate the slow pace and suggested that he and two of his companions should leave the road they were travelling and take a short cut across the meadows. There had been some good natured arguing and two of the company had agreed with pleasure to join him and laid wagers on the first to reach the manor.

They set off at a good pace and he led from the first. They burst into the fields taking a low hedge and dashed towards the dip at the bottom of the hollow. With the Duke still in the lead and the others digging in their spurs to keep up with him he skirted a band of trees and raced up the rise on the other side. Gaining the next meadow he increased the lead and then without warning, veered sharply towards the crumbling walls of a shepherd's disused hut. Unbelieving, the others turned their horses reining in as they did, but the Duke kept on and spurring his mount set him straight at the wall. The great horse gathered himself for the leap but before the horrified followers, a hoof caught in the crumbling stone and with his rider came crashing down.

By the time the two men reached them the horse had rolled on his back and with legs flailing the air had the Duke helplessly pinioned beneath. With much effort they pulled the terrified horse clear, but the Duke did not move and his head was lying at a twisted, unnatural angle.

The courier stopped, halted by the whiteness of the lady's face and the tears which she did not heed.

Poor John, poor John, something was repeating over and over in her head. My poor John. Years of campaigning in France and to be killed in a bid to win a wager. It did not make sense to her.

Making a great effort she bade the young man rise and gratefully took the cup of wine that the steward proffered.

'Tell the household to come to me here,' she said dully. She would have to break the news to them that their lord was dead and that they now owed their loyalty to the three year old child that was the only outcome of their brief union. Now she would have no way of soothing John's troubles and helping him to cope with the morass that the country's affairs had come to. A small voice, through her grief, told her that he was beyond her aid and his despair and bitterness too, and had gained a peace which was everlasting. Could it be that a recklessness had suddenly possessed him and that the horse's stumble had been more than accident?

She stood up as a subdued cluster of men and women in their greys and russet fustian shuffled into the room. A widow again, she must not let them see her grief and shock for they looked to her for guidance and support. Her duty was to the living.

2

As soon as was possible the Duchess made her plans to return to the manor at Bletsoe. She sent word to her cofferer and keeper of the wardrobe, Ralph Lannoy, that she and her family would be returning to take up permanent residence.

The funeral at Wishbone Minster had been a tremendous ordeal. The Court had come from Sheen and she had been strained to accommodate the young King and so many of her husband's supporters and kin.

The preparations for feeding such a large company and the finding of beds for the chambers gave her little time to think and she was glad of it.

Looking back, when the house was stilled again she recalled the reserve that she had sensed. They had given her of their sympathy and Henry had been genuinely grieved for her loss, but with it all there was an undercurrent. She realized a little the tension that had surrounded John and many times she caught the speculative looks of the mourners. She had accepted the sympathy of Cardinal Beaufort gratefully but at the same time had known that he and Gloucester, uncle to the King, were on uncomfortable terms.

She was greatly relieved to leave the nightmare of Kingston Lacey behind her and return to her manor in the rolling countryside of Bedfordshire. Her sons had come to be with her and she found in their young manliness great comfort. John, being the eldest, felt his position keenly. He was with his mother as much as she would allow, trying with his presence to help her. He regretted that his age necessitated his return to Warwick.

He, and his brother and sisters, were especially kind to the small Margaret, for they remembered almost too vividly what it was like to lose a father.

With their mother they shielded her as much as they could from the unhappiness of it all and saw that her days were fully occupied. They organised expeditions and took her hunting in the neighbouring copses with bows and arrows improvised from the willows round the brook.

Before John returned to Warwick Castle, his mother called him to her and told him that she was accepting the offer of the Earl of Suffolk to be guardian to Margaret. A descendant of the de la Poles, a merchant family of Suffolk who had successfully manœuvred themselves into prominence, he had been a constant companion of her late husband in his campaigning days in France. In his will John had directed that Suffolk should, as a strong and loyal supporter of the Lancastrian house, make his daughter his ward. The Earl had some influence with the King and John had considered him well placed to watch Margaret's interests.

John was a little happier as he saw that his mother had decided to comply at once with his stepfather's wishes and that she could be sure of a reliable supporter. Two days before he and Oliver were due to leave to resume their duties Suffolk sent word that he would present himself at the manor on the following day. John would be able to see for himself the protector that had been provided for his half-sister.

Suffolk had lately returned from France, with Edmund, John Beaufort's brother, who had succeeded him as Duke of Somerset. They had been, secretly, to the Court of Rene of Anjou, to negotiate the marriage of his daughter Margaret, with King Henry. It was rumoured that when Suffolk and the girl met they had been swept into an overwhelming passion which had made them oblivious to all else that went on in the world. When the proxy marriage had taken place at a ceremony in Nancy Cathedral, they had gazed into each other's eyes in complete abandonment to the concern of the onlookers, who had their King's interest to consider. Margaret, the Duchess of Somerset, reserved her opinions until she knew more facts, and anticipated that the story had been embroidered to endanger the cause of Suffolk by the Yorkist faction who considered when the secret became general knowledge, that too high a price had been paid for Anjou's daughter. If it were true that Maine had been surrendered for a dowerless girl, it must be that she had other qualities to outweigh this lack.

The newly created Marquess of Suffolk was a large somewhat overbearing man, with curled, flaxen hair. He sat his horse, a strong chestnut stallion, easily, the light grasp on the reins showing his perfect control. His armour was covered with a bright surcoat bearing his heraldic device. He brought with him a train that filled the small square courtyard at Bletsoe, dispelling with their raucous voices and clanging accoutrements the quiet that usually prevailed.

Margaret watched them from her window, with nurse at her side, fascinated by the movement and colour. She could hardly wait

34

for the summons to join her mother and her guest in the hall; she knew that this visit was in some manner connected with herself and that her mother regarded it as important that she should look her best and behave in a seemly way. Nurse had taken extra time and trouble to dress her in her most becoming dress of red velvet with sleeves, almost touching the floor, lined with white.

When at last she went down, the hall seemed full of people. Lady Somerset took her by the hand and led her up to the tall, well made man and she bobbed a curtsy. Almost at once Suffolk, returning her curtsy, brought forward a stocky, square-cut boy, who had been standing beside him. Margaret saw that this was his son, for he was as fair and stolid as the older man, and copied his every action. He bowed gravely over her hand, and spoke, unsmilingly, some appropriate greeting. When the St. John boys came and led him to a corner where a young hawk was chained to a perch his relief was obvious.

Suffolk, as he resumed his chair beside the fire which burnt in the hall through winter and summer, watched his new ward as she sat on a stool at her mother's feet. Her eyes regarded him levelly and she smiled without coyness so that he was amused at her childish dignity. What a match this would be for his son, if he kept on the right side of his King and did not overplay his hand with the mother. He had already realized that the widow of his friend was a strong capable woman perfectly able to see to the correct upbringing of her daughter, under his protection, which for the moment anyway, could be from a distance. There was much yet that she could be taught here at Bletsoe before she came to Court to further her studies and broaden her outlook as befitted her rank.

He spoke to the child of her home and her brothers and the peaceful quiet of the countryside in which she lived and then sent her to join the other children.

As the Marquess talked with her Margaret's mother was filled with pleasure to know that it was not his intention to take her daughter away from her at this tender age.

'I know, madam, that a woman such as yourself who has had as much experience in the rearing of a family is the best person to see to the immediate upbringing of my ward, and with your permission it is my intention to leave her with you at Bletsoe, at least for some time to come.'

'Thank you my Lord Suffolk, you have indeed made me very happy. Now that I know you will furnish us with your protection that we can hope to live here unmolested I shall do my best to give my child every opportunity to grow up into a useful, well educated woman . . . '

'Ah, there madam, if you will forgive me interrupting you, you have touched upon a matter to which the King and I have given some thought. Although I hesitate to speak to you upon such a personal subject, as John's friend I feel perhaps it gives me a certain right to mention it. His Grace thinks that although the Lady Margaret has become my ward, it will not be possible to look always to her safety here at home, and your widowhood, in itself, adds to this complication. While in no way wishing to push you into a new alliance it is thought that for your safety, and especially that of your daughter, you should consider taking another husband.'

He stopped, his face reddened with the ordeal of the delicate subject that he had felt constrained to discuss.

The Duchess, secretly a little amused at his embarrassment murmured in agreement, 'You are quite right, my lord, but you will understand my reluctance to take this further step, having already suffered the loss of two good men.'

Even as she spoke she realized that the continued stay of her youngest child at

Bletsoe probably depended on her remarriage and she hastened to add that she would give the matter her immediate and serious thought.

Suffolk, glad to have made this point turned the conversation to lighter matters and gossip of the day. It was inevitable that the marriage of the King to Margaret of Anjou should be mentioned but Lady Somerset sensed at once his withdrawal at her name. Drawing her own conclusions she dismissed the topic as soon as was comfortably possible, only enquiring, womanlike, if the Queen were fair.

The Marquess assented somewhat surlily, and added that the King's new wife was possessed of many virtues and that His Grace could count himself fortunate when he had her strong support. He added that the gentle scholarly King needed a woman of vibrant personality to bring him to life, but the widow of Bletsoe found herself wondering if the monkish recluse who spent most of his time at prayer or meditation would be happy or able to cope with a woman's disturbing proximity. Much as she would have liked to pursue the subject, she knew that she would only antagonise her guest with her interest, and she wanted that less than anything else. She could tell that Suffolk would not be pleasant as an enemy and she had no wish to upset her daughter's guardian. She tactfully turned the conversation to more general discussion of the many problems that beset land-owners in these troublous times and was relieved when Ralph Lannoy came to lead Suffolk to his apartments and servants entered to lay the boards for dinner.

Her sons, after bidding the Marquess Godspeed and escorting him to the main highway for Bedford, took their own farewells of their mother and sisters. They were happy that Margaret's future had been cared for and that they could take up their service to the Earl of Warwick with the load of responsibility to the Bletsoe household considerably lightened. They viewed with mixed feelings their mother's announcement that the Lord Suffolk had considered it wise that she should remarry. They were old enough to understand that marriage for a woman meant other than the acceptance of protection and entailed the bearing of more children, which would place further burdens on her. Seeing that the Lady Somerset saw only the advantages and appeared certain that this was a wise course of action they gratefully accepted her verdict and rode off for Warwick.

So it was that the household at Bletsoe settled down into a tranquil home, where the little girl who was to do so much to unite the warring houses of Lancaster and York, lived out the rest of her short childhood, while the undercurrents that caused those factions, seethed and bubbled, until eventually they clashed in a whirlpool of trouble that engulfed all the nobility of England.

3

Margaret Beaufort was eight years of age when her guardian deemed it was time for her to come to Henry's Court. She had grown into an attractive little girl, with soft brown hair that escaped beneath her cap to fall to her shoulders. Her eyes were thickly lashed and the country air had bloomed her cheek with a glow of health. Though she was happy to be walking or riding in the fields and looked forward eagerly to the infrequent visits of her half-brothers when they took her with them to hunt or hawk, her tutor reported that she had the application to learning of a girl twice her age and had already outstripped the others at reading and writing. The thirst for knowledge was a vital part of her life and she liked nothing better than to sit and listen, almost forgotten in a dim corner, to the tales told by the many guests that her new stepfather, Sir Leon Welles brought to the manor.

The growing tension between the rival Houses of Lancaster and York had been kept from her, at her mother's wish, as much as possible. The Queen had as yet produced no child and the Lady Margaret's position as heiress to the Lancastrian inheritance made her especially vulnerable. Lady Welles, while recognising that the newly created Duke of Suffolk must have judged that this was the appropriate time to bring his ward to Court was not completely convinced that it was so. Although she hated to admit it, even to herself, she was not absolutely happy with Suffolk himself; she was content that he was in an almost invincible position but regretted that it seemed as if he had climbed to power as much over fellow Lancastrians as Yorkists.

The matter of the Anjou marriage which he had negotiated when Margaret first became his ward, had caused much trouble for him with the Duke Humphrey of Gloucester, uncle of the King and Cardinal Beaufort, Margaret's and the King's great-uncle, who had bitterly opposed it for its giving away of hard won territory in France. However, popular acclaim for the match had endorsed Suffolk's work and the marriage was celebrated at Tichfield Abbey by Bishop Ayscouth of Salisbury and when it was announced that a two years truce with the French had been acquired with it, the populace went wild and Suffolk received a tumultuous reception.

It was the price that England had to pay for

this cessation of hostilities which caused the friction between the older statesmen and Suffolk. It had meant the surrender of all England's claims in the counties of Anjou and Maine, and Gloucester and Beaufort saw in this the beginning of the end of her hold on the continent of France. One by one the fair provinces across the. Channel had slipped out of England's grasp during this long, unremitting struggle which had been sapping her strength since the reign of Edward III. It seemed as if it were for nothing that English manhood under the King's father had fought and struggled in the mud at Agincourt. All those hard-won territories were now traded for the hand of a princess who held William, the then Marquess of Suffolk in as much esteem as did the rest of the people. For it could not be denied that Suffolk was popular and that Margaret of Anjou doted on him.

Lady Welles knew moments of unease when she recollected that the Duke of Gloucester and Cardinal Beaufort had died within six weeks of each other in the spring of 1447. Although she could not bring herself to believe, as many people did, that Suffolk had been instrumental in their deaths and might even have been guilty of their murder, she could not help wondering what manner of man this was to whom she was entrusting her daughter.

His influence with the King was undoubtedly great and favours were heaped upon him. This, Lady Welles, comforted herself, was proof that Suffolk could not be involved in the deaths of the two statesmen, because Henry could not have looked with pleasure on the murderer of his kinsfolk. However, a small voice whispered that the King looked for good in all men and refused to believe that evil existed. He had been so bewildered by the loss of the two men on whom he had leant since he came to the throne as a nine month old baby that he had been glad to turn to anyone for support and the canny Queen had seen to it that Suffolk had been there at the strategic moment. She had never neglected to further the cause of the man who had been her only friend and ally on her arrival in a hostile England, and would have had little difficulty in convincing Henry of Suffolk's innocence should it have ever been necessary.

Sir Leon had told his wife on his return from a journey to the court at Windsor the month before that the Queen seemed genuinely fond of Henry in the way that a mother would watch over and safeguard the interests of a dreamy child, but that when she was with Suffolk she became all woman. Her haughty, proud nature was drowned in his supremely powerful maleness and under his influence she became soft, desirable and malleable. This the Yorkist faction were quick to exploit and showed scant respect for her in the names they bandied about, losing no opportunity to bring the Lancastrian Government into disrepute.

The Yorkists were especially bitter that Richard of York had been replaced as Regent of France, by Edmund Beaufort, the Lady Margaret's uncle. This they realised was entirely due to Suffolk's influence with the King and it was little wonder that they hated Margaret of Anjou and hoped that she would prove the downfall of Suffolk. Lately it had seemed that this move had shaken the country's confidence in him a little for an attack on the French held fortress of Fougeres had treacherously broken the truce and renewed the war.

Lady Welles knew that he felt no fear for the future and when she tried to explain her concern to her husband he drew her to him and laughed away her anxieties as being indicative of her condition, for she was near to her time with their child. She prayed to God that this was the truth and that He would protect her precious daughter in her new life.

Margaret was so preoccupied with the preparations for the journey that she hardly realised that she was to be parted from her mother for the first time in her life. She could not visualise life without the wise influence of Lady Welles and did not fully understand that it might be some long time before, if ever, she was allowed to come home. Lady Welles had asked her what she would like as a parting gift and had brought out some chains and trinkets for her to choose, but Margaret had begged for an illuminated Book of the Hours and a special one with strong leather covers had been made for her. She opened it twenty times a day to gaze at the intricate lettering set in scrolls of tiny flowers, leaves, birds and figures and could not find adequate words with which to thank her mother.

Chests full of rich clothes and bedding, with Margaret's own linen and plate had been packed. She had helped nurse to stow away the silver cups, ewers and dishes engraved with the Beaufort portcullis and set with precious stones, while she questioned her closely about life at Court. The woman searched her memory for any little detail that would please the child but had to confess that she could not remember very much as it was so long since she had attended anyone there and fashions changed so rapidly. The only thing about which she was fairly certain was that the present Court was not very gay. The King, since his marriage, had made several royal progresses for the purpose of showing his bride to his people and he visited frequently the scholastic foundations he was creating in Cambridge and near Windsor. Apart from this he spent his time cloistered with monks deep in discussions on theological themes or in his chapel, praying.

This did not daunt Margaret who felt a certain sympathy for her kinsman because learning was so much part of her own life and she liked to say her prayers, but she did hope that there would be music and some dancing and that there would be other children because she had never been without young companionship. Her sisters teased her that Suffolk's son, John de la Pole, was no doubt at Court and would be asking her to dance, which they were convinced would be like standing up with a carthorse. They thought that there was a chance too, that the young Earl of March, son of the Duke of York, might occasionally be of the Household. Rumour had it that although he was of the opposing faction, he promised to be extremely handsome and very tall. When Margaret heard he was younger than she was, she pulled a face and vowed that when she married, if she ever did, it was going to be with someone much older than herself, at least Oliver's contemporary, as she had no time for babies.

Nevertheless, with all her grown up talk she was very glad that her mother was to accompany her to London. For one thing it delayed the inevitable parting by at least a week.

It was late summer when the party set out for Westminster. Heralds had been sent ahead to make arrangements for them to stay at Chicksands Priory and Hatfield House but it was still a matter of much organisation to assemble the collection of horses, sumpter mules and litters. The steward stood in the courtyard with a long list in his hand and checked it against each load that was brought from the house. His manner plainly implied that it was fortunate that his lady and her daughter did not make a journey to London too frequently and that the sooner the noisy throng were off the sooner he could settle to a tankard of ale in peace. The escort provided by Suffolk were in high spirits; a hand picked band, who having served in France, were well able to sense and smell out danger for their charge. It was their boast, repeated rather too often for those who had not been across the Channel, that having survived the terrible aftermath of the war in that devastated land they would not be frightened by any misguided vagrants or robbers who might be lying in wait for them. They regarded this duty as a pleasant relief from routine and infected the other travellers, who were in varying stages of fear and anticipation, with their enjoyment.

At last the heavy chests, boxes and bedding were considered sufficiently padlocked and roped well to the patient beasts and the entourage moved off. Margaret was sitting pillion behind the bailiff with her arms encircling his ample waist and, as they came into the lane and passed the small dwellings clustered at the manor gate she turned in the saddle and took a last farewell of her home. She thought it had never looked so friendly and safe as the distance between them lengthened, and in the morning air she shivered at the unknown frightening prospect of her new life in such different surroundings. However, the gaiety of the men-at-arms and her mother's frequent calls from her litter slung on poles between two horses, for her to regard this or that point of interest, soon overcame her momentary unease and she was enthralled by what she saw.

The Ouse flowed with them in broad stately quietude, while the swallows dipped and wheeled close to the surface. They passed the 'Falcon' ale house where the lantern glowed dimly in the light of day, showing that the innkeeper was still abed and not yet about to attend to her duties. The escort made pointed remarks about it being a pity it was so early that they had not yet worked up a thirst and the more strait-laced of the women made disapproving clucks that men should have no more to occupy their minds than drinking.

The tower of the church at Milton Ernest showed through the thickly leafed trees and then they were fording the river at London End, the shallow water running smoothly over the huge flat stones which had been placed there no one knew how long before. Margaret who was irresistibly reminded of nurse on the long distant day at Kingston Lacey, glanced toward that homely, familiar figure who was comfortably seated behind a stalwart and gallant soldier who good naturedly smiled at his companions' quips about their knowing that they had always realised what he needed was a nursemaid. Nurse, her plain headress slightly awry, worn out with several days of packing and other harassing preparations for this journey, nodded her head toward the solid back in front of her and dozed at intervals.

Margaret was entertained by the story the bailiff told her about the Saxon tower to the church at Clapham. He pointed out to her the windows in the highest part which were to a room which had been used as a refuge many times, the most audacious being when the Danes came to sack the nearby town of Bedford in 1010. Their saucy standard bearer, who had been named Trowed, brought his bride to be with him, and so that she should come to no harm in the fighting which followed, placed her in the room. This act had become a legend in Bedfordshire to this day, the man told her.

They trundled over the green at Goldington and once more crossed the river at the newly constructed bridge which had no less than seventeen arches and came in to the outlying streets of Bedford. The houses were huddled together as they came up to St. Paul's, where a busy market was in progress.

Margaret was glad that they were to break their journey here for a short while to eat the food which they had brought with them. She was lifted down to the ground and stretched her cramped limbs. She stood on the soft grass by the river, which they had to cross again later to the other part of the town. Their party attracted much attention and they were quickly surrounded by pedlars and dark women eager to sell them fairings. The soldiers looked on benignly as the women were tempted to buy the gaily coloured ribbons and favours, while Margaret watched, large eyed, a man with a small monkey on his shoulder juggle with three balls of wood. A group clustered round a slant-eyed man who begged them find the pea under three walnut shells, but although they guessed time and again they were always wrong and the small, wrinkled pea was under one of the other shells.

Margaret left her cold meat and bread almost untouched and was reluctant to leave but the sergeant-at-arms was anxious to press on as they were still some distance over hilly ground from the priory and the journey for the next day was a long one. As they crossed the bridge a swan with a string of brown cygnets caught Margaret's attention. Outside the porch of St. John's Church another group, mostly children, were gathered before a red and white striped booth where a puppet show was in progress. The sergeant himself enjoyed seeing the outrageous behaviour of the man doll and so permitted the company a brief halt to watch.

Too soon, however, he was urging them on their way and Margaret slept a little, rocked into sleep by the continuous gentle sway of the horse's movement.

As the sun was sinking they turned off the main highway and took a sandy, pine edged track towards the priory gate. The wind had turned colder with the coming of the evening and sighed softly in the high trees and all the company were glad to be at the end of the long day, with a friendly hospitality awaiting them.

The priory was a religious house of the Gilbertine Order which had, in separate communities, both monks and nuns and was well fitted to cope with the Bletsoe party. They were met by lay brothers who took away the servants and horses to good quarters and stabling and led the menfolk through the cloisters to the hall where a large fire welcomed them. The women they handed over to the Prioress who received them in her private room and offered them wine before sending them to eat in the refectory.

Margaret was so tired with the fresh air, unaccustomed exercise and the day's excitements that when she went to the small room where she was to sleep with nurse, she at once fell into a complete, dreamless slumber.

They were awakened with the first light and accompanied the nuns to the chapel, where they made their prayers and joined with the women in their devotions. After a quickly eaten bowl of bread and milk their company reassembled in the courtyard and free of sleep rejoined the road on their way to Hatfield. The air was crisp and soon revived them as they took the sharp hill out of Cotton End and before long they resumed the easy fellowship which had been engendered on the previous day.

The undulating hills of Bedfordshire gave way to the leafy lanes of Hertfordshire and the sergeant issued discreet orders to his men to be extra vigilant for an ambush. The banks, covered in brambles and convolvulus afforded excellent cover for lurking robber bands. The compact villages were small and neat and the fast flowing Mimram, as they rode down into Welwyn, was merry and sparkling in contrast to the stately Ouse. They joined the Great North Road after they had rested at midday and fell in with other travellers, who stayed with them until the Bletsoe party turned off in Hatfield for the palace.

The royal manor had been set at their disposal by Henry and as they wound up the long ride Margaret could see in the darkening light of evening that it was a large rambling house bigger than her own home, but at the same time, inviting and well proportioned. She was happy that they were to rest here for two nights to enjoy the surrounding woods and the sloping lawns.

Later, she sat with her mother in the solar, and talked of the exciting days which they had spent and the unknown interests which lay ahead. Lady Welles had stood the journey over the rough roads very well, but was glad of this opportunity to move about and ease her cramped body. The success of their passage had, in some measure, overcome her anxieties for her daughter and she now looked forward to the visit to Court, which would be her first for some time.

They arrived in the Palace of Westminster two days afterwards in the late afternoon. Margaret had had her first glimpse of the broad Thames and the City of London from the top of Highgate Hill and was filled with a quickening sense of urgency to be among the crowded streets. When they threaded their way over the cobbles and between the tall, overhanging houses however, she hung closer to the comforting familiarity of the bailiff's waist and felt very small indeed. Their herald had judged their arrival accurately and a small posse of troops rode out to escort them over the last mile to the gates of the palace. The courtyards and the chambers and rooms surrounding them were overshadowed by the bulk of the great hall and the soaring majesty of the abbey. How far away and fairy-like

Bletsoe seemed to her now, as they were met at the door and she was lifted down and stood waiting for Lady Welles to alight from the litter. Hand in hand they went in and Margaret's new life was beginning.

Apartments had been set aside for them and while these were being made ready with the beds and hangings that she had brought with her, she and her mother were received by the Queen in the private solar.

Speaking in French, and looking immensely handsome and commanding despite her youth, she greeted them with studied cordiality tempered with restraint. As they were offered comfits and wine, Lady Welles, watching the proudly held head and obvious air of authority which she had gained in only four years as a Queen, formed the opinion that, despite her having celebrated her nineteenth birthday less than six months ago she was a power with which to reckon. The eyes, practically the same colour as the dull gold of her brocaded headdress, were fiery and calculating and it was difficult to imagine that they ever softened with tenderness or compassion. Her dress which was of a tawny green flecked with gold was slightly out-moded but showed the abundance of her figure to perfection. It was not difficult for the older woman to imagine the delight that the

56

bold Suffolk had in this girl in whom was an obvious latent animal passion. Lady Welles hoped sincerely that Margaret would not have to be much in her company for the sensitive, affectionate child with complete trust in the adult world would be unable to understand the arrogance and self-seeking which the Queen displayed in even such a short acquaintance. Margaret of Anjou gave every appearance of a spoilt child who had grown to womanhood expecting the same attention to her wants that she had had when she was younger and could be expected to make life difficult for anyone who crossed her.

'So you are my Lord Suffolk's ward?' she was asking Margaret. She lingered over the name as if it gave her a sensual pleasure to speak it. 'You are welcome here to learn the ways of the Court and fit yourself to take a husband. I trust you will look with favour, madam,' speaking to Lady Welles, 'on the suit of my lord's son.'

Margaret Beaufort turned with quick, indrawn breath to her mother, but she only smiled and murmured some non-committal reply about there being plenty of time to arrange the matter of her daughter's betrothal and that all suitors would be fairly assessed on their merits when the occasion arose. Margaret, now looking at the floor, missed most of the rest of the conversation as she thought over how she would account to her brothers if she had to become the wife of the lumbering boy who had visited them at Bletsoe when she had been little more than a babe. She hoped fervently that she had not been brought to Westminster for these ends, for it was not unknown in these days for marriage contracts between children to be made with high-handed disregard for the feelings of the interested parties. However, she knew her mother sufficiently well to trust her not to make any unfavourable plans for her future without warning her first, and she had not seemed particularly anxious to agree with the Queen's suggestion.

'Have no fears for your daughter, Lady Welles,' the young woman was saying. 'She will be well looked after here and proper attention will be paid to her studies as you have wished. My husband,' the first reference to Henry since they had been admitted. 'sets great store by learning and there are many scholars and men of wisdom attending him. We have already spoken with one Bernard Frognale who will include the Lady Margaret among his pupils while she is here.'

'That gives me good heart,' replied Lady Welles. 'You may think that it is unnecessary for women to be able to read and write, but having been twice widowed as I have and having had the management of large estates, it has been essential for me to check documents and bills of trading to see for myself that my inheritance is not being allowed to dwindle so that when it is in turn handed over to my heirs they may receive their due and just share. When God is pleased to bless your union, Your Grace will realise the responsibilities and anxieties that one feels for one's offspring. I can rest assured that with Your Grace's interest and my Lord Suffolk's protection my daughter will be well provided. Thank you, Madame.'

The Queen inclined her head, a slight lowering of her heavy lids concealing any emotion that might have been roused at the mention of an heir and Lady Welles made as deep a curtsy as she was able, and Margaret, watching her closely sank to floor as she had been taught. She was strangely thankful that the interview was at an end and she could escape from this unusually disturbing atmosphere to their room, where nurse, and the well known furnishings from home, awaited them.

The Palace of Westminster sprawled over a vast area of land and was big and as self-contained as a village. It was easy to get lost and Margaret was glad that she had her nurse with her. Her mother had left for Bletsoe two days before and it was overwhelming to be alone in a strange place where every face was, as yet, unfamiliar. While her mother had been with her she had not been shy of meeting my Lord Suffolk and his friends but she could not be certain that she would be at ease when she encountered them on her own for their bluff manner and restlessness differed considerably from the conduct of those she had lived with at home.

With King Henry it had been completely different for he had appealed to her at once. When she had recovered from the surprise at finding her kinsman a comparatively young man when she had expected to find a middle aged one, she had lost her nervousness and they had talked quite freely.

Henry VI was a thin, pale man with a slight stoop who smiled continually. His clothes were in complete contrast to the flamboyant dress of his courtiers and Margaret thought he was more like a monk than a King. Once looking down she was intrigued to discover that his feet were covered with strong country boots that would have been the pride of her mother's bailiff. He questioned her gently about her life at home and really listened to her answers, which was something she hardly expected as she had soon discovered that adults at Court were preoccupied with their own affairs and had not much time for children. She told him with pleasure about the manor and the people there and added shyly that she hoped he would visit her family as the clean, country air would suit him well. She had to admit that the small, chilly room in which he sat before a table heaped with manuscripts and books did not compare very favourably with her room at the palace or indeed with any at Bletsoe, and she wished that Lady Welles could look after him and bring some colour into the aesthetic face. A large table stood against the wall spread with papers, which at first glance to Margaret, seemed as if they were covered with a tangle of lines and patterns. Henry saw her look and fresh interest seemed to enliven him as he drew her to inspect them. 'These are the plans for my new college at Eton,' he told her. Margaret saw them, as he described them to her, that the squares represented rooms and halls and she caught some of his enthusiasm as he enlarged on his plan to make this watery meadow a home of learning for boys. Realising her interest he asked her if she could read and write.

'Why, yes, Your Grace, my mother has sent us to lessons with the priest since we were five years of age and although I don't like learning

Latin very much I am trying to master it.'

Somewhat astonished to find that anything female had thought for more than clothes and fripperies Henry remarked dryly that it was a pity he was not thinking about building a school for girls; at which outrageous suggestion they both laughed merrily.

'When next we visit Windsor little Margaret, it would give me much pleasure to show you the progress in the building. Most of the dormitories and other rooms have been completed and work is starting on the chapel where the boys can praise God in His goodness.'

Henry returned to his chair and Margaret thought he looked suddenly more tired than when she arrived.

'You are most welcome to our Court and I shall look forward to seeing you again. God go with you.'

Now she and nurse were finding their way to the small room close to the Jewel Tower which had been set aside as a classroom for herself and several other children where they received daily instruction from one of the monks who lived at the abbey. As they hurried over the worn stones in the cloisters two young men came towards them, deep in conversation. The elder, who was dark, well proportioned and of medium height was listening to the other with amusement tempered by affection. When they came abreast of Margaret he noticed her and turned his head towards her; their eyes met and he smiled. Unidentifiable happiness swept up in her and she smiled back, then looked down abruptly to cover the confusion she felt. Quickly as they had come they were gone, but in that brief moment some of the home sickness vanished and she thought that besides Henry there was at least one person in this enormous place who had noticed her for herself.

She longed to ask nurse if she knew who the youths were, but something held her back as if she wanted to keep this comfort to herself. Anyway the woman was too occupied in finding their destination to have time for ought else and she stopped a servant who was staggering under a yoke hung with heavy wooden buckets filled to the brim with water. Cursing roundly until he noticed the child, he set the load down, while water slopped over on to the pavement.

'I'll lead you,' he said. 'If you're but lately come here, you'll not find it easily alone.'

Gratefully they followed the man, turning this way and that, up and down short flights of stairs until at last he stopped before a low, wooden door.

'Here you are, ma'am.'

Margaret thanked him with a smile. It seemed easier to be happy today and the servant went off muttering to himself that it was a pity that more of the gentlefolk did not follow the young lady's example and realise that the low born were at least human and not animals only fit for servitude.

A Benedictine monk, cowled in black, greeted Margaret and gave her a place on a bench with two other children. Nurse took herself off, glad to have an hour or two to spend with the new gossips she had made at Westminster.

At first Margaret listened to the elderly monk enthralled. Bernard Frognale had much more to teach her than the priest at Bletsoe, but from time to time she found it difficult to concentrate and she gazed out of the small, high window to watch the round, white clouds scudding across the sky. Now and again she saw in her mind the smiling face of the young man she had encountered in the cloister. She felt relaxed and happier than at any time since she set out for London. The monk, seeing the dreamy expression on the fine drawn, intelligent face recalled her to the lesson, and coming out of her reverie with a start she applied herself with extra vigour to the tasks set, for it would never do for reports of inattention and sloth to reach her mother, her guardian or His Grace.

Nevertheless, it was good to be released from the airless chamber, which smelt of dusty scrolls and dried ink and join the others on their way to eat in the hall. The great place was filled with the bustle of a large company taking their seats at the boards which ran the length of the room, and the noise was deafening as Margaret sat with the other young people and their nurses below the dais. A hush fell as the King entered, followed by his Chancellor and his esquires. Almost at once the Queen came in with her steward, John, Viscount Beaumont and a train of ladies that included Lady Scales, Lady Margaret Roos and Lady Isabel Dacre. Suffolk hovered in the background and after Grace which was pronounced by the Chancellor took his seat on Margaret of Anjou's left.

Margaret Beaufort watched the company as she had done every day since her arrival, fascinated by the magnificent pattern of colour they made against the dark stone wall behind them. Candles set in huge candelabra gleamed on the white coifs and gauze veils of the elaborate head-dresses of the women, but she knew that today it was not the beautiful gowns or rich tunics that interested her, but one face only. She began her search to the far ends of the right hand table without success and her food was taken away, untouched, by a page while she scanned the left side. She was beginning to fear that she would be disappointed when, with a small shock of surprise she saw that he was sitting only one place away from the King. As she watched, the King leant forward and addressed him and their immediate neighbour and they talked gravely at some length. Nurse at this point noticed the untouched food and she was forced to turn her attention to her platter, but while it prevented her looking at the high table it did not stem her thoughts and her quick perception told her that there was something unusual about the two dark heads she had seen bent towards each other. It was not until she was falling asleep, however, that night that she realised that the odd thing was that the shape and colouring were similar.

4

Lady Welles was safely delivered of a son in the October after she had taken Margaret to Court, but her fears for her daughter's well-being did not disappear with the baby's birth. There were many people coming and going between the household at Bletsoe and the palace and disquieting rumours reached them about Suffolk's position. It appeared that the Commons had lost confidence in him since the fateful attack on Fougeres which had ended the truce bought by the Anjou marriage. Added to this there were unsupported beliefs that Suffolk, with Lumbley and Adam Moleyns had been tyrannising the countryside at home and extorting vast sums of money for their own use. Lumbley resigned the treasuryship and Moleyns gave up the Privy Seal.

Nurse reported that Margaret was well and happy and that Lady Welles was to rest assured that no breath of her guardian's difficulties was being communicated to her. In fact his lordship did not bother them over much and they rarely saw him other than when they were called to visit the Queen and he was present. His Grace the King took far more interest in the child and she was making favourable progress with her studies. If nurse or anyone else considered that the situation warranted their return home she would inform her mistress immediately.

This comforted Margaret's mother a little, but when in the November Parliament was recalled and almost at once charges were laid against Suffolk, she was again filled with anxiety and chided herself for ever allowing Margaret to go away from her.

Margaret had settled down well and was quite unaware of the growing feeling against her guardian. There were other children to talk with and games to play and the time did not go too slowly. The dark young man that she had seen in the cloisters had left Court for she had not met him again, and his bright image had faded a little, but she still bestowed on him a certain amount of hero worship.

Christmas, the first she had spent away from home, saw a relaxation of the tension, for the Commons were in recess and a spirit of goodwill prevailed. Suffolk had, as yet, made no defence against the charges brought against him and all seemed, for the moment at least, forgotten.

The King sent one of his personal squires

to escort Margaret with nurse and her page to visit the City of London. This was a wonderful day and one that she never forgot. They set out quite early in the morning, warmly clad, in a small, painted wagonette, taking the route through the Strand, where she saw the site of her great grandfather's Palace of the Savoy, which had been totally destroyed in 1381 during the great revolt of the peasants. They passed by the towering walls of Baynards Castle with its wharf at Puddle Dock, crossed over the Fleet river and came into Ludgate Hill, where they were crushed in a great crowd who were also making their way to the clearing outside St. Paul's. Margaret was so excited to be in among so many people, all good humoured and talkative that she had no time to be afraid. They clambered down from the little cart, and left it with a friendly boy outside an inn in Seacoal Lane, and finished the journey on foot. The boy told them that a Miracle Play was to be performed and that the Mayor and Aldermen were coming to watch.

As they pushed their way with the growing throng they could see above the heads of the crowd, in front of the great doors of the church a high scaffolding. The King's squire elbowed his way to a vantage point and the good-natured Londoners made room for the country woman and the child. They were all absorbed in the crowd around them and the preparations that were being made for the play. Magnificently dressed men in the extreme of fashion, with points to their shoes so long that they were secured to their calves with thongs were directing a mass of men with pieces of scenery and properties for the play. Even the mummers and jugglers who had come to Bletsoe and to the palace at Westminster paled beside these gesticulating producers in their bright doublets and hose. If it had not been for the page they would have missed the procession of the Mayor and the Aldermen as they were escorted to wooden benches in the forefront of the crowd.

Margaret craned her neck to watch the scarlet robed figure with a great gold chain as he took his place. The squire told them that this was the newly elected Mayor of London, Thomas Chalton, who would hold his important office as first citizen of the city for one year. He came of a wealthy merchant family who, with others like him, were the virtual rulers of the city. Between them they, and other members of the great Merchant Companies carried out the extensive business which made London a thriving port. It was their ships that crowded the nearby wharves waiting to load and export overseas to the Hanseatic ports wool, corn and cloth. The squire told Margaret that they lived in the tall houses that she could see around her and that they lived in a state which could compare with her own. On their way to great St. Paul's they had passed booths and shops, crammed with gorgeous silks and goods that she had never seen before, and these she heard, came from Italy and the East. The squire promised that on their return he would take them through Cheapside, where there were many jewellers and goldsmiths.

Just then a hush fell on the crowd as an actor could be seen making his way up the ladder to the platform. He announced that as it was the time for the celebration of the Nativity of Jesus Christ it was the pleasure of the performers to enact that scene. Amid much clapping he departed down the other ladder, while more actors clad as shepherds of their day climbed the scaffold and took up their places round a pot which they hung on a trivet to represent a fire. They were scarcely settled when apparently from above them two youths in white robes with wings attached to their backs came down to startle them with their announcement of the birth of the Saviour. It did not need much imagination to conjure up the cold, pastoral scene for the breath of the players was clearly visible and Margaret was glad of the press of bodies to keep her warm.

She watched in awestruck wonder as the Mother of Jesus arrived in the courtyard on a little grey donkey which was mercifully not called upon to climb the ricketty ladder to the stage. The Mother and St. Joseph were met by the innkeeper and his wife who led them to a corner where straw had been laid, while offering them food. The angels arrived in the same mysterious manner as before and Mary was led to the front of the platform where it was revealed that she now held a bundle fashioned with swaddling clothes to represent the infant Lord. The angels fell on their knees and at the same moment from behind the scaffold an unseen choir began the carol 'I sing of a Mayden'.

Several of the women in the crowd behind Margaret sniffed and glancing up at nurse she saw the kind face puckered in sentiment. The angels took their places behind the Virgin and Child, and up the ladder came the procession of the shepherds, while the choir broke into 'The shepherd upon a hill he sat'.

Having made their adoration and handed over to St. Joseph a newborn lamb, they joined the angels while from the other side came another trio of men, whom Margaret recognised by the splendour of their robes as the Three Kings. They carried in their hands boxes of gold which they presented to the Infant as they prostrated themselves before Him.

All these having departed the Holy Family settled down to rest, but St. Joseph was awakened as an evil looking man appeared out of the shadows and announced that he was King Herod. He went as quickly as he had arrived, but it was long enough for St. Joseph to understand that this was a portent of evil and he hastily woke Mary and carrying her Babe they left the stage and mounting her on the donkey went away. Up on the high platform came the bereaved mothers who had had their first born slain by Herod and Margaret was glad when their anguished waiting was over and the angels returned and announced that the scene was now set in Egypt and that the Holy Family were about to join them there. Almost at once the now familiar donkey with its precious burden appeared and remounted the stage, where they were joined by all the cast while another carol was sung quietly and reverently from behind.

The crowd began to break up, knowing of old that this marked the end of the performance.

Disappointed, Margaret looked up to the young man who had escorted them 'Is that all?' she asked.

'I am afraid it is, Lady Margaret. But there is more for you to see yet before we return.'

He led them behind the huge church into the narrowness of Cheapside and Margaret was instantly carried away with the display in the booths that lined the street. She would have lingered at each stall, marvelling at the gold and silver work that was displayed, but nurse was beginning to tire and she announced that her feet were ready to give way. Grumbling a little she waited long enough while they entered one dimly lit shop where a portly shopkeeper brought out some silver-topped rattles with ivory handles for Margaret to choose one for her new brother. Candles guttered in their sconces and played on the muted gold and silver. It was as enchanting as a magician's cave and the child was reluctant to leave, but she knew that it had been such a happy day that to make nurse cross would only spoil it, and anyway she was beginning to feel hungry herself. With the gift safely wrapped they said their farewells, and made for Seacoal Lane and the wagon.

She was very quiet as she huddled close to nurse on the journey home, reliving the highlights of the day. Of all that she had seen she thought she liked best the little donkey as it bore its sacred Burden and she resolved as she said her prayers that night to say a special word to Our Lady who had borne so much for us. The Thames had ebbed since they had left this morning and it flowed thinly between the muddy banks and the day began to darken. A few seagulls swooped on refuse the receding tide had left and the ferryman replenished the lanterns to hang at the sterns of the boats they used to take passengers across to the Southwark bank.

When they arrived in their own apartments it was to discover that a messenger had come from Bletsoe bringing her gifts from her family for St. Nicholas' Day and her eyes filled with tears as she took from their velvet lined boxes a pair of silver-gilt cups chased with marguerites set with precious stones. How her brothers would have enjoyed the play she had seen today and the magnificence of the Mayor and the court of aldermen. She gave way for a moment to an overwhelming wave of homesickness and she clutched the exquisite cups to her, but it would not do to give way to the miseries and she looked round the room to find a suitable place to display her new treasures. A small oaken table against the wall seemed the very place and she put them down on the polished surface and sank against her bed to admire them, head on one side. They looked at home immediately and she brightened at once, calling nurse, who was vigorously rubbing some new life into her feet, to come and admire them.

During the festive season a real effort was made to shut out the crisis which threatened the palace and a round of feasts and entertainments took place. Margaret went with the other children to the abbey on Christmas Day and joined with them in the singing of carols and the playing of traditional games. On the night of the New Year a whole ox was roasted in the courtyard of the palace and they watched from windows above while the soldiers and servants of the palace danced and made merry. She had to admit that they made an awesome picture as they pranced in front of the leaping flames and she was reminded of some of the ghoulish stories that she had heard from the boys who delighted in making her flesh creep. She was happy to go into the solar where men and women of the Court were playing chess and a new kind of game with fifty-two pieces of card on which were depicted kings, queens and knaves. She watched fascinated as the brightly coloured pictures were thrown and stacked beside the players.

As she answered the other children's call to join them in front of the fire where they were roasting chestnuts she was quite happy and thought what a great deal she had to write and tell her mother when the courier next returned to Bletsoe.

This Christmas peace was rudely shattered when news was brought that the ex-Chancellor, Moleyns, had been murdered at Portsmouth by some discontented sailors, while he was trying to take ship for France. At once the old tensions reasserted themselves and faces about the Court wore the familiar look of strain. Parliament hastily reassembled and the anxieties which had been lulled by the remembrance of the Holy Babe's birth became apparent again.

One day, late in January, Margaret was sitting in the Queen's solar with a group of the ladies attending her grace. A girl had been singing quietly, while she accompanied herself on an eight stringed lute, and the child had been filled with unaccountable longings by the sweet music, when the Queen had sharply commanded the girl to put down the instrument and join the other ladies in their stitching on the immense tapestry. This was a wall hanging for the Jerusalem chamber in the abbey, but Margaret had not thought that its completion warranted such urgency that no time could be spared for the making of music. Glancing hurriedly at the Queen, she thought she looked pale and not very well and now that she remembered it all the ladies, who usually chatted with her, were very quiet and withdrawn. She had not been told about the murder at Portsmouth but she was sensitive enough and had been at Court long enough to realise that perhaps something was amiss.

At this moment a waiting woman burst into the room announcing that the King was approaching. The Queen was on her feet in an instant for it was unprecedented for her husband to seek her out. The other women rose, and Margaret caught anxious glances from one to the other.

The Queen moved quickly to Henry's side as he came into the solar, and even Margaret was struck by his ghastly pallor and the drawn look on his face. He took Margaret of Anjou's arm and leaned upon it. The Queen knew at once that Suffolk's defence, which was expected to commence today, had proved inadequate and that Henry was shocked by the accusations against the man in whom he had placed such trust. She could not support that the women craning to catch every word, should hear ill of her favourite and calling for wine to be brought to her bedchamber she led Henry within.

As they disappeared other gentlemen arrived and the ladies clustered round them, like sparrows round a piece of cake, unable to wait to hear the reason for the King's distress. Only Lady Suffolk and Margaret remained seated.

Northumberland could be heard recounting the scene in the Commons when Suffolk had been accused of plotting with the French to invade England, for which it was affirmed that he had fortified Wallingford Castle as a place of refuge for the invader.

'But that is impossible,' Lady Clifford cried. 'My Lord Suffolk has ever had his country's interest at heart and waged the war against France with all the means at his command.'

'This is what he tried to plead with them, setting forth his long list of service at home and abroad, but the Parliament would have none of it, indeed they further accused him of sending monies to Charles, King of France, to enable him to reopen the war, which had resulted in the capture of the Earl of Shrewsbury and Lord Fauconberg.'

Lady Suffolk, unseen, crept out of the room, her plain face contorted. Margaret, beginning to feel afraid, watched her go, the poor creature who always seemed so ill suited to be the wife of the dazzling Suffolk.

But Northumberland was continuing with a long list of the indictments that had been laid against the Duke and there were shrill cries of disbelief from the women. Though Suffolk was not popular, he was Lancastrian, as were most of the people assembled in this place, and he was one of them. To accuse him of treason was to strike a blow against their faction and incriminate all.

There was silence again as Northumberland went on, 'Ah, but that was not all. There was matter even more serious than this, which struck at His Grace himself.'

'Against His Grace, how come?' This from Lady de Roos, a staunch friend of the Queen and therefore quick to champion her paramour.

'It appears,' went on Northumberland, 'that for some time he has been aiming at the throne for himself!'

'That's a lie,' shouted a friend of Suffolk's. 'How could he possibly make any claim whatsoever in that direction?'

'He made no claim,' answered Lord Willoughby of Eresby, who was known to have Yorkist sympathies.

'Well, how could he reach for it then?'

'Far more subtly than by arms or litigation, but by marriage of his son with the little Beaufort.'

Margaret did not hear the reply for the blood was pounding in her ears and hot angry tears stung her eyes. She remembered vividly the Queen speaking of John de la Pole when she had first arrived at Westminster and her mother's calm reassuring reply. She longed to be able to fling herself into that comforting lap to blot out the half-understood words she had just heard. Unable to help herself she covered her face and sobbed, when suddenly she felt a pair of strong arms lift and carry her from the room. She buried her head in the comforting warmth of the broad shoulder and cried as if her heart would break.

As they came out into the cloisters she stopped her tears and opening her eyes looked up into the face of the dark young man she had thought so much about.

He set her down on her feet and proffered a large handkerchief.

'Are you better now?' he asked smiling down at her. 'I could not let them break your heart with their excited jabbering.'

Margaret nodded dumbly, sniffed once or twice and gave him back his handkerchief, then trustingly placing her hand in his, led him towards her chambers.

'Please take me to nurse,' she said quietly, wishing that when she had met her hero again her face had not been blotched with weeping.

'They did not know you were there, you know,' he said kindly. 'The news made them forget that the Lady Margaret was of their company.'

'You know my name,' Margaret said slowly, wondering.

'Yes, your fame has even reached me!'

'Now you are laughing at me.'

'Never that,' he hastened to reassure her. They were almost at the door of her room and she was at a loss to know what to do next, for she wanted him to stay, even if only long enough to ask his name.

'You know my name,' she said quickly, amazed at her daring. 'But I do not know yours.'

'I am called Edmund of Hadham, Lady Margaret, and I am your devoted servant.' A swift upward glance assured her that there was not even a twinkle on the handsome grave face and she sighed.

'Thank you for that, and for bringing me away. I am a little confused with all this talk about the Duke. You do not think — '

'Yes,' he prompted.

'You do not think, do you, that anyone can

make me marry John de la Pole?'

'You will not have to marry anybody that you do not wish, I am quite sure, and after what has happened in Parliament today it is very unlikely that my Lord Suffolk's son would be given the opportunity of betrothing you.'

'Oh, thank you,' she breathed.

Edmund knocked on the door and nurse came to open it. She was startled to see a strange young man with her charge and greatly alarmed when she heard what had happened. She thanked Edmund warmly for his action and took Margaret in.

Looking back over her shoulder Margaret was just in time to see Edmund still standing where she had left him. She smiled and taking off his hat he made her a deep bow.

Nurse, very agitated was offering her some wine and bidding her sit by the fire while she rubbed her cold hands.

'We'd better be getting ourselves back to Bletsoe if this is the way things are going to turn out. Your mother would not be able to rest at night if she knew what was happening to her lamb.'

The next morning nurse was summoned to an interview with the Queen and Margaret was accompanied to her lessons by a serving woman and her page. This youth was distantly connected with her family as he came from a cadet branch of the Beauchamps and had been at Court some time. His knowledge of personages was bound to be better than her own and Margaret meant to make the most opportunity of nurse's absence to make enquiries.

She purposely left her cloak behind and half way to the classroom claimed she was cold and asked the woman to go back for it. Somewhat unwillingly the woman hurried off, knowing that nurse would not approve of Margaret being attended by her page only.

As soon as she was gone Margaret turned to the lad and demanded earnestly.

'Tell me quickly, all you know of Edmund of Hadham.'

The boy was startled and somewhat surprised for he had thought his lady a mere child for all her bookish ways and quick brain and had not thought to hear her enquiring about the young men of the Court. He hesitated, then glancing down at the frank eager young face, saw that her interest in his reply was vitally important to her.

'Why, my lady, he has been knighted recently with his brother Sir Jasper of Hatfield — '

'Yes, yes,' Margaret interrupted, 'but where does he live, what does he here, who are his parents, and how old is he?'

Out of the corner of her eye, down the long passage she could see the woman returning with the cloak.

'As for his age, he would be nineteen or twenty and his father was a very handsome gentleman who was Squire of the Wardrobe to the King's mother, Princess Katherine de Valois.'

It was too late to ask more for the woman was up with them and setting the fur edge wrap around her shoulder. Flashing them both a grateful smile she entered the room and bobbed a curtsy to the monk.

As she took her seat with the other children she sensed that they were regarding her with unusual curiosity and she wondered what they knew of her guardian's disgrace and her part on the matter. She was relieved when they were set a particularly complicated Latin text to transcribe and she, and they, were fully occupied.

Throughout the day there was an air of tension in the palace. Reports and alarms were bandied from hall to solar, from kitchen to pantry to stables. It was said that Londoners had tried to lynch their erstwhile favourite when he had attempted to leave the palace. The mob had rushed up to the great gateway shouting that Suffolk was the cause of the loss of the French possessions which had been gained by the outpouring of their blood. There were screams of vengeance for Henry V 'The Christian Champion, The Flower of Chivalry' who had led them to victory and whose conquests had been lost by the mismanagement of this jackanapes. Open accusations of adultery with the Queen had been shouted at him and he had hastily retired to the safety of his quarters with 'Now is the fox driven to his hole' ringing in his ears.

The toppling of a great man brings uneasiness to all who have owed allegiance to him and there was much speculation about what would happen to the countless followers and retainers of Suffolk if it were finally established that he was guilty. Lady Suffolk kept to her room, unable to face friend or enemy.

The Queen was outwardly calm. Her bearing gave no hint of the inner turmoil that she felt at the dilemma of protector and counsellor. Only her serving women knew the extent of her grief for her lover. She turned her attentions to the suffering King, and when he appeared that evening to dine he still looked drawn and beset with care and pathetically ready to lean upon his wife. His physicians were never far away.

In the audience that nurse had begged with the Queen, she had been only too willing for word to be sent to Bletsoe that it was advisable that Margaret should go home. Although it was so early in the year and the roads difficult Margaret of Anjou would not allow that this would make a journey difficult for the child and her party. She promised that a strong escort would accompany them and that arrangements would be made for easy stages. It was quite obvious that she was distracted by what had occurred and waited with gnawing anxiety to see how the Commons would punish the man who meant so much to her. To be rid of the responsibility for the Lady Margaret relieved her of one headache at least, for it was rumoured that Henry was ill and suffering a breakdown with shock.

Nurse left the chamber happy that her task had been made so easy for her.

5

In under four days a courier arrived fom Bletsoe with a letter summoning Margaret home. Nurse hurried delightedly into the preparations for the journey and hardly noticed that her charge was distrait and quieter than usual.

In the schoolroom Bernard Frognale found it difficult to interest her in the lessons and forgave her, putting down the lack of concentration to the strain of recent events. She had told him that she was leaving the palace and returning to her mother. After an hour he called her to his side and set her some reading and translations to take with her and bring to him on her return.

'When will that be, sir?' she asked, grateful to be released.

'Who knows,' the priest replied. 'Perhaps when a little of God's peace comes to these fractious nobles and they can spend time in quietness rather than at destroying each other. The seeking of power is surely the greatest evil that can beset a man for he loses sight of all else in his self-aggrandisement. It is better for you to go to the understanding and safety of your own home for the moment. Work hard, my child, and do not waste the plentiful gifts that God has bestowed upon you; to be well occupied is to approach His wish for us. His blessing attend you.'

They set off in the earliest, grey light of a chill morning, well wrapped with furs against the cold. The town still slept as their small cavalcade clattered over the cobbles, where even the runnels were frozen. Generous rations of spirits had been doled out to the men and nurse had slipped a spoonful into Margaret's milk.

The child found her own feelings difficult to understand. She felt a sadness at leaving the Court because Edmund was there. He had heard that she was to make the journey to Bletsoe and had presented himself to tender his good wishes for a safe passage. He had brought her a small velvet muff lined with fur as a parting gift and she had been unable to thank him, for the pleasure it had given her had almost choked her.

On the other hand the relief at rejoining her family and being with her mother filled the future with joy. There was the excitement of seeing her new brother for the first time and she longed to tell her mother about her new found friend and hoped she would not laugh at her young dreams.

After five days of miserable cold and slow, difficult travel the party arrived with much rejoicing at the manor in Bedfordshire. Mother, daughter and stepsisters were reunited with affection. Lady Welles had spent hours on her knees in the chapel, braving the cold winds again and again to pray for the safe homecoming of this well beloved, important member of her family, and tears came into her eyes and she clasped her to her bosom. Much as she loved her large number of children, this one, resembling so closely her good-looking father, had a special place in her heart, and she had hated every moment that she had been away. She almost blessed the bad news about Suffolk so that Margaret could come home.

Fresh despatches had been brought for Sir Leon and the news in them was grave, in that the Commons now intended to make a formal indictment in eight separate articles against the Duke and it was considered extremely unlikely that he would miss paying the supreme penalty. Henry intervened at this point and decided that the case should be put in respite for a period. The Welles of Bletsoe, deeply perturbed at the plight of Margaret's guardian and what it could mean to her future, breathed a little more freely, but waited in considerable trepidation for the next move from the Commons. It was not long in coming and on March 9th they presented two more charges of malversation while in office and embezzlement of money paid in taxes, with a special note to investigate the action of Suffolk in prevailing upon the sheriff of Lincolnshire not to serve a writ upon a henchman of his called Tailboys who was being sued by a number of women for the murder of their husbands.

The future looked exceedingly black for the Duke when Henry, who was ever merciful, intervened again and ordered that Suffolk should be banished from the realm and from that of France for five years from the 1st of May. At this Suffolk vanished and was reported to be in hiding at Wingfield. No word came to Bletsoe concerning his ward.

Lady Welles had questioned nurse closely about the incident at Westminster which had prompted the homecoming of Margaret. In the telling the woman did not forget to mention the young gentleman who had so thoughtfully saved the child from the unpleasant scene.

Margaret brought specimens of her lessons to show Lady Welles and the mother was pleased to see, that at least in some directions, her visit had not been wasted. She asked quietly if Margaret had spent an appropriate time at her devotions and was assured that this important aspect of her life had not been neglected.

With her mother she went to visit her baby brother in his room. Nurse accompanied them and disapproved strongly of the pagan custom, as she called it, of immersing the boy in water to cleanse him. The fresh-faced young nurse who was caring for him, replied a little tartly, that the room was as warm as an oven, which it certainly was, as even the windows were sealed to allow no cold air to penetrate, and that it was the modern custom to ensure cleanliness. When the child was dried and clothed Margaret was given permission to hold him. She cradled the sweet-smelling bundle in her arms and buried her face in the soft folds of fat at his neck.

'He's lovely, Mother, isn't he?'

'I think so,' replied Lady Welles.

'And he looks like you, too!'

'It's to be hoped so, after all the trouble I went to get him.'

Lady Welles laughed and arm in arm they went off to sit in the solar.

Suddenly Margaret blurted out.

'My lady, have you heard of Sir Edmund of Hadham?'

'Why, yes, certainly. Have you?'

'Yes, I do know him a little. He is kind.'

'So,' said the mother, smiling secretly to herself, for this must be the young man of whom nurse had spoken. 'How, especially, was he kind?' she prompted.

Flushing a little Margaret said, 'It was about some talk I overheard in the Queen's solar concerning the Duke of Suffolk's son and myself. I was troubled and he came and took me away to nurse.' Hesitating, she went on, 'They were saying that Lord Suffolk sought to marry us, and do some harm to the King thereby.'

Ignoring the last Lady Welles took her daughter's hand, noticing the expression on the child's face when she spoke of Edmund.

'That was indeed kind and thoughtful of him.' In her experience of life at Court, concern for the feelings of others was not paramount and she warmed towards her daughter's champion.

'Mother,' Margaret asked in a rush, 'who is he? Please tell me. It seemed so ignorant not to know and I found it hard to ask.'

'When you find it difficult to ask questions, things must be stressed indeed! But when you say you do not know who he is, you must surely realise that he is half-brother to the King.'

Margaret looked up at her mother, her eyes

wide with amazement.

'Oh!' she exclaimed. 'That accounts for why I thought their heads looked so alike.'

She thought about this new knowledge and then a puzzled frown appeared on the clear brow.

'But I thought that Henry is an only child?'

'Yes, that is so on his father's side, but after he died in France, his widow, Katherine was neglected as if she no longer mattered. A Regency was set up to reign until her child was old enough to govern for himself and his uncles took him away from her to have complete control of him.'

With the memory of her own baby brother still very close, Margaret expressed indignant sympathy for the bereaved Queen.

'What happened then?' she asked.

'The King's uncles sent her to Hatfield House — where you and I stayed, you remember — with a small household and kept her, virtually as a prisoner. At first she was very sad and lonely for she missed her baby, more so as she had not had a very happy time as Queen, for the King, her husband had been preoccupied with the war in France and had never paid her much attention. Even at the child's birth she had been out of favour, for against his wishes she had gone to Windsor for the event, and he had had some superstitious belief that things would turn out ill.'

'Did they?' Margaret enquired.

'Well, the King did die, as you know, but that would have happened wherever the Queen had produced the baby, and no blame should attach to her for that. If Henry seems sometimes to have ill-health that could hardly be her fault either, but is inherited from his mother's father, no doubt. No, I think she was much maligned and a very unhappy young woman, so that it was no wonder that when a knight called Owen Tudor, who had been appointed Squire of her Wardrobe, fell in love with her and courted her with kindness and a gentleness that she had not realised existed, she returned his affection.'

Margaret sat thoughtful, her warm nature aroused at the absorbing story.

'That's an odd name!' she said slowly. 'Tudor!'

'It is Welsh,' her mother told her. 'Owen Tudor claims descent from the oldest royal family in Wales.'

'Please go on.'

Lady Welles hesitated for a moment for she was not quite sure how to present the rest of the story. She had never been absolutely convinced that the pair had been married but it would not do to tell her sensitive child that her hero might be a bastard. As Margaret looked at her to see why she waited she continued with a rush.

'They ran away and kept their marriage secret, for had it been discovered they stood a very real risk of losing their lives, for it was, and still is, a great crime to wed the widow of a King. However the risk proved well worth it for they found complete happiness in living shut away in the country together and they had five children — '

'Edmund is the eldest of these?' Margaret interrupted.

'Yes, he is the eldest,' Lady Welles replied. 'Jasper — have you met him, too? — is the next, and there is one other son and two daughters. There were many attempts to find them and eventually they were discovered and brutally torn away from each other. Once more the Queen had her offspring taken from her. This time she was confined in a nunnery at Bermondsey, where, it is not to be wondered, she died of a broken heart. Owen Tudor was banished and although he tried again and again to find Katherine he never succeeded.'

Margaret's eyes filled with tears and they ran unheeded down her cheeks.

'What of the children?' she asked in a subdued whisper.

'When Henry reached manhood and it came to his ears that he had other brothers and sisters, he made every effort to trace them. He was very concerned that his uncles had purposely allowed them to vanish into obscurity for fear of any claim on their part to the succession; he is, as you know, very tender-hearted and could not bear to imagine that ill had fallen his mother's children. When some monks came to him with information that a certain Abbess named Catherine de la Pole had three unknown little boys in her charge at Barking, he made investigations and when he discovered that they were his half-brothers had two of them brought to Court, where he has heaped land and favours upon them to compensate for the slight on his mother's name. The other boy chose the life of a monk and has been placed in a monastery.'

The mother, looking down saw the droop of the head and she drew Margaret to her.

'Don't fret, chicken,' she said gently. 'Edmund is quite happy now, especially since Henry revoked Owen Tudor's banishment and reinstated him in his lands. The boys spend quite a good part of the year with their father.'

'Yes, I do think Edmund is happy, but what of his poor mother, and you did not tell me

97

what has happened to the girls.'

Somewhat uneasily, Lady Welles recalled that much searching had not revealed their whereabouts and it was commonly supposed that they had been quietly bestowed upon some grateful nunnery with a handsome dowry to ensure secrecy. She reassured her daughter that she was quite sure that Henry, as their half-brother would do all in his power to see to their welfare.

'Sir Priest will be here later to start you with your lessons again,' she said, changing the subject.

The child, at the mention of learning, brightened at once and her mother quietly decided that she must find plenty to occupy her time. When she was not studying Margaret could be with her about her housewifely duties, for it was never too early to learn the gentle art of keeping house.

Later Lady Welles confided to her husband that the small daughter they had sent to Court had returned more grown up than they had realised possible. With a twinkle in his usually grave eyes, Sir Leon agreed that Sir Edmund would make an extremely suitable match for Margaret.

Six weeks went by and the tranquillity of Bletsoe enfolded Margaret and her family in its accustomed peace. The daily routine caught them and soon it was almost as if the visit to London had never taken place.

Early in May a courier arrived from Henry bearing news which only too vividly recalled the disturbing few months she had spent there. Lady Welles was in the still room when the steward came at his master's bidding to ask her to come to him in the solar.

Sir Leon held out the despatch for her to read as she entered the room. She read the hastily scrawled words and sank into a chair. Although they had been prepared for the shock of Suffolk's disgrace and banishment, they had been lulled into a false sense of security as time had elapsed and they had heard no more. It had always seemed to them that their child's guardian would be further saved by Henry's intervention and they were completely taken aback with the news that Suffolk had been murdered while he was taking ship for France.

The messenger, who was waiting in the shadows of the dark, panelled room was able to furnish more details than the letter afforded.

It appeared that the Duke had set sail and was only a few hours out from the English coast when another boat had come out of the early morning mists and ordered his ship to lower its sail and heave-to. The newcomer,

The Nicholas of the Tower, was full of rough, swarthy sailors and they forced Suffolk to leave his ship and clamber in with them. Once aboard the *Nicholas* he was dragged, without further word, to a block which they had set up and was held down while he was beheaded. Later his body was thrown upon the shore at Dover, where it was discovered and buried, at the King's command, at Wingfield, where he had previously been lying hidden.

When they were alone again and the first shock had subsided they found they were able to talk quietly about Margaret's future. They both determined that they must send urgent application to the King and Margaret's Uncle Edmund, Duke of Somerset, for guidance in the selection of a new guardian. They knew that to approach the Queen at this juncture would be most unwise, and they wondered how she was enduring this final blow to her overriding passion for the late Duke. Lady Welles expressed the sincere hope that the King would be able to put her with child, although from all accounts the gentle monarch did not look like the sire of a large or robust family; it would be as well, also, if the hoped for infant delayed its appearance for ten months or so in order to quieten any suspicions that Suffolk's child had attained the throne after all.

Until such time as an heir did appear Margaret remained in the vulnerable position as heiress of the Lancastrian faction, a position made more difficult by the absence of a strong and reliable sponsor. Although not willing to think or speak ill of the dead, they were secretly a little relieved that Suffolk, who had, it turned out, fully earned Lady Welles' mistrust, was no longer a major concern in their daughter's future.

To Margaret, when the news was broken to her, it made very little difference. She had never been completely at ease with the flamboyant man whose ward she had become and she joined in masses for the departed soul of the Duke and forgot all about him in a short time.

With Edmund it was altogether different and the morning and nightly prayers she made kneeling at the small altar in the house chapel always contained a hope for his well being and a wish that it would not be too long before she saw him again.

6

It was the autumn before Henry sent word to his young kinswoman that he wished her to come to Court for a short time so that he could acquaint her with her new guardian. Now that she was the sole heiress of the Lancastrian House, the King knew as well as Lady Welles and her husband that a strong protector must be found for her. Henry had suffered from the disaster of his faith in Suffolk, not least because it was openly believed that his death had been at Yorkist instigation and that the King's position was threatened. Although it was fairly definitely established that the marauders who had boarded Suffolk's ship had been fanatical pirates from the West Country who hoped to extract a vast ransom from the Duke's followers, it was impossible to prove that they had not been backed by the growing army of Richard of York's supporters and the King, longing only to be left in peace to read his books and build his schools and colleges, was shattered and made completely miserable by the knowledge that anyone wished him ill.

The Queen, however she had been personally

wounded by the death of the man who had enthralled her bodily since she had been a girl, awakened from the misery into which she had been plunged and turned to Margaret's Uncle Edmund, Duke of Somerset, as her new champion for Henry's and her own cause. She saw, instinctively, that Richard of York, while disarmingly talking of only wishing to help Henry, coveted the throne for himself, in the belief that his claim was stronger than the King's. This strengthened her determination to keep it a Lancastrian monarchy and she threw her energies which she had previously lavished on Suffolk, into this immense task, for it could not be denied that the situation was one of mounting tensions. Richard, Duke of York, had been sent to Ireland as her governor, but there was no certainty that he would remain there and a supporting army could very easily be built up for him in his absence. There were too many well-trained followers of all houses of the nobility, idle at home, with bow fingers itching to take up any quarrel to hope that peace would be maintained at home.

It was with relief that Lady Welles accompanied Margaret to Windsor where they had been summoned, for the anxiety of the times were communicated to Bletsoe. Sir Leon had been ordered to the Calais garrison and the mother had felt defenceless in the protection of her child. Her sons came to be with her as much as they were able, but during the last months John had gone to join his stepfather in France and Oliver was continuing his studies at Cambridge. She realised that she would not have them at her side as she would have wished as they grew fast to manhood. It was most necessary that her daughter became a ward of a man who would furnish protection and render assistance with her upbringing.

When they came into the straggling village of Eton from the north the great round tower of the castle seemed wreathed in white mists and the river flowed turgidly grey and chill. As they crossed the drawbridge and entered the courtyard scurrying figures passed quickly from doorway to doorway reluctant to stay in the damp air but their herald had announced their coming and they were quickly taken to small, well-warmed rooms in which cheerful, sweet scented fires were burning. They were relieved that food was brought to them here and that they could take to their hastily assembled beds without being called to pay their respects to the King that night, for they were tired and wearied with the damp cold.

It was to be two days before Henry sent for them. They dined the next day in the hall and

Margaret scanned the faces around but saw with disappointment that Edmund was not of the company. Henry did not join the high table either and his Queen sent her page to fetch them to her chamber, where she apologised for her husband's absence explaining that he suffered a slight indisposition and sent them away with books for the child to look at and a piece of tapestry for Lady Welles to occupy her time of waiting. Margaret of Anjou appeared to Lady Welles to be considerably thinner than when she had last seen her a year ago and she had lost much of her seductive sensuality, but her eyes still flashed with amber fires although it was now the political situation that aroused the deep running emotion. She left Lady Welles in no doubt of her concern for the unrest which was developing and her determination to see that Henry was not ousted from his throne. She told them that her husband wished to speak personally with them on the subject of Margaret's guardian and then went on again with her extensive catalogue of the shortcomings of the Yorkists. Lady Welles felt convinced that whereas a peace loving woman might have helped to ease the differences between the two Houses, Margaret of Anjou would never accept mediation and would be ruthless in her desire to keep the throne in

Lancastrian hands. She knew that they were given this short interview and courteously received because Margaret was a niece of Edmund, Duke of Somerset, who was now firmly established as advisor to Henry and the Queen.

Margaret stood at her mother's side, watching as far as good manners permitted, the strange woman who was Queen of England. Although she had not seen her for some months, young as she was she could sense some change in her which in no way drew her to Margaret of Anjou, and she was as relieved as she had been before to make their curtsies and depart.

Back in their own rooms they discussed what they should wear when they did present themselves to Henry and they had decided on the deep green velvet edged with miniver for Margaret when Henry's chamberlain came to request their presence for an audience on the following morning.

Lady Welles spent an almost sleepless night, turning over and over in her mind what lay before them on the morrow. So much depended on the man who would be chosen. Like Suffolk he could be desirous of pushing his personal affairs with a match for Margaret and his own heirs or he could even think it better for the child to enter a convent and be completely safe, in sanctuary, from all power seekers. Somehow, the girl, although pious and obedient, did not seem the right material for a nun and her mother hoped that this easy solution for protection would not occur to the new guardian.

Looking round the circle of their acquaintances who Henry might pick upon to succeed Suffolk, Lady Welles had not been satisfied that any of them from Buckingham to Warwick could be entirely altruistic in the guiding of Margaret's affairs and she relied upon Henry to make a good choice. She had also written, privately, to the Duke of Somerset, asking him to use his considerable influence towards a worthy man. Sleep still would not give her respite and pulling her chamber robe around her went to the new styled fireplace and threw on fresh sticks and logs. The merry flames warmed her and huddled in a velvet seated chair she dozed a little, dreaming of cold white cells where Margaret would be gratefully accepted as a member of a nunnery only too anxious to receive her fortune as a dowry.

The next day they were escorted through long, draughty passages and up some steep and winding stairs to the room, set high in the inner walls of the castle, where the King lived while in residence. From the small windows it was possible for him to look out across the river and meadows to the new school he was building.

The chamber was bare and comfortless as a monk's and only a small fire burnt on the hearth so that Margaret was glad of the fur on her gown. She hoped, childlike, that the cold had not reddened her nose and that it would not run, for there were several people in the room. She and her mother knelt to the King who greeted them with unfeigned pleasure. He was extremely pale and his shoulders drooped more than usual under the plain robe. His table was littered with plans and documents, which he had been discussing with an ample gentleman in a dark brown mantle, who he introduced as John Hampton, Surveyor to the College of Eton. With him also were two monks who were emissaries of William of Wayneflete, Bishop of Winchester, the Provost of the school. Henry liked to have first hand information of the progress of his scholars and he was endeavouring to catch up with the backlog of his interests that had accumulated during his recent illness.

'Perhaps tomorrow, Lady Welles, you and your daughter will accompany me when we go to inspect the progress on the building of the chapel. Master Hampton tells me that much has been accompished since I was last here. I shall be happy to have your company, Lady Margaret, for your own bent for learning gives me much pleasure already.'

Margaret looked down, fidgeting from one foot to the other. It was embarrassing to have her scholarly pursuits mentioned, making her feel she was a rarity rather like the parrot that had been brought to Bletsoe by a party of mummers who were proud of its ability to talk.

'Did you know,' the King was continuing, 'that our great-uncle, Cardinal Beaufort, was very encouraging to me when I first thought of building a school here?'

Margaret murmured that she had not known. In fact she was somewhat surprised to hear that the warlike statesman of family legend had had time for the gentler pursuits of learning.

The King continued at some length about his plans for this school and a college that he hoped to start in Cambridge, until Margaret, while quite happy to listen, wondered if he had forgotten the reason for her being here.

Eventually, obviously buoyed by his hopes for the future success of his projects, he rolled up the plans and handing them to the surveyor's clerk dismissed them all with his usual gentle good manners.

As the door was closed behind them he

called over her shoulder.

'Edmund!'

Margaret wheeled on her fur lined slipper and Edmund who had come in unnoticed and had been standing at the window, caught the full radiance of her obvious pleasure as she saw him. Despite her youth he was struck by the charm of her delight as she extended her hand and he bowed over it.

While Henry called for some wine, he greeted Lady Welles who had been studying the young man quietly since he had come into the chamber, liking what she saw since they had met last. She admitted to herself that much married as she was he was most attractive and could well understand her daughter's admiration for him. There seemed to be a perpetual smile about his mouth which looked as if it could not harden in anger, while the cleft in his chin accentuated the strength of the jawline. She thought he would be a man difficult to rouse to opposition but one who would hold firmly to beliefs when he considered them right. She liked particularly the gentle way he spoke with Henry, striking happily the balance between deference and brotherly affection. His courtly manners were natural expressions of the long lineage of French royalty from which he came, while the strength was

110

perhaps an inheritance from the Tudor side.

Lady Welles drew Margaret near to her and nodded when the page handed her wine. The child sipped it while she watched and listened.

The King was telling them that he and his advisors had given much thought to the question of finding a new guardian for Margaret. Many men including Lord Roos, Lord Dacre and the husband of Lady Scales and others had been put forward as possible successors but none of them had possessed all the qualifications for this important task. Lady Welles could fully appreciate Henry's reluctance to sponsor anyone who might emulate the late Suffolk.

'Edmund, as you know, is my brother, and I have spoken with him on the matter of Lady Margaret's wardship and he agrees with your uncle and me that a worthy man must be found. We know well that Sir Leon has sufficient with his own family to care for.'

Lady Welles smiled her agreement. One heiress was sufficient for any man. Margaret leaning against her mother's knee, listened while she watched Edmund covertly. He was as pleasant as she had remembered and it was her turn to almost forget why she was here. It was enough to be with Edmund in the same room. She was aware that Edmund was listening gravely to the King, but did she detect a faint twinkle of amusement? She hoped he was not laughing at her because he had heard Henry talk about her academic bent and was weighing her up as a book worm. To counteract any suggestion that she was dull she flashed a brief smile to him when their eyes met.

Edmund was so intrigued by the charm of the luminous eyes and the upcurved mouth that he smiled back at her with great tenderness. So lost was she in the heart stopping moment that she almost missed the all important part of Henry's decision about her future wardship.

'So, Lady Welles, my brother has agreed, without any prompting to accept your daughter as his ward, and you can trust him to look to her interests from this day.'

Margaret's mother, who had realised a few minutes before that this was the probable outcome of the interview thanked Henry and Sir Edmund with much sincerity for the undoubted wisdom of the choice. She was frankly overjoyed that Margaret should have someone so close to the throne to be her champion and that coupled with this knowledge of future security was the undeniable affection that Margaret had for the young man.

The child found to her dismay that she was near to tears and quite unable to lift her hand, for not in her wildest dreams had she ever given consideration to Edmund being appointed to look to her estates and safety. The political side of it completely escaped her while it meant to her mother that here was a man for whom there could never be a deflection to the Yorkist faction, and who through the question of his birth could never be self-seeking. She only knew quite simply that here was a man in whom she had complete trust. Recovering her composure she curtsied.

'Thank you, Your Grace,' then coming up to Edmund she again bent her knee and looked up.

'Thank you, Sir Edmund.'

Lady Welles asked if any plans had been made for Margaret's immediate future.

'From what I can hear of it,' Edmund said, 'the Lady Margaret is doing well enough at Bletsoe.'

Margaret thought, he had heard about the studies but he went on, 'May I say, Lady Welles, that I am sure that you are the best judge of what is right for her. You understand so very much more than any of us can what she needs to know and she is fortunate to have a mother who has given her the opportunity to learn, as well as fit her for the usual accomplishment of womenfolk. With your permission I think it wiser for her to stay with you — '

'From what I can hear of it,' Henry interrupted, 'Edmund's chief task will be dissuading would-be suitors, for I know you have been plagued with many of these already, Lady Welles.'

This was news to Margaret, but it touched on a subject which she saw, as Edmund looked at her, he remembered as well as she did. They smiled again in comfortable companionship of shared events. Afterwards he recalled with some surprise, her face, and was amazed that having received languishing, desiring looks from half the bored women at Court, her childlike appeal should stir something in him which the over-painted beauties had never been able to accomplish.

Henry called for a page to escort Margaret to her rooms while he, with Edmund and her mother, called lawyers who were waiting outside to settle the legal aspect of her wardship.

Regretfully, but entirely happy, she left them and returning to her chamber through the chill passages, curled in front of the fire, thanking God for his great kindness in giving her the perfect guardian.

The day chosen for the visit to the college at Eton was fine and sunny, set like a rare jewel in the sombre pewter of autumn.

Margaret rode out early accompanied by a groom and other of the younger members of the Court. The beauty of the day exhilarated her and the pony she had been given answered readily to her well tutored hands. The groom had some difficulty in keeping up with her as they set the brisk pace.

The bare branches of the oaks stood out in sharp contrast to the pale blue of the sky and the charcoal burner fires gave off an acrid steely smoke which mingled well with the pungent smell of the rotting leaves as they slowed down on the homeward stretch. Coming to the meadows where the castle showed strong and impregnable against the skyline they fell in with some other riders, among whom was Edmund. Seeing his ward among the young people he rode over to them, and saluting her gravely took her bridle and kept beside her.

'Are you for the college today?' he asked. 'Henry forgets in his own enthusiasm that everyone might not relish climbing over heaps of stone and wading through mud to view his new buildings!'

'Yes, I am glad to be going,' she replied.

'Then you will have to put up with me, too,

115

for Henry thinks that while my ward is here I should prove to her that her interests are mine.' Glancing swiftly from under her warm hood, she saw the laughter in his eyes as he added, 'Does my ward object to my accompanying her?'

Looking away she murmured that she was happy that he could spare the time to go with them and arriving at the stables at that moment she was spared further comment as he threw himself from the back of the fine chestnut he was riding and put out his arms to help her dismount. Nestling for a brief instant against him she caught the half remembered sense of comfort that he had given when he had caught her up and removed her from the Queen's solar on the unhappy day in winter.

The sun glowed on the warm brick as later the party from the castle cantered into the quadrangle of the college at Eton. There was much activity amongst the piles of Caen stone, rubble and mortar as they entered. After a curious glance or two from the workmen, who were afraid to stop work for fear of a fine, they started on a tour of inspection. John Hampton who had bustled out of a small door as they approached came to greet the King, surrounded by a bevy of clerks. One of these he despatched to bring the master masons to present to the distinguished visitors. These men, who received three shillings a week for their labours were considered the principle part of the building force. Many of them were Italian or had been to Italy to study the methods used there and they were in constant demand for their skill in working the stone. Although the new style bricks, which were being employed in England for the first time since the Romans left, threatened their precedence a little, they were too firmly emplanted in their occupation to fear losing their hold.

Henry led them first to the inner quadrangle where was the home of the Provost, the library and the hall. He told them that the college under its full title of 'King's College of Our Lady of Eton beside Windsor' was endowed mainly from the revenues of the alien priories suppressed by his father. When he had first started the foundation almost ten years before it had consisted of a provost, ten priests, four clerks, six choristers, a schoolmaster, twenty-five poor scholars and the same number of bedesmen. He had, however, he explained, recently dispensed with the men and increased the number of boy scholars to seventy. Lately other boys, who could not be accommodated in the long dormitories which he next showed them in the outer, large quadrangle, were taking lodgings in the village of Eton and attending the lessons in the upper and lower schools. He told them that there was a connection between the college and his newly commissioned King's College at Cambridge, where he hoped the Eton boys would progress to complete their studies.

As they entered the half-completed choir of the college Henry said that this was to be the beginning of the large chapel he hoped to build. The added enthusiasm he displayed and the pleasure in his face told his listeners that it was here that the real heart of his interest lay. He was building to educate the young to be able to appreciate for themselves the wonder of God's goodness to mankind. He left them to attend to some minor detail and the surveyor took up the story. Margaret listened with interest as he told them that the bricks were baked in a kiln fired with thorns and sea coal in a yard near Slough and that the stone was brought over from Normandy in deep-hulled ships. If they ran short of the hard stone they sometimes were able to obtain supplies from a quarry at Boughton near Maidstone, in Kent. The men, who came from all over England to work on the building received fourpence a day as wages. This he hastened to explain to his audience, whom he knew were among the wealthiest landowners in the country, might not seem overmuch for a day's hard labour, but they were freemen, and beer only cost them a penny-halfpenny a gallon and four quartern loaves not much more. This was the first time that Margaret had heard of wages and the hard fact that food had to be bought, for there had always been such abundance in her own home that she had thought that all folk received it as their just due in life. She found it worried her a little that beer and bread should be all that these men could give their families and she determined to ask her mother to tell her some more about how other people lived when they had an opportunity to be alone.

Henry rejoined them and they made their farewells and remounted to ride back to the castle. Henry was obviously gratified by the favourable comments and the interest which the visit had invoked for he looked much better than when he had given them the important interview. Margaret wondered, for the first time, why the Queen had not come with them to Eton but forgot it as they clattered over the drawbridge into the courtyard. Edmund went with them into the hall and asked, if they were leaving on the morrow, he might accompany them on at least part of their journey, as he was bound for Cambridge to meet his brother Jasper on some business of the King's.

Lady Welles was delighted to accept his protection and company, for she was anxious now that the matter of Margaret's guardian had been settled, to return to Bletsoe, where much demanded her attention before the Christmas season, and his ward was equally happy to know that he would be with them.

7

Life at Bletsoe, after this all important visit to Windsor soon resumed its harmonious round and the preparations for St. Nicholas' Eve, which fell just before the feast of Christ's birth occupied the minds of all who lived there.

It was hoped, from the letters that came from Sir Leon, that he could be spared from his garrison duties and the St. Oliver boys were already at home. It was fun to have her half-brothers at home again and Margaret saw them, unknowingly, with a different eye. They had grown taller and were filling out into sturdy young men, but whereas before she had always considered they were the finest looking boys she knew, she wondered what it was that made them suddenly appear gawky and clumsy. She listened as attentively as ever to their tales of their prowess with the bow and the lance and the seemingly endless stories of the fishes they caught and the better ones that eluded them, but she found her attention wandering. As far as they were concerned sport and jousting made up their lives, although they were more than ready to tease her about her new guardian. To Oliver especially, who had found a new sophistication in his army career, the position of his half-sister as ward to a young man hardly older than himself, the subject had never ending possibilities. Not all of which he communicated to Margaret. When however, in an unguarded moment, she confided that she was pleased with the change, they would not let her forget it and dashing Welshmen were mentioned at the most embarrassing times.

They were curious too, about the new Duke of Suffolk, whom they remembered as a fair, lumbering child visiting them nearly seven years ago, and they wanted to know if any more had been heard of his late father's plan to betroth them. Margaret replied, indignantly that she knew nothing of this and added that she hoped her mother would resist any further move to unite her with this family for whom she had no special fondness.

Quickly on this thought came the swift comfort that she could trust Lady Welles, with Edmund, not to pledge her hand in a match which might prove an unhappy one for her.

John asked her, quite seriously, if she had heard any other rumours of her betrothal, for it was a subject that interested them in its endless ramifications, for although she had no idea of the importance attached to her by the Lancastrian House, they were very cognisant of the place which she held. Margaret shook her head and told them that the bailiff had reported seeing a large trout many times lately under the reeds in the bend of the Ouse close to the manor. As she knew it would, this change of subject completely took their attention away from her and they clattered out of the room in search of rods and tackle.

Settling down with a piece of embroidery in front of the large, hot fire, she admitted to herself that she had given thought at times to the question of her betrothal for although in the usual way she would not have considered it, the very fact that it interested other people, brought it to her notice. Somewhat perplexed with the whole subject she was glad when her mother came into the solar, followed by two prosperous looking men, who she recalled as the merchants who paid half yearly visits to the manor to deliver and receive Lady Welles' long lists of requirements for her larder and storeroom.

They lived in Bedford and had connection with the shippers and importers who owned the tall houses close by St. Paul's. Although the manor was largely self-supporting as far as meat, corn and fish were concerned, and game could be had for the taking, wine, sugar and spices had to be bought as well as oranges and dates. It was also usual for Lady Welles to place an order for the silk and damask that she would be requiring for the warm months of summer, when the merchants came at this time. For although all the woollen cloth for every day clothing was spun and woven at Bletsoe, finer cloths had to be obtained from London.

Margaret was fascinated by the bolts of stuffs that the men unfolded to show her mother and the heady names of exotic goods from the East that rolled off their tongues.

The feast, after a celebration of Mass attended by all the family, including her stepfather who had arrived late on the previous evening, was a sumptuous affair, garnished by the fruits and other luxuries that had been brought by the Bedford merchants. Margaret was sure that the gleaming silver and fine napery was equal to anything to be seen at Henry's Court and in the act of putting a particularly succulent piece of meat, dripping with well seasoned gravy, to her mouth she was uncomfortably reminded of the uninteresting diet which she had heard at Eton, was the fare of the labouring classes. She was somewhat relieved to know, that here, in Bletsoe at least the serving men and women and freemen of the village had enough and more to eat. Beggars, also were never turned away hungry and dole was always available for them at the gate-house. She had watched the itinerant troups, who had come to the door grasping their thin rags about them, clutch with dirty hands at the bowls that were pushed out to them and had, with childish relief, gone back into the comfort of her home and forgotten them.

She found she had lost her appetite a little and pushed the plate away from her. Although she would not have admitted it, she was also disappointed that she had received no word from Edmund on this, the first St. Nicholas' Eve since she had become his ward. She had not looked for his gift among the small pile that had been beside her place at the table, but would have welcomed a letter to say he had not forgotten her. She had been delighted with the presents from her family, who had given her a chain to hang at her waist with a small pair of silver gilt scissors attached and an illuminated book of Christmas carols. They in their turn had been happy with the gifts she had brought for them and kept concealed until this day.

She watched them all now, decked in their finest robes and was proud of the distinction of their looks. Her heart filled with affection for each one of them. She took one of the golden oranges piled high on a dish in front of her and peeled it slowly, savouring the moment.

When she went to her chamber it was very late and she was sleepy with delicious fatigue. In no time she was between the linen sheets and pulling the warm blankets around her ears, while nurse yawning hugely, took herself off to bed. She lay for a time watching the fire and the shadows it threw on the walls before she drifted off to sleep.

She was never quite sure afterwards where dreams began or consciousness returned, but she saw quite plainly in the dying embers of the fire, a fatherly figure in a cope and mitre, that she recognised easily as a bishop. Strangely, she was not at all afraid and when he spoke to her was not greatly surprised.

He told her that it had appeared to him, during this especial Feast for the Young, that she had been troubled in her mind concerning her future, so he had come, wishing to spare her further disturbance. He promised her that she would never be forced into any alliance that was not pleasing to her and that she could trust Sir Edmund completely in this matter.

'Edmund,' she spoke his name, drowsy with slumber and saw that the bishop had disappeared. Struggling in a half state of waking and sleeping she tried to recall the moment but it eluded her and she slept.

In the morning, as she dressed, the remembrance of the dream returned with startling clarity and she hugged the secret knowledge to herself. Going about the house throughout the day with a far-away expression, and not hearing a single remark that was addressed to her, Lady Welles, herself exhausted from the arrangements of the preceding day, hoped she was not to be further burdened with a case of sickness on her hands. She attributed the dreamy look to the late hour at which the dinner had finished and the richness of the dishes and made a mental note to see that simple fare was provided for her daughter's consumption.

Sitting, in the later afternoon, in a comfortable chair with her feet cushioned on a small stool, she was enjoying a well-earned rest after all the extra work she had been called upon to do. The girls and Margaret were with her, Elizabeth and Margery, talking over highlights of the feast and the relative qualities of several of the young men who had joined them from neighbouring manors. Unheeding, Margaret sat in the window embrasure gazing out, until she startled Lady Welles by coming to kneel at her feet.

'My lady,' she said quickly, and rushed on, afraid she might not be able to continue. 'Last night I had a vision.'

Now Lady Welles was really concerned, for visions were the direct consequence of high fever.

'A vision!' she echoed bringing her tired brain to deal with this new problem. 'My child, you were overtired and you probably had something to eat which disagreed with you; let me send for nurse to help you to bed. A good night's rest will soon have you better.'

'But I am not ill, my lady. I just wanted to tell you that in this dream, or vision, or whatever it was, someone — I think it might have been St. Nicholas himself — told me that I need have no fear of having to wed the Duke of Suffolk.'

'The Duke of Suffolk!' this was really quite beyond the exhausted Lady Welles, and the girls hearing mention of a wedding were eagerly coming close to catch this interesting conversation.

'I had no idea,' went on her mother, 'that you were concerned about this matter in any way.'

The girls exchanged sidelong glances for they had heard the teasing that Margaret had received from Oliver and John and wondered uneasily if they should have mentioned the matter to their mother, but they need not have worried for with complete simplicity, their half-sister was looking up at her harassed mother and saying, 'Yes, you see, St. Nicholas told me that I was to trust Edmund not to do anything that would make me unhappy.'

'Oh!' said Lady Welles on a long drawn breath and was wondering how to further answer this sometimes unpredictable child of hers, when mercifully the steward came to announce that messengers had arrived from Sir Edmund and asked that she should receive them.

Only too happy to grant this request Lady Welles directed them to be brought at once to the solar. Two young men, one of whom was Edmund's squire, entered and bowed over her hand. He told her that they should have arrived on yester eve, but had been hindered by the ford at London End which was flooded over. Turning to include Margaret he apologised for this unseen delay which meant that his master's gift to his ward was a day late in its delivery. He took from his pouch a small box, which, with her mother's permission he handed to Margaret. The child took it with fingers that trembled with excitement and she gasped as fumbling with the clasp, she looked inside.

'Isn't it lovely, Mother?' she asked as she held out the box. Her mother and half-sisters exclaimed with delight as they saw the brooch of reddish gold and rose diamonds which was fashioned in the shape of a small marguerite. Margaret was lost for words as she gently took out the jewel and pinned it to her dress.

'Oh, thank you,' she said to the young squire, 'for bringing this to me. Mother, he will not have to leave before I have had time to write to Sir Edmund, will he? He is very clever, don't you think, to have had it made for me in my own emblem?'

'Very, dearling,' agreed Lady Welles, delighted with the thoughtful gift for her daughter's sake and also for the care which she recognised Edmund had for his ward. He had certainly made her a very happy girl.

If the heiress of the Lancastrians was happy it was not the case with the fortunes of the other members of the House.

In the June of the year that had seen the murder of Suffolk, Bishop Aysgough, who had officiated at the marriage of the King and Margaret of Anjou, and had been a friend of Suffolk, was brutally dragged from his church at Edington and murdered. He was the Bishop of Salisbury, a diocese where Lollard preachers met with attentive audiences, and had served as a chaplain in the royal household. His only crime could have been that he represented a body of Churchmen against whom was a growing resentment for their wordly outlook, and one, who in daily contact with Henry had not acquainted the King with the defects of the advisors around him.

On the same day that Aysgough met his death a band of rebels marched towards London and met in a vast concourse on Blackheath. Their leader was a Kentish man named Jack Cade, who sometimes called himself Mortimer, the family name of the Duke of York. The rebellion undoubtedly had the support of the Yorkist faction who fanned the real grievances that the ordinary citizen had against the Government, into open revolt. The worrying sign for the Lancastrian party was, that whereas the Peasants' Revolt, over sixty years before, had been backed only by the serfs and the poor, this one had the support of the middle class which was emerging. It was not for nothing that sons were sent to the many new grammar schools to learn their lessons. The memory of Suffolk and his misdeeds against his tenants in the East Anglian counties was uncomfortably fresh and allowed no glossing over of misappropriations and crushing of the rights of the common man.

Blood was shed and heads adorned the parapet of London Bridge before the rising was put down and Cade was captured and killed. York, from his virtual banishment in Ireland, watched these events and decided that the time might be ripe for his return. He arrived when Lancastrian feeling was high against the instigators of the Cade rebellions and he set in motion an accusation against Margaret's Uncle Edmund, who had inherited her father's title, but not his strength of purpose.

There was undoubtedly some truth in the Yorkist claim, against the Duke of Somerset, of mismanagement in France, which resulted in the loss of the Bordeaux region, with its largely pro-English population. The cooling of the sympathy of the Gascony peoples was coupled with serious damage to the very cordial relations with Bordeaux in the wine trade, which further antagonised the merchants in England who dealt in this commodity.

Faster than ever before there was growing up round the Duke of York and his son, the Earl of March, a group of dissenters who were no longer satisfied with grumbling behind closed doors but were longing for action. The Commons were ready to throw in their support with York and among other grievances, they contended that the Lancastrians were not the lawful holders of the throne as they had seized it from Richard II and that Richard of York's claim, was a good, if not better than Henry's. It was feared among York's followers that as the Queen had still not produced an heir, it was not impossible that Somerset would work upon the gentle King to name him his successor. Once again it was apparent to thoughtful Lancastrians that the late Duke of Suffolk had very seriously undermined the power and security of the throne.

Lady Welles could only be extremely thankful that Margaret was no longer under his jurisdiction.

The situation in France worsened but the threat which York implied with his return to England was sufficient for the Government to recall Somerset as it was felt that the monarchy was directly challenged. When York was granted an interview with the King in September he protested his loyalty, although demanding that certain reforms should be made in his name. None of the nobles of the realm, least of all those with Lancastrian sympathies believed this hypocritical avowal.

The Lancastrian cause was at a low ebb when in the December, York, gaining the control of the House of Commons with a surer grip by backing the Speaker, was able to have the Duke of Somerset committed to the Tower on several counts of mismanagement of public tax money for use in the Royal Household.

This proved a setback of only small duration for Somerset was soon released. The tension did not in any way relax, however, and the country watched to see how the struggle for power would develop.

York returned to Ludlow and waited for what he considered was the appropriate moment to strike with force. Promises had been made with the reinstatement of Somerset but they were only half fulfilled and no real attention was given to the growing chorus of dissention. On the advice and with the support of the Earl of Devonshire and Lord Cobham, York in the January of 1452 began a march on London.

Henry, galvanised into action by the Queen moved a large force towards the north-west to meet him, but when he reached Coventry it was to discover that York had been notified of his approach and had wheeled his forces into taking another way. The King's company, numbering Edmund and his brother Jasper among them, hastened back towards London and, having the right to march through the city encamped themselves on the Blackheath.

York not being so fortunate took his men over the Thames at Kingston Bridge.

Everything pointed to a settlement by a show of arms but Salisbury and Warwick, with the support of the Bishops of Ely and Winchester intervened and the Duke of York, with the banner of the White Rose, held over him, advanced to the Royal Tent and on being given permission to enter, threw himself prostrate at Henry's feet.

All present waited with bated breath for York had blatantly committed an act against the King. Henry however, never able to be vindictive forgave him on the understanding that he would make a public avowal of allegiance to him in St. Paul's.

Undoubtedly York would have been further punished had it not come to Henry's notice that York's son, the young Edward, Earl of March, was coming to his father's aid with a company of eleven thousand men. Though not promising York anything further about the Succession Henry assured him of a position on the Council.

Later in the year, Henry, with the childlike trust that he showed all his life, forgave the Duke sufficiently to become his guest, having previously given amnesty to all the offenders in a general pardon on April 7th, and stayed with him at his castle at Ludlow.

If Henry was prepared to forgive and forget, it was not so with the other Lancastrian leaders, particularly Somerset, with whom his short term of imprisonment still rankled. They saw to it that York was not summoned to the Council until 1453 when the situation at home and abroad had deteriorated in a disastrous manner. York lost no time in filling London with armed men and issuing circulars with pointed accusations against Somerset and his administration, especially in France.

Henry, distraught with the worry of these fractious men, leaned heavily on the Queen and his half-brothers, who repaid him with their constant and loyal support. He in his turn loaded them with honours and riches. Margaret of Anjou received permanent endowment of lands which had been assigned to her as her dower but from which she had not so far benefitted and Edmund and Jasper were declared of legitimate birth and were summoned as the Earls of Richmond and Pembroke, respectively. Edmund was now the premier Earl of England and he and his brother bore the royal arms of France and England, differenced with blue borders and the royal martletts of the Confessor's shield.

Lady Welles received this news with quiet

satisfaction, more relieved than she knew that the slight doubt of Edmund's birth had been cleared away. Margaret was happy that her guardian had been honoured by his brother. Edmund had fulfilled his commitments to the Bletsoe household in full measure. He had sent well-trained men from his own retainers to implement the men-at-arms at the manor to guard the life and property of his ward: and had given strict instructions that Margaret was not to make journeys without his knowledge and then only under a heavy guard. He had come to the manor as often as his duties with the King allowed and showed a real and sincere interest in the welfare of Lady Welles' daughter. In every way the King's choice had been an excellent one and however troublous the times became the Bletsoe household trusted Edmund to protect them.

The situation in France reached a climax when Charles VII opened a campaign against the English in the spring of the same year, bringing to bear on the forces from England three separate attacks from all directions. All the skill that the veteran campaigner, Lord Talbot, employed as counter measures were useless and the French were victorious. Added to this loss were the untimely deaths of Lord Talbot and his son, Lord de Lisle in the fighting which left the English completely demoralised.

In the summer Henry sickened by the misery to which his realm had been brought, went suddenly and completely out of his mind.

The Queen, with her supporters, tried to keep this last death-dealing blow within the confines of the Court but it was not long before the secret was out, adding fresh power to the Yorkist cause. An insane King was a poor figurehead for a country which had attained such illustrious heights under the kingship of his late father, and his rivals lost no time in pushing this point home.

Margaret of Anjou made every effort to break through to her husband, but it was a hopeless task. It seemed as if the gentle Henry, unable to support any longer the tension which was thrust upon him by his quarrelsome lords, slipped quietly away beyond their reach to some dream state where it could trouble him no more.

It was especially hard for the Queen to bear as she had found that after more than eight years of marriage she had at last become pregnant. With this knowledge she strove to establish herself, with her characteristic energy, as Protector of the Realm. The negotiations were long and protracted and before anything was settled she had borne a son, who arriving on October 13th, St. Edward's Day, was named after the saint.

Despite this, carried on by growing support in the Commons, York was declared Protector instead of the Queen, and his first act was to commit Somerset to the Tower where he was to remain, without trial, for a year. Margaret of Anjou took refuge at Greenwich, away from a London which became increasingly hostile and looked helplessly into the black future, which contained little for the wife of a helpless lunatic who was without the support of her strongest ally. It was impossible for her to take any real pleasure in her child, who grew into lusty infancy while his father took no more notice of him than of anyone else who tried to rouse his interest.

The new Earl of Richmond was considering moving his ward to the safety of his brother's castle at Pembroke in the remoteness of Wales, when as suddenly as he had sickened Henry recovered.

He shook off his madness as if it had been a long, refreshing sleep and demanded to know what had been happening while he had lost consciousness. His baby son filled him with delighted wonder and he liked nothing better than to dangle him on his knee and watch his childish progress. The King sent messengers to Canterbury with a large offering in gratitude for his recovery and the great blessing of the long awaited heir. It was now his fervent hope that the child's coming would put an end to the constant warring of his nobles.

He returned to sanity with more strength of purpose that he had hitherto shown. He released Somerset and relieved York of the Protectorship, while relieving Salisbury, York's brother-in-law from the Chancellorship and giving it to Archbishop Bourchier. The Queen, accepting Henry's recovery with unfeigned delight, set about strengthening their position, for it could be that her husband might succumb to a further attack. She sought about to obtain all the help she could receive from sympathetic landowners and rejoiced in the reversal of their fortunes. The House of Lancaster took new heart.

8

Margaret woke one morning in the spring of
1455 and stretched luxuriously in her bed.
She was not going this morning to the priest
for her daily lessons for it was a Saint's day
and her mother had suggested a rest for her.
She had been studying with great concentration and although Lady Welles was as devout
a believer in education as ever she drew limits
when too great a strain was being placed on
the student.

Margaret had matured with poignant
beauty and although not very tall carried
herself with grace. Her breasts were full and
rounded and her hair glimmered with
unexpected lights and the expressive quality
of her eyes had deepened. The young men
who came to the manor were captivated by
her good looks and unaffected charm.
Although she was attentive and well man-
nered to everyone the admiration she received
seemed to go unnoticed. It was almost as if
she held herself in check, keeping herself in
reserve.

The spring, and the trembling new life had
caused a restlessness in her which she had not

thought possible. She controlled the longings which assailed her with an adult will, which resulted in extra hard work and long hours spent on her knees in the chapel. Sometimes when alone she was overcome by storms of weeping which she was at a loss to understand, for she had never been a melancholy child.

In some inexplicable way she found it was when she thought of Edmund that she was most troubled. She had not seen him now for almost a year, although he wrote and sent his emissaries to her with regular details of the accounts of her demesnes and their revenues and he had not forgotten her Saint's days. He was, at the present, as he had been since the summer of last year, with Jasper in the west of Wales consolidating the Lancastrian interests there with the Duke of Buckingham who also owned vast estates in Brecknock and Newport. Much of their effort was spent in securing the support of the Herbert family, who, possessing great power in Wales, were wooed by Yorkists with equal fervour. In his last letter he had told her that it was believed that the Duke of York had gone north to muster another force in readiness to withstand Somerset, who had returned to the Queen's side with more determination than ever to finish him. For this reason it was vital that he and Jasper rallied every wavering supporter.

When he had last come to Bletsoe Margaret had been dismayed to discover that she had lost the friendly ease with which she had been used to talk with him and had developed a tongue-tied shyness. She had been extremely conscious of her hands and the tightness of her dress over her chest and for the first time had been glad when he had left the house. It was after this day almost twelve months ago that she had developed these fits of the miseries which she had confided to nobody. They had, however, not gone unnoticed by her mother, who wisely did not mention them, but provided extra interests to keep her occupied. Once or twice she had gone with her mother's bailiff, when the situation had seemed easier, to visit a small estate of her own at Collyweston near Corby. The manor was about two days journey and she had been accompanied by some of Edmund's retainers. She had enjoyed the change of sharp hills which were a contrast to the garden-like surroundings of her mother's manor, and expressed a lively interest in the working of the slate quarries which made with some small blast furnaces the source of the estate's wealth. The steward at Collyweston was pleased to have her

143

interest and confided to his wife after her first visit that it was unusual to find a young woman who so readily picked up the talk of best markets for good quality slate as if she had been born to it and coupled it with being exceptionally good to look at. He was surprised to discover too, that she asked endless questions about the welfare of the men who worked the quarries, and that when she had returned home he had been instructed through her guardian, the Earl of Richmond, to increase the daily earnings of the workers by half.

Now, on this lovely spring morning she rose and dressed unhurriedly, choosing a sapphire-blue riding habit edged with fur. She broke her fast with a mug of milk from the dairy and a piece of white bread spread with butter and honey and then went down to the stables and had a groom saddle her mare. The man was glad to be asked to accompany her for she was fearless on horseback and had not been out much recently.

As they trotted out into the fields the sharp clear brightness of the day caught at her throat. The hedgerows were green with new shoots and white thorn filled the trees with garlands of fresh blooms. White clouds moved swiftly in the sky and birds, busy in the rearing of their young, swooped on pieces of straw and twigs. She breathed deeply of the sweet air, filling her lungs with its goodness, and thought as she had many times before that if man spared the time to look at the loveliness of the world around him and took some of it into his make-up he would have less time to think of petty grievances and half the troubles of the present world would be averted.

They took the field gate which led out into the lane in the direction of Kimbolton and coming out into an open heath gave the horses their head. The brisk wind freed her hair from the cap on her head and she snatched it off and struck it into the saddle bag. She felt emptied of thoughts as her mind was absorbed in the task of guiding the horses as they gathered speed. They rode for almost two hours exhilarating in the exercise. At last, reluctantly, she turned for home. The groom came up with her and as she turned to smile at him he thought she had never looked lovelier and that despite her reputed bookish ways she would be an enticing woman. Close by the stream, where the wood gentled down to the water's edge she saw a patch of early kingcups bright in the trees' shadow. She dismounted and gathered an armful for her mother and then continued at a more leisurely pace to the manor, in no hurry to leave the freshness of the outside. She slid from the mare's back and stood watching the boy summoned by the groom to rub her down, then gathering the flowers walked slowly inside.

Suddenly she was anxious to find her mother and tell of the pleasure of the ride and humming under her breath ran the last few steps into the hall, bursting into the dark chamber.

Edmund, standing in the hall with Lady Welles, saw her all woman for the first time in that moment, as with eyes shining and cheeks whipped to rose, she pushed the kingcups into her mother's outstretched hands.

'Margaret,' Edmund said gently.

She stood quite still, shocked into immobility at the sound of the well remembered, well loved voice. Well loved! Yes, that was it. Her heart pounded, stopped, raced on again, while her hands flew to her cheeks. Recovering her composure she bent her knee in a deep curtsy, fighting to control the great joy that was welling up in her. Edmund! He was here and she had not known.

He stepped towards her and lifted her to her feet. She stood near to him, and with great effort raised her eyes to his face. He was smiling down at her with a look that she had not seen before and she smiled back, her beautiful eyes tender with affection. She was lost, oblivious of her mother, drowning in the timeless wonder as he put her hand to his lips. As she felt the hard warmth of his mouth she turned her hand and caressed his cheek. From then on for the rest of her life she loved him with an unwavering devotion and her heart became his alone.

The day passed in a whirl for her. It was almost as if the coming of Edmund had released a dam and set in flood a kind of living that she had not known existed. Before his arrival the day had been lovely, now it was remarkable in that the sun had never shone so brightly or the house looked so welcoming and well cared for. The furniture seemed polished with a lustrous patina and the hangings glowed in richness of colour and design. It was not as if she even consciously noticed this change for she was drawn to watch and listen to Edmund as if within her was some metal to which he alone possessed the magnet.

He too, was deeply affected by this new facet of the ward he had not seen for so long. He had been moved by the charming gesture she had made in touching his face. He gave her his undivided attention, drawn by the fresh loveliness of her beauty and some other attraction which he was at a loss to define. It

147

was sufficient to be near her, to hear her speak and to watch her play the youthful hostess to himself and the retinue he had brought. If he had had time to notice he would have seen that his young squires followed her around like a couple of puppies, vying with each other for the privilege of retrieving a lost kerchief or opening a door. She thanked them sweetly but was unaware of their admiration. She only knew that she and Edmund were in the same house and there had never been any emotion she had experienced to match the awareness that each had of the other.

Later in the day the family sat together in the solar. Lord Welles, about to go to the Calais garrison, was talking earnestly with Edmund, whom he had kept by his side since they had come up from the hall. He was particularly concerned to discover if Edmund thought that the situation was more stable now that Henry had recovered his sanity and whether the campaign which Jasper and he had been conducting in Wales to consolidate the support of the Nevilles and the Herberts had been successful.

Edmund was able to say that at least all the Lancastrian supporters in Wales were on their guard while Jasper and he had been rousing them with the knowledge that the Yorkists were fortifying their estates from Builth to Denbigh. Edmund said that he was fortunate in being in a position to call in at the Bletsoe household, breaking the journey to Windsor where Henry had summoned him to escort him and his Queen to Leicester where the next Council was to take place in early June. He understood that the Duke of York would be present at this meeting and that it was hoped that complete accord would be reached.

While he answered Lord Welles with the attention that the older man commanded Edmund hoped that he appeared intelligent and well-informed for Margaret was sitting on cushions in front of the apple wood fire which burnt brightly in the hearth. She had on a dress of azure velvet, cut wide from the shoulder to waist and filled at the low bosom with white samite powdered with silver stars matching the broad band at the hem. She was playing quietly on the lute, while her sisters sang; the words, which he tried to catch, came he thought, from a poem of Geoffrey Chaucer's. While courteously listening to Lord Welles he gave a brief thought to the odd quirk which had made Chaucer a relation by marriage of the Lady Margaret. This man, who was unsurpassed for the beauty of his writing had been married to

Phillipa who was sister to Katherine, wife of John of Gaunt and great grandmother of she who played the plaintive melody.

Lord Welles asked Edmund guardedly about the Queen, and the young man dragged his mind away from the girl who sat by the fire and told him that since Henry's recovery Margaret of Anjou had been fired with new enthusiasm for their cause. Now that she was able to share the delight of a son and heir with her husband it seemed as if she had been compensated in some measure for the overwhelming loss she had suffered at Suffolk's death and had regained some of the zestful good looks that she had had so abundantly while he had been there to guide and comfort her.

Lord Welles, listening, looked up and caught his guest off guard, as for a moment he turned his eyes towards the group at the fire. Inwardly somewhat amused, he thanked Edmund for satisfying his curiosity and sought his wife and her ladies.

Edmund's squires rose as they saw their lord alone, but he signalled to them to continue their game of chess and went to join Margaret. She went on playing, betraying only by a swift lowering of the eyes that she knew he was there. When she came to the end of the song she put down the lute and her sisters went to stand over the young men at their board.

A little shyly, but not conscious, as she had been when she had last met Edmund nearly a year past, of moist hands or inarticulate speech, she asked him too of the hopes for a real peace. It had suddenly become tremendously important to her that there should be no open warfare.

Edmund reassured her as far as he could, stressing what she already knew well, that Henry desired nothing more than to live at peace. When she asked him if the support that York was whipping up in the country was a universal feeling of hatred or discontent for the Government he replied that he and Jasper had gained the impression that the ordinary freemen were indifferent to whosoever sat on the throne as long as the crops ripened and the price of corn stayed the same from one month to the other. Abundant catches of herrings to salt were far more important to the man with a family to feed than the rights and wrongs of two factions who were the country's greatest landowners. It was the growing band of the half-educated who were the malcontents, and it was to these that York was appealing.

'So you enjoyed your visit to Collyweston?' he asked her. 'I was happy to receive your

151

message that you considered that the men working the quarries should receive a better wage. How did you arrive at that decision?'

'Do you remember the day we went with Henry to the college at Eton?' she said.

'Why, yes, of course I do.'

'The surveyor told us then of the small amount that the men earned each day and I could not forget that I had so very much more than they. Our pigs were better fed.'

He told her then that he and his brother made special provisions for the servants and underlings on their estates. Plague and the sweating sickness were all too prevalent and the misery that came in their train to the sufferer and his dependants was painful to see. Jasper and he considered that it was unfortunate that these humanitarian ideals were not shared by more of the nobles of the realm. It was much more common for the wealthy to misuse those who owed them fealty.

Margaret listened to him voicing her own unspoken thoughts fascinated that his outlook was broader than even her own mother's sense of responsibility. She was glad that she had had the opportunity of Lady Welles' wise guidance and the teaching of learned men to impress upon her the need to realise that the common man had feelings which were as fine as those of more gentle birth. She felt that even if she were years behind Edmund in experience she could at least appreciate and comprehend the depth of his new approach to those under his charge.

They talked on quietly together, discovering in each other the pleasure of a ready and complete understanding. He had heard much of her scholarship and before this visit had privately considered that she had probably grown bookish and something of a prig.

This he had at once discovered was very far from the truth. Indeed she was educated far beyond any young woman he had met and spoke an excellent French, although she confessed that she found Latin more difficult. She used her knowledge to give her a reasoning at once human and lively and he was as fascinated with her unusual wisdom and wit, when it flashed out, as he was with the tender droop of her head as she half-turned from him to gaze into the fire. He watched entranced as the warm light played on the creamy skin of her neck and shoulders.

Margaret, looking at the browned, beautifully shaped hand which lay on his knee beside her, longed to cover it with her own and found his proximity immensely disturbing.

Lady Welles called the women to her and

Edmund sprang to his feet and helped Margaret to hers. Stooping swiftly he kissed her on the brow and emboldened by the gesture she looked at him and they smiled.

'Until tomorrow,' he said softly.

She joined the other ladies and went out of the door with them, speaking to no one.

Margaret found each day of his visit more wonderful than the last. Her beauty unfolded as petals of a rose in the sun and the reserve she had previously shown disappeared.

The Bletsoe household took to Edmund instantly and he was made most welcome. The charm he possessed and the indefinable quality which set him apart from most of the men of high rank of the day, endeared him to them all. Lady Welles had arranged a feast for the last evening of his stay and messengers had been sent to neighbours and friends inviting them to attend. Word had also been sent to Windsor to Jasper, who had gone straight there when Edmund came to Bletsoe.

On one morning of Edmund's stay a party from the manor set out on an expedition to the cell of an aged hermit who lived in the hamlet of Riseley. He was reputed to possess the gift of second sight as well as the cure for simple ailments such as warts and chapped skin. It was believed among the young folk that he had been known to concoct a potion

154

for the relief of lovesickness and many a married woman had reason to thank him for his skill with herbs.

It was almost as if the weather shared Margaret's new enchantment. The spring winds were warm and the trees were bright with the resurgent leaves. Margaret was gay as Edmund rode beside her down the lane to North End. The fields bordering the road were thick with the spears of new wheat pushing through the heavy earth. In the quiet of Galsey Wood primroses nestled in the dried leaves of autumn and wood anemones swayed in the breeze. It was a day of promise.

In the village of Riseley they passed the church of All Saints which was surrounded with wooden scaffolding and they heard the noise of busy hammering of workmen engaged in rebuilding and extending the chancel. Over the porch Margaret showed Edmund the stone figure of a pelican in her piety which they recognised as the emblem of the Blessed Sacrament. The main thorough-fare of the village was long and straggling and as they passed children came from the low cottages to watch.

The hermit's dwelling was set into an overhanging bank which had once been part of some ancient earthwork. A groom went to the entrance and a bent figure looked out of

155

the darkness and asked them their business. His voice was frail but cultured. Margaret's half-sister, Margery, replied that they had a guest, who having heard much of his skill and wisdom, was desirous of making his acquaintance. At this the brown-cowled head came up and Margaret watched as the piercing, deep set eyes went straight to Edmund.

The acolyte's face was pale and the skin tightly drawn over the high cheek bones. His mouth was thin but curved slightly at the corners to counteract any impression of harshness. Without speaking his gaze travelled from Edmund to Margaret and then returned to Edmund. The girl, for no reason, shivered, and she glanced to see if a cloud had covered the sun. It shone as brightly as ever and she was suddenly horribly frightened. For a full minute the old man held them with his searching eyes as they stood as if mesmerised. Making the sign of the cross, he turned from them and walked quickly inside his shelter.

Bewildered and embarrassed the party broke into excited chatter to cover the awkward moment. Edmund, seeing Margaret's wide-eyed look of perplexity caught at her bridle.

'Come,' he said cheerfully, 'I'll race you back to the wood.'

The mare whinnied as she dug the spurs

lightly into her side. As they gathered speed the unexplained melancholy lifted, although it did not go completely, and she could not regain the light-hearted gaiety she had when they set out.

When they came to the wood Edmund slowed his horse and turned to wait for her.

'Show me the church of your home,' he asked her and they continued at a more leisurely pace past the house and on to the lane which led to the Bedford road. Arriving at the path to the north door he dismounted, helping her down, then tethered the horses to a branch of a young chestnut tree.

As he joined her almost at the church door he saw to his dismay that she was weeping quietly. He knew that she was thinking about the incident at the hermit's cell at Riseley and he hated that she should be upset over a trivial incident. He put his arm round her shoulders and drew her head to rest on his breast. Now she cried in earnest.

'Don't cry, sweetheart,' he said gently. 'Come with me into the church, for I have something I want to tell you.'

Inside the stone chapel it was cool and dark and it took Margaret a moment to get used to gloom after the brilliant bright of the day outside. They dipped their fingers in the stoup of holy water by the door and still with his arm about her shoulder went to kneel at the steps where the nave met the chancel at a slight angle to symbolise the droop of Christ's head upon the cross.

Edmund took away his shielding arm and they prayed silently until he turned towards her and took her hand into his.

'Margaret, look at me.'

The eyes she raised to his were still full of tears and the generous mouth quivered. He took a strand of her hair from under the velvet cap and wound it round the fourth finger of her left hand. Margaret looked down, startled, at the ring it formed. Her heart thumped and the melancholy vanished.

'Little Margaret, will you be my wife?'

'Edmund,' she whispered 'Oh, Edmund, thank you.'

It seemed as if all her life had been leading up to this moment as he took the hand with the ring of her hair and held it to his mouth. Although she was amazed that this should happen she knew that it was what she had always hoped, ever since that long ago day when she had seen the vision of St. Nicholas. In the few days that he had been at Bletsoe all the childish hero-worship of her guardian had matured into deep love for Edmund. His every word or gesture was sufficient to melt her heart and each time their eyes met she

158

was pierced with unknown longings. It was as if she had always been part of him and he had been ordained as her protector.

Unwinding the tress from her finger they went out of the chapel and walked down to the manor. They did not speak a great deal but she asked him shyly what her mother had said to him when he had told her the purpose of his visit, for she knew that he would have spoken with Lady Welles about so important a subject before mentioning it to her.

'Your mother very gladly gave her consent, I am happy to tell you. She seemed to see no objection to your guardian becoming your husband also!'

'Let's go and tell them,' she said, all the early morning's happiness returned as she picked up her skirts and ran towards the house.

'Edmund I'm so happy I am sure I shall wake up and find it is a dream.' She stood on the steps leading into the manor and waited for him with hands outstretched. He took them in his own, smiling at her youthful exuberance which was in complete contrast to the downcast look she had had such a short time before.

The family were awaiting them in the solar. Lady Welles had been secretly a little anxious since the others had arrived back and told her of the odd happening at the cell. She was relieved to see the radiant Margaret as she came in with Edmund.

Going to meet them she said, 'So Edmund has told you why he is come, dearling?'

'Yes, oh yes,' Margaret replied. 'Isn't it the most wonderful thing?' then blushed as the others laughed a little and crowded round them to kiss them and wish them well.

'So now you know that the feast is to be for your betrothal and the secret is out,' said her mother. 'I had a hard task not to tell the others, I can promise you.'

From this time Margaret's life revolved round Edmund. She grudged every hour that she could not be with him and went reluctantly to bed at night. She tried not to think of the separation that was so unhappily near and was plagued with nightmares about the hooded hermit. Once she awoke sweating and in such fear that she almost called out to Betsey Massey, who had been her own serving maid since nurse had retired to comfortable gossiping, and slept in a small chamber beside her own, to come to her with a light. She decided against disturbing the girl and wrestled with her anxiety alone. She found to her dismay that she was shivering violently and that her mind was filled with forebodings. She prayed with all the reserve of strength that she could muster and after a while her limbs relaxed and she became calmer. She recalled the vision of St. Nicholas that she had seen in this very room and was comforted by the remembrance that he had foretold that she should marry Edmund. Marriage with him was her ultimate joy, and hugging this knowledge to herself she slept.

The manor was seething with preparations for the betrothal feast of its lady's daughter with the King's half-brother. Men and women bustled from one place to another on seemingly endless errands while vast quantities of food were brought from the store rooms and made ready in the kitchens. Messengers had been despatched to the Beaufort fisheries at Ware to bring trout and salmon. The cottagers brought supplies of eggs and cream from their cows, for Margaret was popular with them all and Edmund had won their hearts with his good looks and ready smile. The Bletsoe household was determined to show that it was fully competent to honour such an occasion.

On the evening of the banquet Margaret was standing in her room while Betsey helped her into the dress of blue-green tissue that she was to wear. At any other time she would have been eager to talk but she could only think of Edmund and the morrow when he

161

would have to leave her.

Smoothing the dress she sat down at the table which was littered with small pots of unguents and sweet smelling salves while Betsey brushed her hair and set the small diadem of aquamarines on her head. The girl, apparently not noticing her young mistress' lack of conversation, worked quietly and efficiently. She handed Margaret the silver backed mirror and looking in it Margaret caught the affectionate regard on Betsey's face.

'Thank you, Betsey,' she said. 'It is kind of you to take so much trouble for me when I sit here without a word. Tomorrow we shall be able to gossip about it all. Do you think that when I go to a home of my own that you would like to come with me?'

'Nothing shall stand in my way, my lady.'

'Nothing!' Margaret echoed. 'Supposing that Richard Stukely wants you to wed him before then?'

'Then he'll have to come along as well or find another wife,' the girl asserted stolidly. 'For as far as I'm concerned there's more kindness and pleasure in being with you than anything else in the wide world.'

Margaret thanked her and was amazed that the girl could so lightly dismiss Richard's claim. She knew well enough that where

Edmund went she would follow, whatever the sacrifice.

At the door she took Betsey's hand and squeezed it impulsively. 'I hope you enjoy the feast, I'll watch for you. My mother tells me that the jugglers and their troupe are newly come from Italy and promise us some surprises.'

Turning the last spiral of the staircase she found Edmund awaiting her. Her heart gave its customary lurch at the sight of him standing there looking at her with tenderness mingled with pride. He took her hands and kissed them each in turn.

'You look so beautiful,' he told her. 'Like a mermaiden breaking out of the sea. It is fortunate for us both that you have no secret palace below the waves, for if you charmed me thither at this moment I must admit that I should be hopelessly lost and drowned for ever.'

'It is a pity,' she sighed, 'that we cannot slip away and spend this last evening quietly,' and was startled at her forwardness in making the suggestion.

To her relief he agreed with her and comforted her with the knowledge that they would not be apart during the evening and that the Council at Leicester would not last too long and he would be back at Bletsoe to

163

discuss the final date and arrangements for their marriage which was planned, for the autumn before Advent.

'Jasper has arrived,' Edmund told her, 'and is as anxious to meet you as I am to show you off. Did you speak with him when you were at Court?'

'No,' Margaret said. 'But I do remember that he was with you, walking in the cloisters, on the first day I saw you when nurse was taking me to my lessons with the monk at Westminster.'

'Yes, I believe he was,' Edmund answered. 'I remember the grave-faced little girl holding grimly to nurse's hand and giving me a shy smile as we passed.'

Margaret thought he had never looked so well as he did now as they smiled at each other again, recalling that long ago day. He was wearing a dull topaz coloured doublet with a simple gold chain at his slim waist and it suited his graceful manliness to perfection. Something new stirred her and swept her in an uprush of longing to be possessed by his strength. Gone for the moment were all the tender feelings of affection, gratitude and admiration, and she was completely swamped by the desire to be held in his arms and know that he was experiencing the same emotion. The suddeness and the unexpectedness of the passionate longing caught her unawares and she swayed a little and turned pale.

'Margaret!' Edmund cried. 'What is it?'

Pulling herself together with an effort she replied that it was nothing, perhaps the excitement, and that it would be a good idea to join the others. He took her hand, full of concern for her and they entered the hall through the intricately carved screens and were engulfed in a host of friends waiting to escort them.

Jasper, when Edmund brought him to her side, she found was stockier and shorter than his brother. He had not Edmund's dark beauty but was more rugged and solid, his face, weather beaten and lined showing character and determination. She knew that he had already acquired a reputation for leadership and was admired by the men he commanded. Bringing all her concentration to bear on him, she recognised his air of authority and sensed that here was someone who could be trusted and relied upon.

Jasper, in his turn, was enchanted by the unspoilt loveliness of the girl who was to become his brother's wife. He admired the choice of her gown which set off the perfection of her rounded breast and the colour of her eyes. Experienced as he was with all manner of women he privately

165

congratulated his brother on his extreme good fortune in betrothing such a girl. He had heard, as had Edmund, that she was an accomplished scholar and had pitied Edmund that he should be tied to a retiring miss who would rather be reading than enjoying the art of making love. As soon as he had seen her and watched her marvellously expressive eyes as they followed his brother moving from group to group, he found he envied rather than sympathised with him. He was drawn to the future Countess of Richmond in a way that was new to him and was happy to find that when they were seated at the board she was sitting between Edmund and himself.

A small band of musicians with gitterns and shawns played from the gallery as the elaborate feast began. The hall was filled to overcrowding with long tables set side by side and the company was gay and clad in their finest attire. The women made covert glances to assure themselves that their head-dresses were quite unique and that no offending sempstress had fashioned two alike. As the supper progressed and the wine was poured freely the elaborate structures of brocade and gauze became something of a burden and difficult to manage so that their wearers would not have cared if all were alike and had been left at home.

Despite this they and their menfolk made huge inroads into the plentiful food. Course followed course, with exotic sauces for fish and meat. The cooks in the cavernous kitchens had not sweated for more than two days in vain. In the centre of the family table stood a marvellous confection of marchpane and sugar made as the Manor of Bletsoe, complete with drawbridge and moat. This Margaret recognised as the handiwork of the man who had made sugar comfits for her when she was small and she called him to her to thank him for going to such lengths to please her. Lady Welles, while conversing with those about her, kept a watch that all went smoothly, for she did not want her guests to go away hungry or without enjoyment.

The company from Italy lived up to their reputation for surprise and produced quantities of white doves from their voluminous cloaks. The birds flew in swooping circles around the hall and returned to their owners where they disappeared as mysteriously as they had come. Tumblers and jugglers followed and delighted the company with a tall pyramid of three strong men at the base, whose arms and leg muscles bulged with strain as they hoisted two more lads on to their shoulders and threw up after them a boy of about nine or so. Women gasped as in one movement the pyramid collapsed and all six were standing in a straight line before them.

Margaret talked with Edmund and Jasper as if they were old friends. Jasper soon knew that besides her comeliness Margaret was wise and understanding. Margaret found that she had not lost the new sensation that Edmund had awakened in her and trembled if their hands met. She was glad when the lute player who followed the jugglers came to her side and began singing her a verse. She had watched him make a round of the comeliest women and sing appropriate snatches to them. Their blushes and lowered eyes betrayed their appreciation of his flattery, and there was much ogling to entice him into a song.

He bowed to her and struck the lute into a plaintive air while he sang so softly that she could only just hear him, an old love song.

'And therefore cometh all goodness,
All honour and all gentleness,
Worship, ease and allhearts lust,
Perfect joy and full assured trust,
Jollity, pleasure and freshness,
Lowliness, largess and courtesy,
Seemliness and true company,

Dread of shame for naught amiss
For he that truly love's servant is
Were lother be shame than to die'

The last chords died away and the lute player bowed over her oustretched hands. The sentiments of the song echoed completely the depth of her feeling for Edmund and she was lost in a dreamy haze of love-longing when she heard Jasper say to Edmund.

'It is not everyday that a King chooses a bride for his brother and he is as fortunate as you are!'

The room went suddenly still for Margaret and she was jolted out of her day dreams as if a bucket of icy water had been thrown over her. The King! — Henry had told Edmund to come to Bletsoe to ask for her hand, and so it was not his own wish at all, but that of his half-brother, who had to be obeyed in all things. Edmund owed him obedience as much for his great kindness as his sovereignty and would not hesitate to do as he wished and come to Bletsoe and ask her to marry him. She who, in her innocence had believed that this was a loving of Edmund and Margaret, saw all at once in the quietly spoken words between the brothers that this was a state affair, a strengthening of the bonds between her house and his.

She was so shocked that she hardly heard when her step-father called the steward to bring the loving cup. The company stood as the silver vessel, heavily chased and studded with precious stones, was brought to him.

Lord Welles came to her side and with a warm smile drank from the cup and passed it to her. With fingers grown numbed and clumsy she took it and putting her lips to the rim, forced herself to swallow a little. Without raising her eyes she faced Edmund as Lord Welles turned his back to protect her from an imaginary assailant. She took the napkin of fine lawn proffered by a page, wiped the lip and thrust the cup towards Edmund. Tears of misery stung her eyes but she opened them wide and held them back as she turned while Edmund drank. She was glad that the ceremony only entailed the immediate family for she longed to escape from the merry atmosphere which had suddenly become a mockery to her. With great relief she saw that the cup was being removed from the end of the table and that her stepfather considered this to be the appropriate time for the giving of the betrothal ring. Her control was complete, and none of the guests craning eagerly to watch guessed that her world of delirious happiness had collapsed around her a short minute before, as she proffered her cheek for Edmund's kiss while he pushed the heavy gold band on to her finger. She refused to meet his look and chattered feverishly with all those who crowded round them. At last, murmuring some excuse, she left the hall.

Once outside she rushed to her chamber, unable to see in the dim light of the stairway, as the tears welled over. Catching the beautiful robe in her hands she rushed into her room crashing the door behind her while grief overwhelmed her. She threw herself on her bed and was torn with anguished sobs. Coupled with the enormous sense of loss was the deep shame that she felt when she remembered the passionate longing that Edmund had engendered in her. She, the heiress of the Beauforts, as eager to be tumbled as a dairymaid at Maying! What was worse it was not as if Edmund had deliberately aroused those passionate emotions. She rolled over on to her side and banged her clenched first into the down coverlet with mortification. She was almost hysterical in her grief when the small, quiet voice of her rational self whispered that after all, it was usual for husbands to be chosen for girls and she was most blessed in that she had always wanted to marry Edmund. Now with her wish granted she was crying for the moon and demanding that as well as wedding her, he loved her. At this, the tears which had stopped, threatened to fall again, but she reasoned with herself that as the heiress of the Beauforts, it was extremely unlikely that she would have been given a free choice of husband and how much worse it could all have been. The thought of the Duke of Suffolk came crowding back and abruptly the misery left her. She was assailed at the same time with doubts about her own behaviour, which suddenly struck her as being highly questionable. She realised that her mother would be chagrined at her lack of manners if it were realised that she had stormed out of the gathering in a fit of pique. She hurried to the garde-robe and poured water into a basin from the ewer. The cold splash of the water on her face revived her and she dabbed hastily with a linen towel. She was glad that she had insisted on Betsey enjoying the feast because she would have been ashamed for her to see her in such tantrums.

With her head held up her determined nature reasserted itself as she left the chamber and crossed the landing to the stairs to join the others — and Edmund.

She had her foot on the first stair when she heard her name. She stood quite still while the blood pounded in her head as Edmund came out of the shadows and led her into the solar. Margaret held herself aloof from him, but he apparently did not notice and going to the hearth, kicked the logs into spluttering flame. Keeping her head averted she knelt on the cushions before the fire. For a while he did not move but stood looking down at her. Then he dropped beside her.

'That was unworthy of you, my Margaret,' the gentle rebuke was so unexpected that she gasped as if he had struck her. Without giving her time to speak he pushed her none too gently down into the cushions. He gathered her to him and she found that she was clinging to him desperately. Her body's delight was stronger than her pride. He kissed her then for the first time with passion; slowly, with his mouth hard on hers until she was weak with longing. Exerting all her will and strength she pushed him away from her. To her amazement she saw that he was laughing softly at her discomfiture and she was about to give vent to her hurt pride when he forestalled her.

'Well, sweeting, perhaps it would be better if I told you what all this is about. But don't sit there with that expression of pent up fury on your pretty face, for it is not as you imagine it at all. It was fortunate for us both that only I realised the effect of Jasper's ill-timed compliment on my bride-to-be!'

'You knew then?' she asked incredulously, at the same time wishing he would take her in his arms again but keeping away from him so that he would think she was unconcerned.

'Knowing you as I do, it wasn't at all difficult to ascertain the cause of the drooping lip and the refusal to look at your betrothed when the cup was passing and I placed the ring on your finger. Somewhat different from the time in the chapel when you were so pleased to accept my humble offering. While the others probably interpreted your cool kiss as maidenly modesty, I was not at all deceived. Although it had possibly not occurred to you until a few moments ago I want you as much as I believe you want me.'

Margaret sat still, frightened to move to break the magic that he was weaving around her.

'You reached your room before I had time to intercept you and closed the door with such finality that even I was daunted. The prospect of rushing in upon you with your maid squealing at my outrageous manhood was too much for me. Anyway, it did not take you so long to think that you had, perhaps, been a little hasty, did it?'

He lifted her chin with his hand, and with an effort she met his eyes at last, secretly wondering at the accurate reading of her reactions. This, she thought, was a power with which to reckon and her own intelligent, just reasoning exulted that the man she was to marry had perception keener than her own.

'Well, did it? Surely you know me better than that, don't you?'

'Yes,' she replied. 'Yes, I do!'

'Margaret,' Edmund went on, 'it has always been Henry's wish that you and I were wedded. It was arranged that it should be so on the day that you became my ward. The lawyers who came to settle the details of my guardianship also drew up the marriage contact. Do you not think that had I not wished it then I should have been party to the matter? I did not have to agree to marry you and there were other suitors that I could have put forward. Henry was eager, with his innocent pleasure in the decision, that you should be told, but it was I, backed by your mother, who asked that we should wait a little before you knew. You were such a child and I thought you had already had burdens enough without being saddled with a future husband who must have seemed senile to you at that time!'

Margaret made to interrupt him, but he hushed her with a gentle hand which she cradled against her face. Perhaps it was better not to admit that ever since she had been nine years old (or was it even earlier?) she had wanted nothing more than to hear that she was to become his wife. The very best of men were prone to conceit. Her mother said so — and she should know!

'You see, Margaret, you touched me so much with your — what shall I call it — affection for me, that, believe it not, I was prepared to wait until the mutual respect we had for one another deepened as I felt sure it would. So it was that, hearing reports of your singular accomplishments and your beauty, which has not gone unmarked in even these turnabout times, I told Henry that I should break my journey to Windsor to wait upon your acceptance of my suit at Bletsoe. Your mother gladly agreed that I should come and you know — you know very well — that from the moment you came into the hall that day last week, I loved you. Loved you as I had not believed it possible, now and for ever.'

He kissed her gently and pulled her to her feet.

'Come then, let's go down to the others before they think we have anticipated our wedding day and run off.'

9

In the first grey light of day on the following morning Margaret stood at her casement and watched the small cavalcade with Edmund and Jasper at its head, file out of the courtyard on its way to Windsor. She waited until the banners faint fluttering were lost and she could no longer hear the jangle of their equipment. She went back to her bed and found that she could neither sleep or rest. She called Betsey who helped her dress and ran to the stables to summon the groom with Margaret's mare.

As on the day that Edmund had arrived she rode out into the waking morning, but was slower to appreciate the beauty around her or the exultation of the exercise. She was quiet with the remembrance of the night's joy, going over and over in her mind the wonder of her discovery that Edmund loved her. Edmund loved her! The little Beaufort — when he could have had any of the Court beauties or daughters of great landowners. Her sadness at being parted from him so soon after she had known he cared was tempered by the happiness that the knowledge had given her and the rousing in her body of the physical need he created. No longer the mating birds and the bursting trees filled her with reproach as they had before, now she felt at one with them, ready to share in her part of the mysteries of the earth's fertility.

She made a pact with herself to look to the future and his impending return rather than dwell on this, their first parting. Her mother had suffered not only separation but the death of her husbands and Edmund had but gone to escort the royal party to a Council, which, it was hoped, would meet in peace. He would be back with her as soon as the King was settled in Leicester.

She found that she had become so wrapped in her thoughts that she had come almost to a standstill and the groom was a little way ahead, watching her in perplexity. She spurred on the mare and avoiding the lane to Galsey Wood, struck out towards Colmworth and did not rein in until they reached the dip before the hill up to the village of Thurleigh. Here they turned round and came homewards at a more sedate pace, the groom as well as the Lady Margaret, hungry after the exercise.

Lady Welles' genius for preparations and management was quickly apparent as the betrothal feast was cleared away and plans made for the forthcoming marriage. Almost over night sempstresses took up their residence in the house while bolts of the silks and brocades that the lady of the manor always had in store were brought out and chosen or rejected. The steward set every available hand to the thorough cleaning of the house and the renewal of worn utensils and hangings. The wedding was temporarily arranged for October and time had an unpleasant habit of slipping by faster than ever the most efficient organiser could account for.

Margaret's mother sent word to her merchants in Bedford that she would have a special list for them and that she hoped that the situation in Bordeaux would allow them to offer her a good selection of wine. She supervised personally the washing of piles of bed linen which had lain, unused, in wooden coffers, since the funeral of Margaret's father.

Margaret quietly resumed her studies with Simon Hovey, the rector of Bletsoe, bringing a new outlook to the gaining of knowledge. When she was not studying she found herself going frequently to the nursery to play with her new half-sister and brother who was now a sturdy five-year-old. She found that she liked to sit at the wooden cradle, crooning half-forgotten lullabies while the baby clutched at her proffered finger and watched her with bright, unblinking eyes until she succumbed to sleep.

Edmund wrote from Windsor that they were setting out for Leicester at once and that he would send more news to her from there. She read this, her first love letter, until she knew it by heart and sat down to answer it. She found that the translations and exercises that she prepared for the priest were much easier to set out than the emotions of her heart. She wrote two difficult pages, dwelling on each word and weighing up its merit, until the letter resembled a treatise on the subject of love. In despair and ashamed of her pride in her accomplishment she threw it on one side and wrote a simple avowal of her constant devotion to her betrothed.

When it was completed and she had sealed it with her daisy emblem pressed deep into the hot wax, she sought out her stepfather to spare a messenger to ride to St. Albans to intercept the party.

Lord Welles agreed that Margaret's own man should go and Margaret, wrapped in a light woollen cloak, watched him set off from the courtyard in the early dawn of May 22nd. He turned in the saddle as he went out into the lane, rousing the sleepy-eyed watch-keeper, and gave her a cheery wave. She acknowledged the salute smilingly and went into her chamber where Betsey had prepared a bowl of bread on to which she had poured steaming milk. The two girls sat in easy companionship, talking quietly at intervals. There was so much to arrange and so many plans for the future and when they had done eating Betsey brought her mistress a piece of fine cambric that she was making into a chamber robe. Margaret picked up the needle but found that her fingers refused to make the small, even stitches. Afraid of spoiling the garment she put it back in her bride chest and taking her Book of the Hours told Betsey that she would go to the chapel.

The sun was warm already and the air in the church struck chill as she crossed herself and went to kneel at the same place she had shared with Edmund only a week before.

She spent nearly half an hour on her knees, praying with devotion and a deep gratitude for God's goodness in making her the intended wife of a man of Edmund's quality. She asked that the Lord would make her worthy of him and grant her the power to keep him happy, for at some moments she felt her inadequacy to give Edmund what a more mature woman would have found easier. She prayed that God would keep him from danger and was startled as she murmured the words for she had no sense of trouble or impending disaster as she had experienced while sleepless at night. It was almost as if the unconscious thought went hand in hand with her love, for he was the reason for her being and without him life would not go on.

Margaret rose from the step and rubbed her knees to bring back the circulation. She met Simon Hovey, the priest, as she came out into the sunshine and they talked over a French translation on which they were working, as they walked together in the churchyard for a while. Simon found that since she had been betrothed she had been able to apply herself with steadfast zeal to her studies and admired her the more for her concentration at a time when most young women would have been too giddy-minded to think of other than fineries and the importance of her new state. He was inwardly satisfied that the man she was to marry was of her calibre and that each would bring to the other exceptional gifts. He was glad to know that the marriage was to be celebrated in the autumn and for some reason that he could not define, he wished that it was sooner.

There was so much they could do for each other.

Many times during the day Margaret thought of her groom as he made his way to intercept the King's party and the loveliness of the day he had for the ride. As she fell asleep later that night she hoped that he had safely delivered her letter and that he had found a resting place either in the King's lodgings or with the monks in the abbey. She hoped that given another fine day the groom might possibly be able to return to Bletsoe on the morrow.

The next day passed much as the previous one had done and when the groom had not returned by nightfall the family at Bletsoe were not particularly anxious as it was a good distance to St. Albans and there was always the possibility of the horse becoming lame or some other minor mishap befalling them. When however, there was still no sign of horse or rider on the third day, Lord Welles, who was due to leave for Calais the following morning, felt considerable alarm. He sent a small group of men from the manor, with two bowmen among them, to meet up with the carrier and escort him home. He chided himself for not sending two men in the first place and had difficulty in keeping his fears from Margaret.

It was twilight on the third day when the company returned with the exhausted messenger among them, incredulous at the story he had told them. He fell from his horse and pushing aside all who tried to stop him went straight into the hall, falling on his knee before the family. He took from his pouch two rolls, one of which he handed to Margaret and the other to Lord Welles.

Margaret's stepfather quickly scanned the hastily scrawled message.

'Good God!' he exclaimed. 'This is hardly possible! Be seated, my lady wife,' he said quietly to Lady Welles. 'This is the most unfortunate news.'

'Not Edmund?' Lady Welles hardly dared breathe the words, but was reassured as she turned to Margaret and saw the girl shake her head. Her young face showed a perplexed bewilderment.

'Not Edmund,' she repeated very low, 'but only by a miracle it seems.'

'This is from Edmund,' Lord Welles was saying. 'Sit you down man,' to the groom. 'Drink some ale and when you have your breath tell us what you know of this business.'

'It appears,' Lord Welles continued, 'that when Henry's party, which was supported by large numbers of men, arrived outside the town of St. Albans, it was to discover that

184

York had mustered the trained men of Warwick and Salisbury, together with the Nevilles and other reinforcements from his recruiting campaign in the north and was waiting for them. Edmund says that Henry was completely taken aback, as indeed all his Lancastrian supporters were, by the menacing attitude of this hostile force. Henry took up a station in the town and although an attempt was made to talk over the cause of this show of arms, which the letter says was the removal of my Lord of Somerset and his replacement by York, it was in vain and fighting broke out.'

'Fighting!' Lady Welles echoed. 'Fighting. What happened after this?'

'Edmund concludes his letter, which he obviously penned in great haste by saying that Henry lost the day and was slightly wounded from a passing arrow. He has now accompanied the King, with the Queen under York's protection to London. As he says, it is not difficult to imagine that Henry needs his protection more now than ever before. What says your letter, Margaret?'

'Only that he will be with me as soon as it is humanly possible and that he will leave Jasper most of his men to help in the safeguarding of the King. He is despatching at once his picked men-at-arms for our manor and wishes me not to go forth unaccompanied.'

Turning to his wife Lord Welles picked up a goblet and filled it with wine. She took it gratefully, glad of its comforting warmth in this moment when the bad news they had received put them again in the unhappy, unsettled state that had prevailed during Henry's madness. But her husband had more to tell.

'The letter also bade me break the unwelcome news that my Lord of Somerset was killed in this encounter and — '

'And — ' said Lady Welles. 'This thing is too dreadful. Do not tell me that others of the King's loyal supporters have died in this senseless way.'

'Unfortunately, I have to tell you that this is the case, for great Northumberland and the worthy Clifford both perished.' The women made small moans of shocked disbelief.

'Now,' Lord Welles spoke to the groom who, crouched on his stool had been listening to the contents of the letter and nodding his head in gloomy acquiescence. 'Perhaps you will tell us what happened after you left here.'

Lord Welles drew up a seat and motioned Margaret and the other women to sit down, while he went to stand behind his wife's chair. He put his arm round her shoulder, an unusual demonstration of his concern for her at this time, for he was not often given to show his feelings. He was deeply shocked at this eruption of a situation which he had believed was resolving itself into one of compromise. He felt most reluctant to leave his household now and take up his duties in Calais, especially when he remembered that Somerset had been the captain there, and that York, realising the importance of the post, would hasten to put it in charge of a good Yorkist.

'My lady,' the groom began, hesitating as he began his story, for he was not used to such an audience. He glanced round at his listeners and when he came to Margaret gave her a faint smile of reassurance. The girl nodded, comforting him as much as receiving help. 'As you know I set out right early, for I had a long day in front of me. The going was easy, though, for the day was fair and the roads hard with no water and I made very good time. At Ampthill I fell in with some other men and they told me that they had seen large bands of men under the banner of 'The Falcon and Fetlock' and the 'Bear and Staff' which I didn't need to be told meant that my Lords York and Warwick were on the move. At first I thought little on't for I knew that my Lord Richmond had gone to meet the King to attend the Council at Leicester and I just imagined that these lords were bound there also. Until, of course, I realised that Leicester was north of them and they were coming away from it. It was a change of plan, I didn't wonder and I pressed on for St. Albans. When I came in sight of the abbey on the hill I was amazed to see the great number of tents pitched in the meadows on the north-east side. Now my heart started to bump a little for there was something not quite ordinary about the ordering of it. Coming into the main street I was horrified to find piles of dead soldiers, with the monks from the abbey, their cassocks girdled about their waists, tending the wounded and comforting the dying. One of them told me when I asked that there had been a battle and that the King had been slightly wounded and was lying in the abbey. He didn't seem to know very much about what had happened but was more concerned with caring for the injured and I pushed on to the abbey, where I knew if His Grace were there there would also be his followers.' The man took a long drink from his tankard, for this unaccustomed talking had made him dry.

'Here was all confusion, but a friendly soldier shared some food with me and said he would speak with his captain and try to get word through to Lord Edmund for me. He was able to tell me, as we sat in the fading of the day what he knew about the happenings. It appears that he had been helping Lord Clifford put up some barricades to prevent a frontal attack being made on the house in St. Peter's Street where the King had made his headquarters. From here the King sent the Duke of Buckingham to my Lord of York to ask him what he meant by barring the road to Leicester. The Court had spent the night at Watford and were completely taken aback when they discovered this mighty force waiting for them. The Duke of Buckingham returned to the King with word from the Duke of York that he in no way wished to hinder his Grace from making the journey to the Council, but he would not move from his position until the King had sent word that he intended to remove my Lord Somerset from the Protectorate. This, from what I could gather, the King refused to do. The soldier had it from a friend, who was posted on the rooftops as a look out, that the Duke of York formed his men up into three long columns. He must have had spies about and had heard of the barricades erected by Lord Clifford, for he made no attempt to come up through the main road, but cut across the gardens at the rear of the houses and pushed his way straight through to the main street. In the confusion that followed the soldier remembered cries and shouts of 'A Warwick. A Warwick' and guessed that it was the young Earl of Warwick who had led the charge. There were showers of arrows, which the men were able to dodge, for they had no armour, but the nobles in their heavy accoutrements were not so lucky and took the full brunt of the attack. The King, coming to find out what all the noise was about, caught a glancing blow from an arrow and Lord Somerset's son, your cousin, my lady,' speaking softly to Margaret, 'caught a dart in the back of his hand.'

The groom paused again and took another drink.

'Don't hurry, yourself,' Lord Welles told him. 'Try to think clearly and remember all you saw. How did you come to Lord Edmund and receive the letters?'

'The soldier was as good as his word and got word through that I had arrived with despatches from Bletsoe. It must have been nearly midnight when the Earl came to me, for I remember a long line of hooded monks going to their prayers with lanthorns swinging in their hands. He looked tired but was happy to have your letter, my lady, and said that I was to sleep where I could and that he would be glad of my help on the morrow burying the dead. He told me then that he and his brother had been searching the streets for the body of the Duke of Somerset, which they had found stripped and mutilated, after hours of looking, thrown into an alley. It seems to me, my lord, from what the men told me that there are mercenaries with the armies of both sides who are practising the foulness that they learnt when they were fighting with the French.'

'I sincerely hope that it is not the case,' Lord Welles interjected violently, for he had all too vivid memories of the atrocities that were carried out by the pillaging armies of both sides in that weary struggle. 'My Lord Edmund says in his letter that the day was lost and that the King is now under the Duke of York's protection, how did this come about? Did not the King's supporters come properly to his aid?'

'Most of them fought most valiantly, my lord, especially the Earl of Pembroke, Lord Clifford and Lord Roos. Lord Edmund went with haste to back up Lord Clifford and was in time to catch him as he fell, before he was embroiled in some close fighting. Then, as suddenly as it had begun, so Lord Edmund said, it finished. With disgrace, he told me, for the Standard Bearer to the King, Sir Philip

Wentworth, threw down the flag and fled. This might not have been the end, but at that same moment the Earl of Wiltshire panicked and fled from the street. Thus the King was left with no more support than from his two half-brothers.'

'Where is the King now, man?' Lord Welles asked.

'He has gone with the Duke of York to London, whither the Queen had fled with her baby son to seek sanctuary and the Lords Richmond and Pembroke have gone with the King to give him their support.'

'Thank you,' Lord Welles said. 'You have told us much.'

'I am only sorry, my lady, that it makes such heavy telling and that I had to be the bearer of ill tidings,' he touched his forehead with his knuckle and stood up.

Lord Welles dismissed him to his much needed rest while the family gathered round to discuss over and over again the shattering events that he had told them.

When Lady Welles had seen the others to bed and had retired with aching limbs to the heavily curtained bed which she shared with her husband, they lay for hours talking about the consequences of the death of Somerset and the rest of the day's news. Now, more than ever before, they knew that the Lady

Margaret was pushed into undesired prominence as the heiress of the Lancastrian House. There was no reason to suppose that the young Dorset would die of his wound in the hand, but in this sad event, even more responsibility would fall on their daughter's young shoulders. With so little time left in which to make plans before Lord Welles departed for Calais in the morning they decided to put forward the day of Margaret and Edmund's marriage for two reasons. The first being that once married Edmund could take his bride to Wimborne or the remoteness of Pembroke Castle, in Wales, which had been given to Jasper by Henry, and had a reputation for withstanding attackers since the days of Strongbow, who built it. The second reason was that in the security of either of these secluded places Margaret and Edmund could set about the begetting and rearing of a large family who could be relied upon to bolster the failing support of the Lancastrians.

Lady Welles spared a passing thought for the Queen, for whom she felt no especial sympathy, but, who, having survived the death of Suffolk was now faced with a future without even loyal Somerset. It was not difficult to imagine that Margaret of Anjou would be searching around for further Red

Rose help and that the field had narrowed considerably in the last few days. Lady Welles hoped that her fancy would light on Buckingham or Jasper, if need be, rather than Edmund. One thing was certain that Richard of York would soon discover that he had caged himself a tigress with exceedingly sharp claws in the defence of her own.

Thanking God that Edmund had been spared to them all they sought comfort in each other's arms and slept.

10

It was almost a week before Edmund was able to leave the royal party in the palace of Westminster and start his journey to Bletsoe. The weather had broken in the meantime and the rain had hardly ceased falling for an hour, making the roads difficult. He grudged the two nights he was forced to spend on the way and if he had been alone would possibly have ridden on into the night, but he knew better than to push his men too far. They were loyal and obedient but this was not the moment to test their devotion. At Milton Earnest he sent a herald forward to warn them of his coming and Margaret was waiting at the gateway for him. He slid down from his horse's back, and oblivious of the onlookers, took her in his arms. She clung to him, her hair damp from the misting rain, too happy to speak, and hand in hand they went into the house.

Henry had agreed to let Edmund stay at Bletsoe until July 9th when Parliament was to meet. Within four days of the Yorkist victory at St. Albans the Commons had been summoned and Sir Thomas Wenlock, who was known to favour the cause of Richard of

York, had been elected Speaker. Edmund had to admit that the Duke of York made every sign of wishing to conform with Henry's desires and had assured the King many times that he had no designs on the throne, but only wanted to see a more settled state of affairs. Edmund also said that though he did not always see eye to eye with Margaret of Anjou, he was with her all the way when she said that she did not for a second believe these protestations, much as he would like to have done. Henry, after his unusual outburst at St. Albans when he had told York's emissary that rather than give up Somerset 'By the faith I owe St. Edward and the crown of England I will destroy them, every mother's son' had reverted to his gentle self and it was Margaret who, at first from sanctuary in the abbey, and later behind closed doors in the palace, was scheming to reconstruct the maimed party of Lancaster. Edmund was not altogether happy that Jasper, sorry for her in her sad plight had agreed to give her all the aid he could.

Sitting with them in the solar on a most dismal June evening, he gave them his account of the fighting which had broken out at St. Albans. It corroborated the story told by the groom and it was obvious that Edmund considered the young Earl of

Warwick a power to be reckoned with in the future. It was undoubtedly he who put Richard of York up to the ruse of stealing through the gardens of Holwell Street and coming out into the main thoroughfare between the two inns of 'The Key' and 'The Chequers' to take the royal party by surprise. Without wishing to embarrass Lady Welles, whom he knew to be related to the Earl, he said that he was a born leader of men, with a commanding appearance, and it was a matter of very much regret that he had thrown in his lot with the Yorkists.

Once he had told them his experience of the battle it was as if he wished to forget it and no one referred to it again. The Bletsoe family were only too eager to let the memory of disastrous St. Albans fade away.

They received, while Edmund was with them a letter from John telling them that he had become betrothed to Alice, the daughter of Sir Thomas Bradshaigh of Haigh in Lancashire and that they hoped to be married without delay. John said that he was very happy and that the Bradshaigh family desired that as many of the Bletsoe household who could come to the marriage would do so. Lady Welles replied that while they were delighted with the good news, it would be impossible for any of them, except Oliver, to make the arduous journey at this time, but she very much hoped that her first born would take the earliest opportunity of bringing his bride to see his mother.

Later, alone in her room, Lady Welles took up her looking-glass and stood in the window embrasure. She twisted her head from side to side examining closely her unlined face. She removed her intricately pleated head-dress and could find only a few greying hairs. She sighed, smiling to herself at her own conceit, for surely she, with her two widowhoods and many childbearings, could have silver streaks without shame. It was the thought of a married son that had suddenly sent her scurrying for a mirror and had made her feel old. Margaret's marriage she regarded as a fortunate fulfilment but John's announcement gave her a sense of being outgrown and unnecessary. She chided herself for being very slightly jealous of the unknown Alice Bradshaigh and determined that when John brought his bride home she would be as welcome as Edmund was. After all, when she thought about it further, she was not yet forty years of age herself and had a baby daughter to heal the wounds of a mother who had never had enough of her son's company. She was grateful, too, that it was not one of the girls, for the marriage of one daughter at a time was sufficient for any household and she had caught several affectionate glances passing between Elizabeth and William Zouche at Margaret's betrothal feast. Lady Welles set her head-dress firmly on her wide brow and shrugging off her momentary miseries went back to her endless round of duties.

If she was slightly piqued at the forthcoming marriage of her son she was happy for Margaret and Edmund. Their quiet enjoyment of each others companionship could only be a source of joy to her and she was relieved beyond measure that her anxieties on the child's behalf were coming to an end. When the matter of putting forward the wedding day for September was raised neither of them had objected but agreed that it was a good time for a wedding with perhaps more settled weather than they were now having.

The only cause for unease she experienced on their behalf was Margaret's complete and innocent adoration of the man who was once her guardian and her future husband. Margaret made no effort to conceal the fact that life had a different meaning when Edmund was with her. Her eyes shone with extra brilliance and she gave him her undivided attention. The older woman had to admit that Edmund did not seem to object to this show of devotion and gave every appearance of reciprocation. They rode, walked and danced together as if they were the only inhabitants of the manor and though heavily chaperoned on all occasions, hardly noticed that they were not alone.

The family supped early on the evening of July 6th for Edmund was leaving for London the next morning. There had been a constant stream of despatches arriving for the past week and the young Earl had been occupied with reading them and sending off replies. Margaret, contrary to the expectations of her sisters and mother, had not been petulant or put out but had patiently occupied the time until Edmund was free with reading and sewing. On this last day he had refused to untie any of the rolls that were still unread saying that nothing was so important that it could not wait until he returned to Westminster.

He and Margaret were sitting, as had become their custom, on the cushions in front of the solar fireplace, where a fire of apple wood burnt in an effort to dispel the damp of the wettest summer for years. Elizabeth was playing chess with one of Edmund's squires while Margery was helping her mother choose skeins of wool for a tapestry Lady Welles had begun for Margaret's bride chest. As it became too dark to see the colours Margery went to pick up her lute while Lady Welles was glad to sit still for a few precious moments.

'Will you be here again before the wedding, Edmund?' Margaret asked him.

'It hardly seems likely, sweeting, but when I am come I shall not go away again except with you as my wife. It is not so long now until September, is it?'

She glanced swiftly up into his face and looked down.

'What is it?' Edmund said, amused at the faint blush on her cheeks.

'Oh, 'tis nothing.'

'When you say "tis nothing' in that tone I am not at all deceived and shall not move from this spot until you have answered my question.'

'If you will not move away from me, why then I am tempted not to speak, for there is nothing that would be more pleasant than to have you stay!'

He took her hand and caressed it gently.

'I know full well that there is something that is worrying that pretty head of yours and I must know its cause so that I can try to remedy it before I have to leave you.'

'Don't remind me of tomorrow, for I

cannot bear that you will not be here. It is not that which gives me misgivings, but something other.' She half-turned from him and gazed into the fire as if seeking inspiration or help.

'Edmund, what do you think of this custom of bedding after the marriage?' It was out with a rush and his hand tightened on hers. So it was this, that had given him some anxious moments also, that was bothering her.

'The thought,' she was continuing, 'of being prepared for your coming by a crowd of well-wishing, slightly tipsy women fills me with horror,' she stopped, her courage at broaching such an intimate subject leaving her abruptly.

'Don't worry about that, sweeting, only put your trust in me that I shall not allow you to endure it.'

She looked up at him, her warm smile enclosing him in a look of complete love as the firelight played on her face and threw it up in sharp relief in the darkening room. Lady Welles, glancing their way caught her expression and the answering gesture as Edmund took Margaret's hand and placed it inside his shirt, close to his heart. Swiftly he bent and kissed her half-closed eyes with great tenderness as two tears rolled slowly down her cheek.

Lady Welles was much moved and her faint unease returned. Fortune did not always smile on lovers who were as close as this and it was recognised that the fickle jade did not bestow especial favours when marriage sealed passionate love.

It was not that Lady Welles in any way doubted Edmund's fidelity, although he was handsome enough to flutter the heart of any woman, even before they had encountered his undeniable charm. He would doubtless be the target of many designing women only too keen to promote misery in the breast of the little Beaufort ... It was something other than this. Something on which, for all her experience, she was not able to put a finger. She had loved her husbands in her own way, but not even with Margaret's father had she ever been at such oneness and had always retained her own complete entity.

Lady Welles clapped her hands suddenly, summoning the pages to bring tapers and light the dips. She pushed away her darkling thoughts making a mental note to ask the apothecary on his next visit to prescribe a potion to cure her of the melancholies which lately seemed to be coming a habit with her.

During the time that Edmund was away she had further cause for disquiet for while it became apparent that Elizabeth and William de la Zouche were fond of each other it was also obvious to her that Margery, her second daughter had a penchant for the young man also. This manifested itself in the droop of Margery's mouth and the long hours she spent locked in her chamber or on her knees in the chapel. The girl had seemed brighter when the Abbess of Salisbury paid a visit to the manor at Lady Welles' request and invited Margery to spend a few months with her community after the wedding of her young sister. She portrayed an almost feverish interest in the forthcoming marriage of Edmund and Margaret, throwing herself unselfishly into sewing some of the many fine garments that were being stowed away in cedar lined chests. With Elizabeth it was completely different and she could hardly bring herself to speak to the sister, who from earliest childhood had been her closest companion.

Their mother saw to it that during the six weeks that Edmund was absent Margaret and Margery spent much of their time together, and there began in those long days, a friendship which was to last her in solid reliability throughout her lifetime. The younger girl knew, without her sister telling her, the cause of her distress, and her own happiness daily drawing nearer its fulfilment, made her doubly anxious to comfort and relieve the sufferer. Margery, unconsciously aware of Margaret's sympathy through the leaden mist of her distress of loving William and seeing him so deeply enthralled with Elizabeth, accepted the girl's sympathy and some of the unheeded love welling in her was diverted to Margaret.

When despatches came from Edmund she sat quietly at her sister's side listening eagerly to the snatches that were read to her, enjoying a vicarious pleasure in the snippets of news and gossip. They discovered too that they shared many of the joys of worship and although Margaret's visits to Simon Hovey were becoming less frequent as the time of her marriage became nearer, they went together to him for instruction. Margery had come in contact with several of the young men who had been up at Oxford and who had become indoctrinated with the Lollardry that was still secretly preached there. She expressed her conflicting fears to the priest and lively hours of discussion on the subject had helped her to take her mind from her unhappy state and fired her with a new interest on an age old subject.

Although Margaret worried a little that her sister was too easily influenced she was on the other hand relieved that she could find something on which to bend her energies. She was sad that these waiting days which for her held promise of deep happiness should be so thwarted for Margery.

Margaret had dreaded the period of separation that would keep Edmund from her side, but she discovered that the time went far more quickly than she had imagined possible. Despite the fact that she had thought she would not be interested in the side of the marriage preparations that usually provided the balm to the young women who did not welcome the bonds of matrimony as she did, she found that the choosing of a gown for the actual ceremony was quite absorbing.

She had known at once, when lengths of stuffs had been brought for her to inspect, what she had wanted and the sempstresses had almost finished the making of the robe. Her mother had suggested the names of three small boys to accompany her to the church and John and Oliver had agreed to act as the customary guards to bring her home from the marriage.

John had been at Bletsoe since the beginning of August with his bride. He had not seemed much changed since before his marriage and was as affectionate towards them all as he had ever been. He was as thoughtful to his mother as was his wont and took a considerable share of the burden of preparations from her shoulders, standing in for Lord Welles until his arrival from Calais. Margaret he teased with good natured amusement coupled with a certain respect which he was at loss to explain to himself. Despite his proffered advice from a much married man to his betrothed sister he found her strangely matured since he had been absent from Bletsoe. He confided to his mother that he had never before realised that Margaret was so attractive.

Alice, his bride, was a tall, cool blonde, self-possessed and exquisitely dressed at all times. She spent much of her time in her chamber, which did not surprise Margery and Margaret as they appreciated the hours that were necessary to present such a polished *toilette*. She was gracious and attentive to her husband's mother and family, but gave the impression that she had no feelings of the variety that beset the rest of the world. For this reason she was not particularly dear to the St. Olivers who were used to the warm-hearted exuberance which characterised the Bletsoe *ménage* and were somewhat intimidated by the girl's haughty manner. Lady Welles was not slow to realise that this poise was an armour which Alice wore to protect herself against her husband's family, for underlying the assurance she had detected an uncertainty which the poised exterior hid well enough. It was quite probable that she had been nervous at the prospect of marrying into a family which had close connections with the throne and had insured her country breeding against the possibility of hurt.

As she stayed longer at Bletsoe, Lady Welles' theory proved correct for Alice unbent gradually and by the time the lawyers had arrived from the Inns of Court in the fortnight preceding the marriage of Edmund and Margaret, was as ready as the rest of the family to share well-stifled mirth at their ponderous ways and dry as dust reasonings. Their dark robes, scant hair and bent scholarly shoulders seemed out of keeping with the union of two young lovers.

When Parliament had completed its reshuffling and had settled down into a surface quiet again Edmund returned to Bletsoe. Jasper assured him that he would give double support to Margaret of Anjou and Henry in his absence and that he would be with him for the marriage day. Jasper had quietly and determinedly placed his substantial armies at the side of the King and Queen and they turned more and more towards him. Margaret of Anjou's interests in him seemed solely concerned with the aid that he was able to give them and she did not, for the moment anyway, seem to regard him as a man to entice. Edmund reasoned that if this did become the case Jasper was well able to cope with any situation that might arise, as it was no secret to his brother that he already had several claims on his heart in the remoteness of Wales, sufficient to keep him from encouraging amorous advances from the Queen.

Edmund felt that the situation was sufficiently under control for him to be able to devote his time to Margaret without any uneasy suspicions in his mind that he had deserted his duty to satisfy the overwhelming longing he had to be with his betrothed. He had not imagined, until this time, that man could experience such need to be with any particular woman. He had smiled, before, at lovers sighing for their mistresses and regarded love pinings and the writing of poems as something for troubadours and courtiers only. Now he underwent a change of heart when he discovered that he could not concentrate on important documents and state papers and his waking hours were filled with memories of gestures and murmured words.

He rode to Bletsoe, impatient to take

Margaret in his arms. Bereft since early childhood of the sheltering love and devotion of his mother he had discovered in his betrothed a haven of belonging. This new emotion, once savoured, he had missed with an almost physical pain and he felt himself incomplete without Margaret beside him.

He arrived at the manor before he was expected and the look of sheer joy on Margaret's face as he came into the solar behind Ralph Lannoy, more than compensated for the six long weeks that they had been apart. He took her proffered hands and held them to his lips as she softly spoke his name and made him a curtsy. The room seemed suddenly full of people as the family, followed by the omnipresent lawyers, crowded in to make him welcome. It was as if all had been waiting for him to arrive and everyone spoke at once. Edmund made a rueful smile at Margaret and his eyes conveyed the message that, once the business of the marriage was settled, time would be hers alone.

It was in fact, late evening before they could talk undisturbed together and they were sitting in their favourite place on the cushions in front of the fire. They held out their hands to the welcome warmth, for the rains which had begun on Edmund's previous visit had poured down on the sodden earth without ceasing and the air even inside the house was damp and chill. Old folks shook their heads and muttered about the full churchyards that would follow if no sun broke through before the long and dark winter.

Now that they could actually speak to each other all they wanted was to sit and savour the delights of their proximity. The many plans that had to be finalised concerning their marriage settlement and the impending move to Collyweston, which they had decided to make their home until after Christmas, could wait until the morrow. The next morning was already set aside for discussions with the black-robed lawyers and by unspoken consent they postponed any reference to the topics that would be thrashed out then.

Turning to look into the room Edmund noticed that the solar was deserted and silently blessed his future mother-in-law for her tact in allowing him a few moments alone with Margaret. He bent and kissed her lightly on the forehead and she raised her eyebrows, startled at the caress, and then relaxed with a sigh of pleasure as she too realised they were unobserved. Still neither of them spoke, unwilling to break the enclosing silence of the long awaited meeting. Edmund took Margaret's hands lightly between his own and pulled her towards him murmuring gentle words of love and affection.

'It is not so long, now, sweeting, until we shall always be together, with no more partings. Jasper is sending almost daily messages to Pembroke urging his seneschal to speed the making ready of our chambers in the tower. The early spring is promised to us as the date we can hope to take up our residence there. Now that my brother, the King, is unhappily beholden to York and the Duke has given his promise to serve him truly, I think it is unlikely that he will go back on his word for the immediate present and we should be able to enjoy living at Collyweston.'

'I hope you like the house there as well as I do, for it has always held a special place in my heart. Why this should be I do not really know, except that it was the first of my very own houses that I ever saw. It is kind of Jasper to put his castle at Pembroke at our disposal.'

'You do not mind,' Edmund said, 'that you will be so far away from here and your mother and family?'

'No,' she replied low, and looking away from him into the fire. 'For where you are, there is my heart also — '

She broke off as Edmund kissed her on her parted mouth.

'And,' she continued a little breathlessly,

'my lady mother will certainly visit us in the good days of summer and bring Margery to see us. A short visit to the sea air will do much to bring the colour to her cheeks again.'

A rustle of silk told them that the family had returned and they joined in the general conversation until it was time to go to bed.

11

The last few days before the wedding ceremony were so occupied that afterwards it was difficult for Margaret to separate one from the other. Hours rushed by with the speed of minutes and no sooner was one task finished than another had to be started. The lawyers at last took their farewells, their clerks staggering under the great rolls of closely written parchment. They had discovered that when the young Earl of Richmond arrived and brought his bride-to-be to their discussions all had gone smoothly. Their naturally suspicious legal minds had been unable to worm out any grasping tendencies in the heiress' future husband and they had gone away satisfied that Edmund would make no more demands on his wife's estate than he had done as her guardian. The lawyers were shaken from their usually cynical outlook by Edmund's insistence that all Margaret's estates should be entailed for future heirs and that his own not inconsiderable possessions should become hers and their heirs at his death.

Politely assuring him, that as he looked in

the best of health, this long away day would see his widow already comfortably provided for, Edmund demurred that with the uncertainties of life as it was today, there was no security that the future Countess of Richmond would be able to keep her estates intact.

With relief the Bletsoe household wished the learned men God-speed and sent a large escort to see them safely to the London road. Almost as they left the guests for the wedding began to arrive and Ralph Lannoy wore a continually harassed expression as he kept everything running on oiled wheels.

With the inconsequence of English weather, two days before the ceremony happily the morning came in with a heavy rolling white mist which gave way to a tenuous sunlight that by noon was warm and heartlifting. Looking for omens, this was seen as a sign that the match was blessed with happy portents and efforts were redoubled to provide a fitting celebration.

Members of Lord Warwick's family arrived and the Staffords from Kimbolton. The young Duke of Suffolk, though he had been sent an invitation, declined on the grounds of pressure of work. As his East Anglian domains were in a continued state of turbulence which had not subsided since the death of his father, this was not unexpected, but did not delude the St. Johns. Lord Welles came home from Calais, where much to his discomfort, he was under the command of Warwick. He was more pleased than he had ever been before to be home and hoped that he would not be obliged to serve in the garrison for some time. As he had done his best to be a perpetual source of irritation to the Lord Warwick he trusted that his lordship would put two and two together and realise his reluctance to serve under him. There were plenty of Yorkist supporters only too anxious to make their number with the growing power of the Bear and who would be willing to take Lord Welles' place.

Edmund and Margaret were fully occupied in the acknowledging of the many and costly presents which arrived from wellwishers. Margery had offered her services in the making of an inventory and her quill scratched through the days recording the gifts. The future Countess of Richmond was secretly somewhat ashamed that so much wealth should be showered on them when there was much want in the country, but she could not help admiring, with her Beaufort eye for the good things of life, the exquisite workmanship of the chalices, plates and rare glass which they were given.

Having inspected a particularly handsome basin for the ceremonial washing of hands before a great banquet, which was set with rough uncut jewels around its rim, she mentioned to Edmund that she would like it if there could be a distribution of silver pennies to all those who lived on his and her estates to mark the wedding day. Edmund smiled at her innocent wish to share their happiness and promised to see that her desire was fulfilled.

Margaret had tried on the dress she was to wear and she had praised the yards of minute stitches that had fashioned it. Her mother, old nurse and the sempstress, with Betsey hovering in the background, agreed that it was the loveliest gown they had seen. The delicate green tissue, threaded with silver designs of daisies, illuminated Margaret's gentle beauty and the tightly nipped waist accentuated the blossoming perfection of her young body. The mermaiden quality that Edmund had remarked upon before was very apparent and the bride looked as if she came from some mysterious underwater world. The pride on her mother's face and the admiration of the sempstress and Betsey told Margaret that Edmund would not have much difficulty in finding her attractive in this dress.

The manor rang with the gay laughter of the assembling guests and there were people everywhere. It was impossible for Edmund and Margaret to find a place to talk quietly. Gone were the precious snatched minutes in front of the solar fireplace and there was no time for rides in the fields. They were needed on every hand for their opinion or consent about this or that. Margaret eyed with disquiet the preparations that were ensuing in her bedchamber. The simple hangings that surrounded her bed had been removed along with the narrow wooden frame and its soft feather filled mattress. Thickly woven damask curtains supported on a tester slung from the ceiling hung round the great bed that had been placed there, and Margaret caught guarded smiles on the faces of the women of the household who came to make up the bed with silken sheets beneath the blankets of finely woven wool. When this preparation was complete, she and Betsey slept in a small chamber next to her mother's room and she experienced already a feeling of disentanglement from the familiar things that had made up her childhood.

Several times she almost brought herself to mention the changes that had been made in her room to Edmund, but on each occasion something caused her to hold back the words.

When she had finally blurted out her fears when he had been with her in July she had been spent with the effort of mentioning the matter to him. Now, although she longed for reassurance, she could not bring herself to talk of it again and comforted herself with the knowledge that Edmund had not failed her yet and was unlikely to do so at this heartfelt request. In moments of doubt, however, she could not see how he would surmount the difficulty for her.

On the morning of the marriage she awoke early and lay for a long time considering the tremendous change that would come about in her life after this day's happenings. She thought of Edmund, the well beloved, the esteemed guardian and she thought of Edmund the lover, the unknown. Although she knew that she loved him with all her being a small voice whispered that overheard snatches of married women's talk had conveyed that bedsport was not always pleasing. She closed her ears to the threat to her happiness and jumped out of bed, calling Betsey to bring her a kersey dress. She stood at the casement while the girl tied the girdle of the surcoat. Idly looking towards the chapel where she intended to go presently to offer prayers to God she saw two dark cloaked figures emerge from the curling mists and hurry towards the house.

'Edmund!' she cried unbelieving and Betsey rushed to the window to draw the curtain to shut out the unfortunate sight of a bride seeing her future husband on the morn of the wedding day before they met in the church.

'Don't let him see you, my lady,' she said quickly, stifling the age old superstition. 'He must wait until you meet in the church for that!'

Margaret laughed gaily, for the fears that beset Betsey were unknown to her.

'Fie, Betsey. It is usually I who am the prude; I had not thought to hear you chide me for immodesty! But worry not, my lord and his brother are out of sight now.'

Betsey wisely held her tongue and allowed her young mistress to mistake her concern.

'Where would the young gentlemen have come from, my lady?' she said anxious to divert Margaret's mind.

'It looked as if they came from the chapel. Surely they could not have been keeping vigil there, all night. Perhaps my lord went to meet Lord Pembroke as he came up the Bedford road, but if that were the case, where is his escort?'

'I'm sure I don't know, my lady, and if I were you I'd not give it too much thought at this moment, for you have other, more important things to attend to. Do you wish me to come with you to your prayers?'

'Yes, please, Betsey. I should be glad of your company to guide me through the mists. Let's hope they soon lift and the sun shines as it has during the last two days.'

Women from the hamlet had been in to the church on the previous day and had decked the entrance and the space in front of the rood screen with small sheaves of corn entwined with scarlet poppies and white dog daisies. Margaret clapped her hands with delight at the transformation of the dark nave and fell on her knees at the chancel steps to offer her prayers and thanksgivings on this most wonderful of all days. Kneeling a pace behind her on the slabbed stone floor, Betsey found herself praying earnestly that no ill would come from my lady's sight of her future husband before the appointed time.

Margaret's sweet smile as they both rose from their knees and went outside, reassured her and she rebuked herself for letting age old superstitions cloud her good Christian upbringing.

All the morning Margaret's small room seemed crowded with the womenfolk of the manor coming to offer her their own personal gifts and advice. Margaret was most touched by a phial of costly perfume from her sister-in-law Alice, who proffered it with a warmth that she would have found impossible three weeks ago. Her half-sisters, coming separately to the chamber brought a chamber robe and a pair of fur slippers. Margery lingered and seemed happier than she had done for some time. It was as if the ordeal she had to face later when Elizabeth and William de la Zouche would be openly together, stiffened her pride and gave her an inward strength. She picked up a hairbrush and brushed Margaret's newly washed hair until it gleamed.

Lady Welles, coming in with a bowl of beaten eggs which she had scalded with hot milk, could hardly reach her daughter for the press of chattering women and, reading the unspoken plea in Margaret's eyes, bade them go to the solar where some delicacies had been prepared for them. Reluctantly they made their farewells of the bride, wishing her well and making arch references to the delights which awaited her.

Lady Welles drew up a chair and Margaret gratefully sank on to the bed while they sipped the reviving drink. She hoped very much that her mother would not take this opportunity to give her her share of embarrassing advice. She need not have worried for her mother remembered too vividly her own first tremulous wedding day and talked idly of this and that event which was taking place in the hall of the manor. It was as if she spoke of some other house or a play she had seen, for none of it was quite real to Margaret. She was vaguely interested in her mother's comments on the outlandish headgear that my Lady Buckingham had chosen to wear and the fact that one of the young bridesmen had a touch of a sore throat, which was causing his mother a certain amount of distress, but she heard it all from a distance. Now that the actual marriage of herself and Edmund would take place so soon, she had become two people, one who went through the process of preparing for her wedding like a puppet on strings such as she had seen on that long ago day in Bedford, and the other who was continually listening for something unknown. It was a strange sensation such as she had not before experienced and she was glad when her mother rose and said that it was time to put on her dress.

'You are rather cramped in here, dearling,' she said. 'But tonight you will be able to spread yourself in your own room again.'

'Yes, Mother,' she replied obediently while her heart's beating threatened to choke her of a sudden. Lady Welles smiled benignly and went out calling Betsey and her own maid to help Margaret put on the gown and the wreath of field marguerites which she had chosen to crown her unbound hair.

At last all was ready and the noise in the manor diminished as the guests crossed to the small church. Her sisters came briefly to the door and blew her kisses, while her brother and the other small boys, sat primly on stools outside her door. Her mother, magnificent in a sapphire robe bordered with miniver, came in and hugged her. Margaret found herself unable to speak and silently proffered Lady Welles a lace edged kerchief to wipe away the tears which flowed down her cheeks. The young mothers, anxiously giving last minute instructions to their offspring to do as they were bidden, went downstairs and Betsey came to tell her that Ralph Lannoy was awaiting her mistress. She picked up Margaret's hand, surprised at the coldness of it, and curtsying low, kissed it.

'Thank you, Betsey,' Margaret whispered. 'Thank you, for all that you have done to help me.'

Then she was alone. Heedless of the new robe she fell on her knees.

'O God,' she prayed 'Bless this day, I beseech Thee. Bless Edmund and bless me, that I shall prove a worthy wife to him. In Thy Name I ask it, O Lord.'

Ralph Lannoy beamed with pleasure as she made her way down to the hall where he awaited her with the bridesmen. Even they stopped their chattering as she approached and clasped the garlands they were to carry with extra zeal. This was going to be more fun than they had anticipated for no one had told them that Margaret was going to look like a sea fairy.

The short distance from the house to the chapel was crowded with the servants and the cottage people who could not ease themselves into the church. They smiled and waved to her, calling out greetings and good wishes. From her dream state Margaret heard them and smiled back at them. She looked so beautiful that there was no envy in the hearts of the onlookers, for Margaret had always been a favourite of them all and it was fitting that she should be decked in the finest attire that money could buy. The silver penny that each one had tucked away beneath their straw palliasses was sufficient reminder that she had not forgotten them on this important day. The smell of the roasting ox in the far courtyard made them sniff appreciatively and hope that Sir Priest would not preach for too long.

Margaret walked up the path to the church

porch with her head bent, for here the press was even thicker. Ralph Lannoy's men held off the crowd with strong arms and with an effort she raised her head and looked straight to Edmund where he awaited her. Jasper was at his side and Simon Hovey, strangely garbed in unaccustomed splendour, stood with his back to the closed church door.

A hush fell on the people as Edmund took her hand and bowed over it. The priest, motioning them to take up their position in front of him, spoke quietly to them both. Although the onlookers craned and pushed to catch a word of what he said he purposely spoke in low tones of the wisdom and truth of marriage which was founded on God's Holy Sacrament and bade them both be ever mindful of Who's servants they were. To Margaret he touched briefly on the wifely duty of Sara to her husband Abraham and that it should be her goal to emulate her good example and to Edmund he spoke sincerely of the need for constancy and the upholding of high ideals.

His short homily finished he bade them kneel before him while they made their vows.

Margaret felt the first fluttering of returning sensation as she heard Edmund, looking deep into her eyes begin the old, time honoured words.

'I, Edmund, take thee Margaret for my wedded wife, for better, for worse, for richer, for poorer, in sickness and in health until death us do part, as Holy Church hath ordained and thereto I plight thee my troth.'

She looked down as she murmured her response, almost unable to speak when she promised to be bonny and buxom in bed but looking up again as she plighted her word also.

Edmund drew from the folds of his doublet the heavy marriage ring and passed it to Simon Hovey who made the sign of the Cross over it before handing it back to Edmund to place on Margaret's finger.

'With this ring,' he said, 'I thee wed and,' as Jasper gave him a salver heaped with gold and silver coins, 'this gold and silver I thee give and with my body I thee honour.'

'In the name of the Father, and of the Son and of the Holy Ghost,' said Simon and the marriage was over. He knocked loudly on the church door which was immediately swung open and he turned into the dark interior bidding them follow him. Margaret took Edmund's proffered hand and was grateful for the strong reassuring clasp.

The church seemed smaller than usual with the great number of men, women and children who were standing crushed together.

The hum of conversation died as the bridal couple came in and walked slowly behind the priest to the inner chapel where they would receive Mass. Margaret's dress shimmered in the gloom, the silver threads catching the faint glimmer of candles on the altar.

The small bridesmen, placing their garlands on the floor, knelt behind Edmund and Margaret as they received the Holy Sacrament. From time to time they made covert glances from behind joined hands to find where their parents had found space and gave quickly concealed grins when they were located.

Lord Welles took his wife's arm as the young bride and her groom stood to receive the final blessing and sip from the gold cup proffered to them by Jasper, the nuptial drink of crushed poppy seed in milk and honey.

'You have much to be proud of, my dear,' he whispered, 'and young Richmond should be a happy man this day.'

As the Earl and Countess of Richmond emerged from the church the crowd, who had been fortified with mugs of wine handed round by the manor servants, broke into excited cheering.

John and Oliver, having taken up their position at the porch door, greeted their sister with affectionate kisses and handed her a wreath of corn to carry back to the house.

There was no time to think as Margaret and Edmund headed the brightly coloured procession through the milling throng to the feast in the great hall. Women, with babies on the arm, pressed forward to get a better view of the bride and her handsome groom, shouting good wishes and wishing them a fruitful and happy marriage. Some of the younger people had broken boughs from the hedges and held them aloft for a canopy over the guests. Following in their wake the good-humoured crowd surged towards the savoury smell coming from the yard. This was a high day and they were going to make the most of it.

In the manor it was some time before the large number of friends had taken their places at the elaborately set tables in the hall. Already pages were moving among them filling their glasses from the ewers of wine and urging them to be seated. All the Beauchamp plate had been brought out from the strong rooms to grace the occasion and the tables were laden with fruit and fantastic marchpane edifices crowned with spun sugar.

Edmund and Margaret took the seats of honour on the raised dais beneath a specially erected canopy of silken brocade. Lady Welles and her husband sat beside them with Jasper and the St. Oliver family, down to the baby girl, who sat on her nurse's knee, on either hand. Edmund had secretly hoped that his father would be present but the old man had sent his blessing and had said that he would wait until his son could bring his wife to visit him on his estate in Wales.

Jasper had greeted his brother's bride with an unsmiling warmth that had touched Margaret deeply. With his solid reliable strength had returned some of the awareness of living which had been numbed in her since the early morning. The banquet began in the late afternoon and showed no signs of finishing until deep into the night. As great mounds of food were eaten other gargantuan dishes took their place, and the noise increased with wine which flowed freely. Margaret, although she ate and drank little, felt stifled with the heat and her head ached with the strain of listening and replying to the continual good wishes that were showered upon them by groups of guests who came up to the platform. Edmund she had hardly been able to speak with and as the evening proceeded and the din became even more uproarious she began to be afraid that there would be no opportunity to escape from the dreaded bedding ceremony. Trying to catch a glimpse of him through a welter of horned and towering head-dresses she was relieved to see that he looked unruffled and her fears subsided. She turned again to the circle round herself and smiled more freely. Knowing she could trust Edmund she enjoyed the troupe which appeared from behind the screens with a chain of little performing monkeys.

At last it seemed as if the guests were satisfied and some of the younger members of the family called for music and started to dance in the centre of the hall. Edmund, smilingly pushed his way to her side, bowed to her and asked her to stand up with him as the musicians began a lively country dance. With his arms about her the numbed unreality of the day dropped from her like a cloak and she smiled up at him, the proudest happiest girl in the land. Twice they circled the hall in the wake of the other dancers, clapping hands and turning inwards and outwards in the pattern of the measure. When they came close together all else was forgotten for Margaret and she was unaware of any other person in the place, so that when a page, carrying a pile of pewter plates, tripped over the outstretched legs of a gentleman sleeping off his wine and fell full length with a tremendous clatter, she was unprepared for the quick pull of her arm.

'Margaret,' Edmund said, bending to speak low in her ear. 'This way!'

While everyone's attention was directed on the unfortunate boy and his painful predicament Edmund led Margaret quickly behind the screens. Snatching a cloak from a peg in the wall he threw it over her shoulders and half-pushed her into the ante room and out to the great door. The courtyard was deserted but she could not resist a fearful glance behind her as they half-ran towards the gateway. Here she expected they would be challenged, but subdued murmurings and giggles coming from the deep embrasure told her that the watch was otherwise engaged and she gave a passing thought to the wrath he would engender if the Captain of the Guard should make his rounds within the hour. Outside the walls a horse stood patiently cropping the grass. He lifted his head and whinnied softly as Edmund helped Margaret into the saddle and freed the reins before throwing himself up behind her.

Edmund dug his heels lightly into the horse's side and turned into the lane towards Thurleigh.

'Where are we going?' Margaret asked, still a little dazed by the swiftness of events.

'To Colmworth, dearling, to the house of

Lady Braybrooks.'

'Oh, Edmund, do you think we were observed?' Margaret whispered, afraid that her voice might attract a host of followers.

'Observed?' Edmund chuckled. 'Not if Jasper and the page did their job properly.'

Her eyes were more accustomed to the darkness now and she glanced back at him to see if he were teasing her. In the dim light she could not be sure but she thought he looked quite serious and she asked, incredulously, if the page's mishap had been arranged and he had to admit that the page had been bribed by Jasper and himself to seek out a man who had drunk deeply of the free flowing wine and was asleep. The boy had been told that the brothers had a wager that even the ear shattering din of metal on metal would not awaken a drunkard and this play acting was to prove one of them wrong. The page had been only too willing to take part and Edmund thought, and he hoped Margaret agreed, that he had been most successful.

'Most,' Margaret murmured and looked again behind her. Edmund tightened his hold on her and assured her that there were no pursuers. She relaxed for a moment but sat upright almost at once.

'But Edmund,' she said, 'it is a good distance to the manor at Colmworth and

Lady Braybrooks may not welcome unexpected guests at this hour as she is a widow on her own.'

'Yes, Jasper reckoned that it was almost seven miles from Bletsoe, but do not fret yourself, sweeting, for I should not take my new bride where all was not prepared for her. Jasper called at the manor before he arrived at Bletsoe this morning and assures me that we are awaited with pleasure. Lady Braybrooks and I had met before and when I explained the nature of my request she was most willing to harbour us secretly for a while.'

Now she was able to nestle back in his arms, glad of the comfort and the thought which had prompted him to snatch the cloak for her because the air was chill and patches of mist hung suspended over the dew ponds and the streams they passed. Once or twice Edmund was forced to slow the pace of the horse, and though she listened with her ears strained, the countryside was as quiet as if they were alone in the world. Once or twice she heard the lonely hoot of an owl and some night prowling animal rustled out of the grasses at the road's edge and disappeared behind them. The stillness and the warmth of Edmund's body lulled her gradually until, soothed and overtired from the exacting day, she drowsed, happy and completely trusting in her bridegroom. He felt the tension go from her and settled the cloak in warm folds around her. Although he did not know the way to the Colmworth Manor very well he judged that they must be over half-way there by now and that they were safe from discovery. Jasper would ensure that a reasonable excuse for their absence would be forthcoming to pacify the guests and would tell Lady Welles of her daughter's wish which was being carried out without danger or risk to Margaret.

Leaving the alehouse on their right hand Edmund took the narrow lane on the left and could see the lights of the manor. When they arrived in front of the tall house the massive front door stood open and an ample motherly woman stood waiting to greet them. Margaret was now fast asleep and was only vaguely aware as Edmund jumped to the ground and taking her in his arms carried her inside. Lady Braybrooks hurried before them, offering warmed milk or some mulled ale as she led them upstairs to a chamber leading out of a small, panelled solar. Edmund smilingly refused his hostess' offer of nourishment and said that he thought his bride's main need was for sleep. Lady Braybrooks nodded her agreement and after enquiring if there was anything else she could obtain for them she left them, closing the door quietly behind her.

The room was small and partly panelled with two window embrasures now well covered with thick woollen hangings. A good fire had been recently made up with dry, well-burning logs and it cast a warm friendly glow about the chamber. Margaret stirred and opened her eyes momentarily as Edmund put her down gently on the wide bed, but she did not waken.

Edmund was somewhat perplexed as to the best way of making Margaret's rest comfortable and threw off his own tunic and hose while he considered the problem. Bending over his sleeping bride he cursed himself for a fumbling fool as he tried to undo the fastenings of her gown. At last he succeeded in loosening them sufficiently to enable him to draw the dress from beneath her. He hesitated when he saw the fine linen shift which clung closely to her gently moving breast and decided not to disturb her further. Touched deeply by her utter trust in him he kissed her on the brow and settled himself beside her throwing his arm over her in a protective gesture until he slept, as she did.

12

She awoke before he did and watched him as he lay beside her, breathing deeply and evenly. His brow was unruffled and his mouth, above the deeply cleft chin, was curved upwards almost as if he smiled. It did not seem at all strange to wake and find him beside her, while the pleasurable warmth of his naked body was no shock. It was as if in the years that she had grown to love him each stage had led naturally into the next and this moment was the culmination.

The white light filtering through the heavy curtains told her that the mornings mists had not yet lifted and that they were wrapped in their hideaway as secretly and safely as a silk worm in the cocoon. She could dimly see her gown lying across the stool and was amazed that he had put her to bed without disturbing her, for she knew that no other hands but his had tended her. She savoured the knowledge, imagining the trouble he must have encountered in the unusual task. Dwelling on all the events of the previous day she prolonged the precious few moments of her first waking beside Edmund until he stirred and opened his eyes abruptly. He looked straight at her and a warmth flooded through her as he whispered her name and drew her to him.

'Dearest little Margaret,' he said again softly. His hands caressed her back, running down her thighs and up into the nape of her neck. There was no urgency in his lovemaking and she lay against him with her head cradled on his shoulder quietly absorbing his unspoken wish to please her, until she turned her face up to his and he kissed her, his mouth lingering on hers. He brushed the soft tendrils of hair from her cheeks, speaking to her soothingly of all the things for which there had been no time during the last hectic weeks. She listened, dimly understanding that even the words he spoke so low and intimately were playing their part in leading them, eventually to a complete fulfilment. Drowsy again he kissed her tenderly until, quite unexpectedly, they both slept.

When she woke it was to find the curtains drawn back and Edmund standing beside the bed with food for her. She sat up as he set down the bowl and brought a soft woollen chamber robe and put it about her shoulders.

'You are spoiling me,' she said smiling happily. 'It is a long time since I broke my fast in bed and it was nurse who brought it then.' Pulling the robe closer round her shoulders she looked up at him.

'Edmund, is this Lady Braybrooks' robe?'

'No, my love, it is yours. I had it made for you and Jasper left it here with some other clothes for you. I knew there would be no time or opportunity to bring anything from Bletsoe and I was sure that a bride without her bride's clothes would be bound to pull a long face. You would not have been too happy to spend all day and everyday in your marriage gown, would you?'

Sipping the milk and looking at him over the rim of the bowl her eyes twinkled.

'You thought of everything, Edmund and I am ashamed that I had any misgivings. How long,' a little wistfully, 'do you think we can stay here?'

'Jasper was to assure your mother after we had been gone a good hour that you were quite safe and that she had no cause to worry for we were well housed. They will think, no doubt, that Bedford was our destination, or perhaps the Buckinghams' castle at Kimbolton; although by the way young Henry Stafford was glaring at me, I do not think I should be very welcome there!'

'Was he there?' Margaret asked. 'I do not remember anything clearly of the day after I first saw you and Jasper come out of the morning mists, until we were riding here. It all seemed like a dream that was happening to someone else with the prospect of it all ending in a nightmare which would have been only too horribly real. I can never thank you enough for bringing me here. My only fear is that they will think me very churlish for running off without thanking them for all they did.'

'If Jasper should visit us you could send word to your mother then and anyway I am sure that there will be so many sore heads this morning that very few will notice your lack of manners. When they do feel like talking their chief topic of conversation is bound to be our destination and the reason for the flight. It is likely to cause quite a stir and, one never knows, might even start a fashion for this sort of thing! It certainly has much to commend it.'

Margaret smiled her agreement but she could not resist a light shiver and pulled the bedrobe tighter round her shoulders.

'Don't let them find us, Edmund.'

'Even in their wildest imaginings they will not think of Colmworth and even if they should Lady Braybrooks will deny any knowledge of us. Besides, it is my belief that your mother will not allow anyone to look for us. Her only concern will be that you have no maid to wait upon you, but that will not worry you, will it?' Margaret shook her head. 'Lady Braybrooks tells me that her people here are curious but they are used to the odd doings of their gentle folk and will doubtless shrug their shoulders at the unexpected arrival of their overlord's daughter.'

'Where shall I find the clothes you have provided?'

'They are in the chest beside the fire. They are very simple but there is no need for other here. Beside I prefer you as you are now!'

She blushed and was glad that he turned abruptly and went out of the room into the solar. She had a brief glimpse of a pleasant square chamber, similar to the bed-chamber.

For a moment she sank back into the soft mattress revelling in the happiness which had so suddenly come to her. It was all so completely different from what she had dreaded and she would have been content to lie there thinking about her good fortune but she could not linger for Edmund would no doubt be waiting for her and would expect her quickly. It would not do to be thought a sluggard on the first morning of their marriage.

She opened the chest and found three woollen robes, one of deep sapphire, one green and one white. The last was finer than the others and was bordered with simple embroidery. She chose the green and put it on the stool with a clean shift while she explored the wooden coffer to see what else Edmund had placed there for her. She was amazed at the care which had prompted him to remember fragrant oils and perfumes as well as linen handtowels and a brush and comb, and a polished hand mirror. There were several shifts and three pairs of shoes, made of the thinnest leather, dyed to match the dresses. She gave a gasp of delight as she brought out a Book of the Hours, handsomely bound in rich blue calf with an M intertwined with an E as the only decoration.

Margaret put it at the bottom of the chest and then folded the other garments neatly and replaced them. She found a copper ewer beside the fire which was filled with hot water and she washed and dressed. She was brushing her hair when Edmund returned. Dropping the brush she ran to him and clung to him.

'Oh, Edmund, was any one ever as happy as I am?'

'Are you really happy, little Margaret?'

'You know I am and you have done so much to make me so that I hope you think I am worth it!'

'I do,' he said simply. 'Come. Put on your

cloak and we'll walk to the priory at Bushmead.'

They came upon Lady Braybrooks in the hall and she asked them if they had everything they required. They assured her that all was perfect and Margaret apologised for her scant manners on arrival the evening before. The motherly woman smiled away her apologies and said she hoped they would enjoy the dish of chicken cooked in herbs which she was preparing for them. It had been a favourite of her late husband's and she welcomed the opportunity to make it for them. They thanked her sincerely for her trouble and said it was their intention to see a little of the surrounding countryside. They went out in the warmth of the late September sunshine and walked on the Kimbolton road, hand in hand.

Coming back in the late afternoon with the fading sunlight caught in the golden leaves of the surrounding chestnuts the manor house, standing on the mound which had been thrown up hundreds of years before by Margaret's Beauchamp ancestors, seemed like a fairy tower. As they stood at the doorway before going in they turned for a moment and watched the darkling light fading over the fields which stretched as far as they could see. Clanking of metal rimmed milk pails and a tuneless whistle coming from the dairy were the only sounds.

They found a low table set for supper in the solar and not long after they came in Lady Braybrooks brought the food that she had prepared for them. She did not stay with them but poured out the pale wine which she had kept hanging in the well and made her curtsies.

They were both hungry and left very little of the delicious dish, enjoying the pleasure of their first meal alone. They talked eagerly at first but gradually the conversation became desultory and she found that she was a little shy and tongue-tied. Edmund did not appear to perceive the lengthening gaps and when he spoke it was in a comfortable, companionable way. He had noticed much more of the happenings of the previous day than she had, and entertained her with recounting them. She was touched to hear that her half-brother John Welles had been in tears on the way back from the church when he had told his mother that he had not realised before that Margaret was now Edmund's and that she would no longer belong to the Bletsoe household. Her half-sister Margery had borne up well under the strain of William's marked attention to Elizabeth and had attracted her own court of admirers. Alice, Edmund then told her, was *enceinte.* Margaret found this hard to believe as news of this kind was extremely difficult to conceal amongst a family, but Edmund promised that it was so, for he had suspected the fact, even if he had not heard her telling her mother-in-law that such was the case.

'Oh, you trickster!' Margaret said laughing, forgetting for a moment the restraint that was growing up in her. 'You would have me believe that you are more clever than I already think you are.'

'Do you think me clever, dearling?' he quizzed her.

'Quite the most knowledgeable man I know,' she said, which was true, although she chuckled quietly to make him doubt it. He was not as scholarly as Henry, nor as learned as the priests who had taught her so much in her young life, but he had a wisdom and deep understanding which she had not found in the learned men she had met. He had none of the harshness which character-ised the men who frequented the Court and were sometimes guests in her mother's home. Perhaps his sympathetic approach came of the blending of the culture of the French royal house with the mystique of the Welsh vision. Whatever it was, she was glad he possessed it and was reminded forcibly of his dead mother who had suffered so much for the man she had loved and the children she bore him.

How different it was for her, who had always been showered with love and affection and had been cushioned against life's tribulations. How fortunate she was to marry, in open ceremony, the man she adored and look forward to bearing his family in honourable respect.

So far away was she, that she was startled when he rose and went into the bedchamber to replenish the fire.

'Come and sit with me here, as we used to do at Bletsoe,' he called.

She went to him at once, the momentary trembling of her limbs stilled as she saw the welcoming blaze and the cushions heaped by the hearth.

'Do you remember,' he asked as he knelt beside her with her head on his breast, 'how angry you were with me at our betrothal feast?'

'Yes,' she whispered, her voice muffled. 'Don't shame me by reminding me of that now!'

'Dearest Margaret, I would never shame you while I live. Betwixt you and I there is no place for dishonour.' He was quiet for a little then went on slowly, 'You are not frightened of me, are you?'

'No,' she replied, understanding instinctively his question. 'No, Edmund, there could be no fear when I have loved you so long.' It was the first time she had spoken of the love she had for him and she was surprised by the ease with which she told him.

He bent to kiss her neck and the light woollen robe fell from her shoulder, which gleamed milky white in the firelight. She took his hand and cradled it against her cheek, while his mouth sought hers. Neither of them moved, until, as on the betrothal eve, he pushed her down into the cushions. But now there was no roughness, only a natural acceptance of a further stage in their mutual knowledge of each other. Lying beside her he kissed the hollow at the base of her throat and downwards to the rounded curve of her breasts while she kept quiet and still, her eyes wide opened and limpid. As he stayed with his face buried close to the beating of her heart she began to caress his head as her fingers ran through and through the crisp, dark hair. A little later she stirred and looking up he saw the great eyes and the mouth half-parted in invitation. He kissed her passionately, while his hands curved over the breasts and slim waist as she low-murmured his name.

It was a long time afterwards that he lifted

her to the bed and came in beside her. He knew now, without doubt, that she desired him as much as he needed her, but he had, with great will power curbed his longing to possess her. The trusting tenderness of her youth tore at his manhood, while her natural sensuality enflamed him. She was so very young to bear his children and he understood only too well the risks of childbirth. That the Lancastrian cause looked to him to provide a male heir, he was certain, for unhappily the young Dorset had died of the wound in the hand which he had received at the battle of St. Albans. With the death of her cousin, Margaret and Prince Edward, the King's son, were the sole hopes of the Red Rose.

Over and above Edmund's loyalty to the half-brother who had succoured him and heaped honours upon him was his love for his bride. Having been taken from his mother when still a child he had known no woman's devotion until Margaret had loved him. He did not want to risk spoiling this in any way. Although he did not doubt for a moment that their mutual passion would be otherwise than completely harmonious, he accepted the fact that her youth would be a deciding factor in this, for she would give herself to him without counting the cost or employing the subtleties of coyness or experience. Here, perhaps, lay his reluctance to take her now, for it was possible in her complete submission he might abuse her willingness and hurt her tenderness.

While he battled with his emotions her even breathing told him that she slept, made drowsy by the warmth of his body as he held her close to him. He smiled in the darkness and silently thanked God that He had resolved the matter for him.

It was not to be gainsaid however and although he might try to push into the background of his mind, their complete mating dominated his thoughts. He was not surprised by her acquiescence and acceptance of the situation for he knew that she looked upon him as the leader and that, if he had told her to do so she would have made a barefoot pilgrimage to the Holy Land. Once or twice he surprised a puzzled look in her eyes as she watched him when she considered herself unobserved, but the days went by in perfect harmony. They walked and rode on borrowed horses, exploring the countryside to the east and north, but avoiding the road which led to Bletsoe. Sometimes they took food with them and did not return to Colmworth until nightfall.

On the fourth evening they dismounted by the stable close to the fish stew and walked into the house, glowing with fresh air, for it had been another beautiful sunlit day.

Lady Braybrooks bustled up to them, commenting on their healthy appearances and telling them she had a supper of roast lamb that she would bring up at once to the solar.

They ate the food with pleasure and when she brought them a flagon of red wine to mull, they thanked her for her kindness in cooking for them and making them so welcome in her house. She beamed on them and said that it was giving her happiness to have them in her home when she was so much alone. Deftly taking up the platters and side dishes she called out a 'good night' to them as Edmund held open the door for her and closed it behind her. He took the poker from the fire irons and plunged it into the red hot embers of the solar fire while he poured the wine into two pewter pots.

Margaret went into the bedchamber and stood for a moment at the small casement, the hangings held back in her hand as she looked out across the fields lying hushed and silvered in the moonlight. She felt restless and perturbed in a way which she had not experienced before. Acting on an impulse she threw off the dress and shift that she was wearing and putting on the chamber robe, girdled it tightly round her waist. She folded the garments and put them neatly in the chest. As she did so she caught sight of the Book of Hours on the nearby table and was reminded that she had not prayed or read a line of praise since she had come to the manor. Discomfited, she hurriedly fell on her knees and said over the well known prayers of thanksgiving and worship and found herself beseeching God for Edmund's happiness, unable to express clearly the exact nature of the benefits she required for them both.

When Edmund came in she was sitting demurely, with ankles crossed, on the stool. She cupped the drink he proffered in her hands while he sat on the cushions in front of her. There was a sudden air of tension between them and neither of them spoke. She sipped the wine, admiring Edmund for gulping down the scalding liquid. He hardly knew that he was doing so, for he had noted at once the tightly belted gown and had not been deceived by the innocent air of his bride. He gave a passing thought to her birth star and decided that it was not for nothing she was born under Gemini's contradictory influences. He kept his eyes towards the fire, not daring to look at her, for he recognised that from the instant he had crossed the room's threshold it was her will, as well as his own, that counted now. He drew out the finishing of the pot of wine as long as he was able but, reluctantly, when he had drained the final drop two or three times he set it down. Almost at the same moment a log fell from the fire with a shower of sparks, some of which splattered the cushions on which he sat. In an instant she was on her knees, beating out the small, smouldering pieces of wood, brushing against him as she did so while the girdle of the robe unloosed. The risk of fire forgotten, they were in each others arms, crying their love names. His last scruples were lost as he had glimpsed the rosy beauty of her body and he was amazed at the passion which had lain dormant and was now awakened into a tensile strength which answered his desire. Mouth to mouth they were drowned in a sea of mutual longing which was breaking in engulfing waves around them and blotting out all restraint. There was no sense of time as they clung to one another discovering with each moment a new facet of delight until at last, it was over and she was crying hot, burning tears against his cheek. He soothed her softly, wonderingly, his hands caressing her back beneath the robe as he kissed away the tears. Although he acted the role of comforter he was as stunned as she by the shattering tide of passion which had swept them together and was humbled by the magnificence of her love. He wondered that he had hesitated to arouse her when she was capable of making him so happy. He blamed his lack of carnal knowledge of women for he had never been able to bring himself to indulge in passing fancies or take mistresses as Jasper had done but was glad now that he came to her as pure as she to him.

She raised her eyes, heavy with consummated passion to his.

'Don't leave me, Edmund, ever,' she whispered, finding her voice. 'You are my life and without you I should die.'

'I have never lived until this hour, my sweet love, and the rest of my life is yours.'

So mouth to mouth and breast to breast they slept, the Earl of Richmond and his young wife, the Lady Margaret on an autumn night in the year 1455.

13

On the afternoon of the next day Lady Braybrooks announced that Lord Pembroke was below and would like to see his brother and his wife.

Jasper came in upon them sitting hand in hand on two stools beside the fire in the solar. He smiled with pleasure as they rose to greet him, embracing them both. Wine was poured and the newcomer drew up a chair to the fireplace. He saw that Edmund resumed his place next to his wife, taking her hand again in his. Margaret gave a look of such yearning tenderness that Jasper's heart contracted and he knew that although she listened politely to what her brother-in-law had to say, she was only aware of the man beside her.

She, in truth, hardly heard what the brothers said for she was reliving the secret transport of her mating with Edmund. She had slept deeply, waking with a feeling of loss to find him covering her with blankets from the bed and then replenishing the fire. She had watched him bending to the task, until he slipped in beside her and took her again in his arms. With a low moan she nestled against him and slept. At the memory of this moment her hand's clasp tightened within his and he turned his head from listening to Jasper and smiled. He too forgot his brother as he went back to the night and thought of the hours he had lain without sleep after he had thrown the crackling wood on the fire she sleeping beside him. Hours, when he lived again the transcending heights of their coupling and had prayed unaccustomed, fervent prayers for the well-being and happiness of the girl who had so completely and joyously given of herself to him.

With an effort he brought his attention back to Jasper who was full of news from Bletsoe, whence the wedding guests had at last departed, leaving a most welcome peace. Lady Welles and all the family were well and recovering from the round of entertaining and sent their loving greetings to the bridal couple. They had given their word that they would not trespass on the privacy of the bride and bridegroom and it was Jasper's belief that several of the younger members of the company agreed with Edmund and Margaret's wish and that many of them had made reservations on the subject for the future. He had come to intrude on their seclusion because word had been received from Windsor that Henry and Margaret thought it advisable that the Earl and Countess of Richmond should not delay the start of their journey to Wales. Jasper glanced towards Margaret as he gave this information for he knew that, although she accepted Wales as their ultimate destination she had hoped to spend some weeks at Collyweston, alone in her own home with her husband, before departing for Pembroke. He saw at once that he need fear no opposition from the Lady Margaret for she only smiled and nodded her head in agreement.

'Her Grace and,' he added quickly, 'our brother consider that there should be no threat to your persons and that Northamptonshire is too close to Yorkist sympathisers. The Queen says that you will realise that it is not long until the winter and that it will soon be difficult, if not impossible to make the journey, and therefore it would be wise to set out before October is finished.'

'We shall do as Henry wishes,' Edmund said, with slight emphasis on the name, for although he recognised that the Queen was the prop behind his half-brother he could never, he knew, bring himself to like the woman. It struck him that if Margaret of Anjou and the late Suffolk had experienced a mutual passion such as he and his wife knew he had a certain amount of sympathy for her on that account because it did not need a wise man to tell him that the scholarly Henry would make a tardy lover. Looking at Jasper he hoped again that the Angevin would not cast her net over Lord Pembroke. He comforted himself with the thought that when he could be spared from Court Jasper had two mistresses in Wales, one of whom had recently presented him with a daughter.

'We shall do as Henry wishes,' he repeated slowly, 'if Margaret agrees, we shall return to Bletsoe the day after tomorrow and make our preparations.'

Margaret's eyes widened, but she murmured her endorsement of the proposal. To herself she was counting the time they had left to be alone together before the world intruded, and it seemed suddenly to be very short. Never again could they be so free and unwatched and she realised with a sense of dismay that her birth endowed her with many privileges but made equally high demands.

Jasper thought, as he watched her, fascinated, how adult she had grown in the four days since the marriage. Her abundant hair, now coiled for the first time, threw into sharp relief the simple beauty of her oval face and the graceful perfection of her neck and shoulders. Her demeanour was controlled and while he had realised before that she had loved and admired his brother with an affection which amounted to hero-worship, he now recognised that this was no childish fancy but a deep emotion which had swept all else from her mind. If he were any judge it was obvious from Edmund's happiness that he completely reciprocated her love.

He stayed with them to share a simple meal and told them he had brought Margaret's pony for her to ride to Bletsoe and that he would send a groom on the day after the next to help transport their clothes.

'There are not many of those, as you know,' Edmund said laughing, 'and send him early so that we may ride to Bletsoe alone, towards nightfall.'

'Very well,' Jasper agreed somewhat reluctantly. 'But be it on your own head if you are waylaid on the homeward journey.'

'No one is likely to be much interested in a man and his maid travelling as we shall be without baggage and we made the flight here so I can see no reason for being unable to return along the same route.'

'You had me to back you up then,' Jasper reminded him. 'But do not worry, I shall leave you strictly alone to make your way back.'

When it was time for him to go Margaret and Edmund walked with him to the door of the manor and watched as he joined the small escort he had left in the courtyard. They waved to him until the party vanished down the hill and then returned to the solar where they stood watching the daylight fade from the fields. Rooks wheeled and chattered in the tall trees surrounding the nearby church of St. Denis until they too were hushed.

'Thank you for giving us another day here,' Margaret said. 'I would not care to return tomorrow.'

'I would rather not return at all,' Edmund told her. 'But wherever we go we shall be together and I give you my word that I shall not leave you unless the reason be the King's business. Did it come to you that Henry must be feeling very dispirited that he wants us gone into Wales so soon? I hope that he is not succumbing to York's domination and returning to his melancholic state. If he does, I think his cause will be hopeless and the young Prince must be trained to take his place by others than his mother, for I do not care for the Queen and her high-handed methods. She can be very cruel and ruthless so it please her.'

'Poor Henry,' Margaret said. 'He is too gentle for the hard business of government let alone coping with an overweening wife.'

Edmund's arm tightened round her shoulders and her head dropped on his shoulder as he touched her face gently.

'Poor Henry indeed,' he said, 'for he is not blessed with a wife such as I have. Come, sweeting, let us go to bed.'

She slipped from him and went into the inner chamber where she threw off her clothes and lay still in the bed with the coverings close to her chin.

She watched, from heavy lidded eyes, as Edmund replenished the fire and pulled off his tunic. It seemed to her that she must look and look upon him until his image was imprinted on her memory. When he had untied the cords of the soft leather shoes he wore, she closed her eyes until he was lying beside her.

They woke simultaneously as the first eerie cockcrow broke the deep silence of the night, and the passion which had been spent only a few hours earlier, carried them again into the deepest toils of sensual delight. Edmund forgot in the transport of their mutual ecstasy his former fears for his bride's youth, for where there was such complete understanding a subconscious reasoning told him that there was nothing to harm her. This loving and giving was an expression in itself of trust.

The sun was warm as they left the manor

after noon and walked towards the tiny hamlet of Honeydon. It was almost as if the approaching autumn was trying to make up in some way for the wet, dreary summer and shorten the winter with peaceful and settled days. The sky was clear and blue and the hedgerows were red with berries and haws.

'The world is so still that it is hard to believe that men will fight for power,' Edmund said as they walked hand in hand. 'Jasper's coming yesterday was a harsh reminder that our cousins of York cannot live amicably with our house. Which makes me think with some irony of the petition that I was preparing to present the Commons before St. Michael's day on your behalf.'

'Petition?' Margaret said. 'I had not heard of this.'

'It is only a small matter,' Edmund said, 'but when the lawyers were here drawing up the marriage settlements they brought letters which they had received from the lawyers of your kinsman Alice, wife to Salisbury and some others concerning the rent of the monastery of Colyngham and Berdesay.'

'Yes,' Margaret said frowning a little at the effort of concentrating, on this lovely day, on anything but the joy of being with Edmund, 'but there is nothing of irony surely, in the revenue which we receive from our estates.

Without them our life would be very different!'

'Most certainly,' Edmund agreed with her. 'But when I tell you that York and his wife, with the Earls of Westmorland and Worcester with Richard, Lord Powys are joint petitioners in this, you will understand what I mean.'

'I begin to see a little,' Margaret said slowly 'but how did this come about, that we who are on opposing sides in this growing dispute, could have a plea to put, together, to the Commons?'

'It appears that Edmund of Woodstock inherited the income from the Monastery of Our Lady St. Mary of Kirkestall from Edward II and divided it at his death between your father's heirs and the people I have just mentioned. From what I can recall from the paper, which I own I did not study very thoroughly as there were other more important matters on hand at the time, I think you will agree?'

She glanced quickly up at him and he bent and kissed her lightly on each cheek.

'Go on,' Margaret said, 'I like to hear you talk of our affairs.'

'It seems,' Edmund continued, 'that the monastery had been in a state of decline for a long time and the Abbot has been paying the rent of twenty-four pounds at Easter and ten pounds at Michaelmas out of his own pocket. Apparently the lawyers of York and the others think it would be advisable to grant the Abbot the patronage and advowson of several small livings in the Diocese of York to help him meet his commitments.'

'That seems a thoughful and just idea,' Margaret said. Then after a pause she went on. 'Edmund, it perplexes me that cousins should fight and squabble in a barbaric fashion as they did at St. Albans and yet have enough humanity to give time and effort to assist people such as this Abbot.'

'Where the Abbot is concerned there is no question of power seeking involved and we all have been trained from birth to look after and manage our estates wisely and justly. You will discover in life that when ambition takes a hold of a man, or a woman for that matter, he will stop at nothing to arrive at his goal. It is this that pushes at York's back now, despite all his protests of loyalty to Henry, and I am convinced it will take him to the throne if the Lancastrian supporters do not rally as they should.'

Margaret shivered. 'Do you think that the Queen feels this in her heart and that is the reason for her haste in despatching us to Wales? Oh, Edmund, what will happen to us if the Duke should become King?'

'Come, sweeting, don't be gloomy on a day like this. Forgive me for it and only think that we are together and that no harm shall befall you while I live. Shall we return to Colmworth now and look in at the church before we go to the manor?'

'Yes, I should like that for it looks very new and shining through the trees.'

Inside the recently completed church, which smelt of freshly worked wood and damp mortar, they knelt and made their own silent prayers and thanksgiving. Mingled with the rush of gratitude Margaret poured out to the Lady Mother she found she was praying earnestly for peace in the land so that their lives and that of all peoples should be free from anxiety and stress.

In the hushed quiet, which was so different from the excited throng which had filled the chapel at Bletsoe, Edmund picked up a strand of her hair and wound it round her marriage finger.

'Do you remember?' he asked her.

'Yes,' she whispered. 'I shall never forget.'

When they came out, closing the heavy iron bound door behind them, the sun was gone and Margaret was glad to pull the cloak around her bare throat.

They had asked Lady Braybrooks to sup with them in their solar on this their last evening and she had shown her pleasure by bustling about more than usual in the preparation of the food. Margaret guessed that fish would be one of the courses for she had seen two of the lads from the manor with nets down by the stew.

She ran up to the bedchamber and put on, for the first time, the white robe which Edmund had provided for her. She brushed her hair and left it unpinned about her shoulders. The mood of despondency which had beset her during the afternoon had lifted and she felt gay and light-hearted. Although there was no looking glass in the room she knew that the dress became her when she saw Edmund's face.

She helped Lady Braybrooks bring up the laden dishes and insisted that the kindly woman sat while she and Edmund waited upon her. She was a little ashamed as the excellent meal progressed and Lady Braybrooks chattered about her absent sons and daughters and dead husband, that, wrapped in her own perfect happiness, she had spared such a small amount of thought for her hostess. When she told Edmund later of her concern he reassured her that Lady Braybrooks was revelling in the intriguing situation and enjoyed having their company in the house.

Lady Braybrooks did not linger with them after the meal was finished and when she closed the door softly behind her Margaret flew to Edmund with arms outstretched and whirled him round the room in her own version of a country dance. He, seeing her gaiety, lost the misgivings that he had concerning their return to the familiar surroundings and the possible dullness of daily routine and abandoned himself to her infectious happiness. He had been afraid without realising it that she would be troubled at leaving this idyllic retreat but, almost as if she read his thoughts she pulled him into the bedchamber and made a place for him beside her at the fire.

'Oh, Edmund, it came to me today that nothing can spoil the bond that binds me to you. Wherever we are the golden line, spun of our love, invisible but strong as steel will be about us, binding us close. I do not mind, now, as I did yesterday, that we are to leave here on the morrow, for it is not the place that makes the happiness but the people, and where you are there is my joy.'

She stopped, suddenly shy at this outpouring of her heart and looked away from him.

'Little Margaret,' he told her as he turned her face towards him, 'I did not suspect when I agreed so long ago to take the solemn, enchanting heiress of the Beauforts as my ward and future wife, that I was preparing the way for the most wonderful happening of my life. I shall ever be in Henry's debt for bestowing this priceless gift on me. I shall never know what I did to deserve it!'

On the next day the groom and another man from the manor at Bletsoe arrived before noon and took away the small oak chests which contained their few possessions. Margaret, watching from the solar window, felt a pang of dismay as this tangible link with Colmworth was removed but it passed quickly and she looked round the rooms that had become peculiarly their own during their short stay and impressed them on her memory.

Later in the day they closed the door behind them and went downstairs to make their farewells of Lady Braybrooks, who curtsied to them and made no effort to stop the tears which poured down her cheeks. She wished them God-speed and continuing happiness in their married life wherever they should find themselves and hardly heard their sincere expressions of gratitude for the part she had played in ensuring that the start had been perfect. She stood at the manor gate, watching and waving until they took the bend in the road at Rootham's Green and then hurried inside calling for the women servants to bring out the copper preserving pan. Absorbed in the process of turning ripe blackberries into jelly she would not have so much time to dwell on the emptiness of the house. At the same time she made a mental note to send to her daughter and beg her to spare her eldest granddaughter to come and stay with her for a while.

Edmund and Margaret made their way at a leisurely pace towards Bletsoe, unwilling to hasten the last precious moments of their freedom. They stopped frequently to watch the rooks flying in great clouds round their high nests and the weeds moving lazily in the current of small streams. Once they picked up chestnuts, half hidden in masses of golden leaves and exclaimed at the burnish of their satin skins. They did not talk very much for there seemed no need and a look was sufficient to carry a world of meaning. As they threw away the chestnuts Edmund caught her in his arms and kissed her lingeringly. She melted against him, revelling in his now familiar strength and masculine smell.

So enclosed were they in each others company that the manor was visible through the trees long before they expected it and they were surprised when they ambled into the courtyard to find it thronged with men wearing the livery of the Queen.

Servants of the household came quickly to their side and helped them dismount. Their flight to an unknown destination had added a piquant relish to the delights of the wedding and all were eager for a glimpse of the young mistress and her husband. Afterwards they would always recall the rapt beauty of her face and his tender solicitude. The women noted the bound hair and the simple dress, but the men only saw the wonderful eyes and the sweetly curved mouth which smiled at them all and included them in a shared happiness.

Ralph Lannoy, considerably more relaxed than when they had last seen him, but still harassed by the soldiery who had been suddenly quartered upon the manor, greeted them with pleasure and told them that Lord and Lady Welles with the Earl of Pembroke were cloistered with Margaret of Anjou's envoy and that his instructions were to escort them to the solar immediately on their arrival. Exchanging slightly guilty looks, they ran up the stairs, but paused long enough to take deep breaths and present a more dignified appearance before making their entrance.

The conversation in the room ceased

abruptly and the group round the fireside broke up as Lady Welles came quickly to Margaret and embraced her in a brief, affectionate hug before extending her hand to Edmund. Margaret was grateful to her mother for her understanding in this emotional moment — and not for the first time — admired her poise. Pages came in with wine and drew up more chairs to the circle while the Queen's envoy Lord Roos was presented to them.

Jasper, with the memory of the enchantment of the isolation at Colmworth still fresh in his mind, wondered how his brother and his new wife would react to the roomful of people. If he had been astonished then at Margaret's maturity and the devotion which encircled them both he was further interested now with their assurance in handling a situation which was disconcerting to say the least. He remembered ruefully his mistresses' behaviour when a change of plan had suddenly interrupted a week of amorous dalliance, but then it would not do to compare a girl strictly and wisely brought up to respect duty, with a Welsh hoyden who probably gave of herself with complete abandon for what she could get out of it. Despite this reservation he did not for a moment doubt that Margaret had been other than a deeply satisfying lover and he found himself envying Edmund his good fortune. Dragging his mind reluctantly from these pleasant thoughts he heard Lord Roos breaking the unpleasant news to the Earl and Countess of Richmond that the Queen had sent him to Bletsoe to urge them to leave without delay for Pembroke. My Lord of Richmond would see from the despatches that he brought with him that Her Grace had ill tidings of the King's health to tell them. Henry had relapsed into madness and the Yorkists were again in the ascendancy.

Lord Roos continued that the Queen considered it was tempting providence to have two such important members of the Lancastrian faction within easy grasp of the Duke of York and his followers and that she considered it imperative that they should depart at the earliest possible moment.

Margaret and Edmund received the news of the recurrence of Henry's madness with sorrow, for their natural affection for him was, at this moment, heightened by the gratitude which they felt towards him for being instrumental in bringing them together.

However, Jasper received further proof of Margaret's strength of character as she accepted without question the Queen's request; putting out of her mind her secret hopes of going to Collyweston or some other familiar place and making preparation to go to the distant and quite unknown Pembroke. It was agreed that all speed being given to the undertaking they could be ready to leave on the day after next.

Lord Roos told them that he had brought some of the Queen's most highly trained troops and they would escort them, under his command as far as Ledbury. Lord Pembroke, he said, had already despatched Richmond's own men to await them there. A train of baggage had left with them and half the men would accompany it into Wales.

While Lady Welles was disappointed that her daughter was to leave her so quickly she was, nevertheless relieved that she should be going to Pembroke's safety. She had no doubts about Margaret's happiness, for the girl was radiant and although she was most attentive to the Lord Pembroke and the Queen's envoy Lady Welles realised that her mind was fixed on her husband. Edmund stood close beside her, without touching her but obviously sustaining her.

In truth he kept his hands firmly clasped behind his back and would not meet her eye for fear of disclosing to the onlookers the depth of their reciprocated passion. For this reason he was glad when assurances had been given to Lord Roos and the women left to make their own arrangements for the hasty departure. He felt he could now give his undivided attention to the mass of details concerning a journey of such length and importance as this one. He was glad of Jasper's unwavering support and found he had already set in motion much of the provisioning that would be necessary.

Betsey welcomed her mistress home with a respectful curtsy and a reserve which she found difficult to explain to herself. This soon melted when she saw that Margaret was pleased to see her and genuinely glad to know that the girl was looking forward to accompanying her to Pembroke. Betsey had already packed most of the clothes that she had considered that Margaret would need in her new life and sent them with the mule train. There remained only the travelling garments to choose and she had set them out in several piles for selection. Margaret shook her head over them all and said that she would take the little wooden chest that had been brought over from Colmworth earlier in the day with the clothes it contained and nothing more. Betsey made no comment but tactfully admired the dress which her mistress was wearing and said it became her admirably. When Margaret showed her the contents of the wooden box she only said that she thought a few more shifts would be a good idea and that there seemed to be room for a book or two. She did not reveal to her mistress that Lady Welles had added to the collection despatched to Pembroke, several bolts of the finest white linen and softest woollen stuffs in case the fastness of Wales proved unable to provide necessary clothing for a baby.

After supper she discovered that everyone who remained in the manor had but one wish and that was to talk with her about the wedding day. Although no one mentioned her disappearance she knew that the unasked questions were lurking behind every smiling face and she was amused and later, exhausted with parrying their interest. Her brother and his wife had departed but she was soon told by Margery that Alice was expecting a child. When she told her sister that she already suspected it Margery was quite taken aback and she was sorry that she had spoilt her story for her. Margery made no reference to her own affairs and had endless stories about the guests to relate. Margaret's unexpectedly hastened departure had given everyone the desire to talk with her without forgetting anything which they would regret when she had gone. Edmund was similarly surrounded by the menfolk and at one time it seemed as if the gathering would not break up before daybreak. However, Lady Welles, remembering how much had still to be done before the party left for Wales, at last stood up and the ladies made their good nights.

When she came to her bedchamber Margaret found that a sleepy-eyed Betsey was still sitting up for her and she sent her to bed, firmly stating that as they had many days of arduous travel in front of them she needed all the sleep she could get and that she could very easily see herself into bed. Betsey, grateful for the solicitude but not deceived, was thankful that she had the sense to put everything to her hand for her mistress and took herself to her small room.

Alone in the familiar but somehow strange room and undaunted now by the huge tester bed, Margaret undressed and sank gratefully into its softness. Her head still buzzed with the cross fire of conversation that she had withstood in the solar and she lay with wide eyes watching the curve of the damask hangings where the light of the dip caught the brocade patterns. As her head cleared she heard the banging of doors and loud laughter that announced the men had finished their drinking for the night and were on their way to rest. A delicious excitement rushed through her, and when not long afterwards, Edmund was beside her she turned to him with a deep sigh of satisfaction.

'I think,' she said, 'that has been the longest evening of my life!'

14

They set out on the morning of the day after when the mists had lifted. While the family made their farewells the noise and bustle of imminent departure came up to them in the solar.

Margaret's sisters and her half-brother and sister were with their mother and Lord Welles as they clustered round her, eager to bestow on her their good wishes for a safe and happy journey. Little Jonathan, so soon to be bereft of his fairy sea-maiden wished loudly that he was old enough to go with her. Margery told her sister that she had only to call upon her and she would come to be with her at any time.

'Take care of yourself, dearest Margery and of our mother, and do write with news of all the small things that I shall be missing.'

Lady Welles said good-bye to Edmund and accepted his assurances that he would guard his wife's life with his own.

'I have no fear for Margaret's safety now that she is your wife and I pray that no such sacrifice will ever be demanded of you. It is a wise thing that you go to Pembroke and although I shall miss the child I shall breathe more freely when she is safe behind the walls of that stronghold. Only promise me that you will send frequent word of how you both are doing for to be without news is surely the hardest burden to bear. Poor Henry, he did a wise thing for us when he gave Margaret into your wardship. It is a pity that he does not find it as simple to govern the country as he does to order his family's private affairs. God-speed and The Blessing of Our Lady go with you.'

When it came time to say her farewells to Margaret they both found it difficult to talk and covered the moments with much advice on taking care of themselves and writing often. Lady Welles hugged her briefly and in an urgent entreaty to Jasper begged him to get the cavalcade under way. He, obviously anxious to be off, hustled them downstairs to the waiting guard and saw them mounted.

As they clattered out of the gateway Margaret turned in the saddle and waved until they were all hidden from sight. She carried for a long time the memory of her mother's upright figure as she gallantly fluttered her kerchief in farewell and was very quiet while they turned onto the highway towards Bedford.

Edmund riding beside her, made no effort

to distract her for he fully understood that his wife and her mother were close in affection and that each would miss the other in a separation that could last for many weeks, months or even years. He knew that their transcending happiness in each other would soften the hardship but this moment of parting belonged to the women and he would not interfere.

The sun was well up before Margaret's spirits lifted and she looked round to where Edmund was riding with Jasper. She raised her hand and he came up with her, pointing out the glory of a bank of trees rich in autumnal colours, which came down to the side of the Ouse. At that moment the air was filled with the chattering of a flock of starlings that arose startled from a field of stubble at their approach. The sun struck flashes of brilliant colour from their wings as they flew off.

The other travellers became more talkative as the day wore on and they urged their horses on the firm highway heading for Newport Pagnell where their route took them across Watling Street. It was planned to spend the night at the hospice at Buckingham and with dark falling early it was necessary to cover as much ground as possible in the light.

It was the first time that Margaret had

travelled on this route and she was a little awed by the tall forests of pine which they entered after midday. But she lost her fear when a herd of spotted deer crossed their path and rushed into the blue shadows ahead of them. She sniffed with pleasure the resinous smell of the countless needles which made a soft bed beneath the trees. Several times she wished that she and Edmund were alone, as they had been on the short journey from Colmworth, and that they could take their own time and enjoy the tranquil beauty of the countryside. She put the thoughts away from her, glad that they were together and that she was not suffering the parting from her husband rather than her mother. The other members of the party consisted of Lord Roos and his esquires besides Jasper and his attendants and several of the Bletsoe servants with a strong escort of soldiery. Margaret realised that Lord Roos and his young men felt a certain amount of diffidence about addressing her and she was glad that Edmund and later Jasper kept her company. Betsey rode within earshot with Margaret's own groom at hand.

As they approached Buckingham and looked down on the huddled roofs of the town the country became less wooded and opened up into rolling fields. Margaret saw their resting place for the night with gratitude for she was tired with the exercise and the fresh air. They were made welcome by the monks and given an ample, simple meal, after which they were shown the sparse chambers they were to sleep in. Margaret saw with relief that she had been given a room for Edmund and herself and that she would not have to spend the night alone. Betsey, being the only other woman of the party was given a narrow cell close by. The two women hurried through their undressing and after Betsey had laid out clothes for the morrow they fell gratefully into the box beds, mercifully covered with a good layer of straw.

Margaret was asleep when Edmund joined her and he lay for a long time beside her, stroking the hair which tumbled round her face. Over her head he gazed through the narrow, glassless slit out into the perfect quiet of the night and gradually shed the strain of the day. Jasper, Lord Roos and himself expected that this first day and probably several more to come were the most hazardous of the journey, when at any moment a Yorkist ambush might intercept them. Absolute secrecy had been insisted upon for all those that accompanied them, but in these days when even families supported differing loyalties a casual word in a homely gathering could spark off an unforeseen chain of events. He was very much relieved that they had come thus far in safety but not until the gates of Pembroke clanged behind them could he know real peace of mind for the well-being of his wife. He felt in that moment totally inadequate to protect her and his heart misgave him that she should have such implicit trust in him. His love for her caught at his throat and hot tears burned his eyes. He buried his face in her hair and she stirred drowsily and turned her face to his.

'Margaret,' he said, almost on a sob, 'Margaret!' In an instant she was awake and they were drowning in love. Now she was the comforter and protector, giving herself without heed until he was safe and enfolded and all his misgivings gone. She whispered soft words until soothed and happy they both slept a dreamless sleep.

The next morning and in the days that followed they stayed close together, polite and attentive to their travelling companions at all times, but obviously only half-seeing faces about them. Jasper knew, watching them without being observed, that they saw nothing unless it was through the others eyes and that though they made no parade of their affection it was the only thing that really existed. Not for the first time he felt pangs of anxiety for an emotion which was as deep as this. He knew, better even perhaps than Lady Welles who had suffered on their behalf before, the separations and temptations which lay ahead. Not a deeply religious man he nevertheless voiced many wordless prayers to Our Lady to protect the lovers from vicissitude and the roving eyes of dissatisfied wives. He chided himself for developing into a sentimental fool and usually vented his anxiety on his advance party for failing to report some distant doubtful object.

The gentle beauty of the Cotswolds touched Margaret in a way that she was not to forget. In later years she could never recall the warm stone villages and the close cropped shelving meadows without a breath-stopping nostalgia. She exclaimed with delight at the trim hamlets of Aynho and Deddington and was lost in wonder as the party reined in on the top of the steep hill which went sharply down into the Vale of Evesham. From here it looked as if all England were spread at their feet and the tiny fields and diminutive houses swam hazily in the warm sun. The weather had remained fair throughout the week since they had left Bletsoe and the winds were gentle so that living became pure joy and it was easy to forget that each patch of woodland and each curving hillock could harbour an enemy. It seemed impossible in these fairytale surroundings that men could be beset with craving after power that turned them into savage beasts preying ferociously on their own kind to obtain what they wanted. Yet a small voice told her that if need arose she would fight for what she valued and in this was not much removed from those who made personal ambition their god. Shaken by this flash of self-knowledge she thought with true clarity for the first time of the many manors and the vast tracts of land that she had inherited from Devon to the Midlands. She realised that whether she would or not, she was, by nature of her birth, absolutely committed to the one side in this dispute and there was no looking back.

They were warmly welcomed at all the religious houses where they sheltered for the night and Edmund privately considered that they vied with each other to provide special comfort for the important visitors who lodged with them. He was worldly enough to realise that they benefited from the largess which could be expected to flow from the Richmond purses.

Jasper, reluctantly, left them at Chipping Camden to return to the Queen's side. On his return to London he found he was unable to forget for long the haunting beauty of the new Countess Richmond and despite his turbulent nature which enjoyed the art of war he was saddened that she was involved so completely in this affair. He resolved to shoulder as much of the burden of sustaining Margaret of Anjou as he could to allow Edmund to settle his wife in Pembroke Castle without interruption.

At Ledbury Edmund's own troops awaited them and Lord Roos came to bid them farewell. They had spent the two preceding days at Tewkesbury in the Benedictine Abbey and had celebrated Mass with the whole company. After the service in the cool chapel they had met in the refectory where Margaret had presented Lord Roos with a silver dish patterned with the Beaufort portcullis and he had been delighted with the gift which she had offered as a token of her appreciation for their safe conduct.

The next day had been one of rest and Betsey had used it for a washing orgy, taking Margaret's shifts down to the river and rubbing them with wooden sticks in the clear, shallow water. They dried quite successfully spread over bushes in the sun and when they awoke the next morning to driving rain Betsey congratulated herself on her wisdom in not wasting the opportunity.

It was almost noon before the rain eased and they were able to set out for Ledbury. The holiday atmosphere of the past few days quickly evaporated and conversation was desultory. The Avon looked cold and uninviting and Margaret was glad of Edmund's hand on her bridle as the grey dusk fell around them some time before they came into Ledbury's wide street.

The great fire in the parlour of the hospice was the most cheerful sight they had seen all day and they ridded themselves of their damp outer garments and huddled thankfully round the warmth. Having seen Margaret comfortably settled Edmund left her to make plans for the morrow with the captain of his own troops. He was pleased to hear from the man that the townsfolk of Ledbury, once they discovered that the troops were not bent on plunder and rowdyism, had received the men billetted on them with good grace and had given employment to some of the men in the local limestone quarries. The captain had thought that the Earl of Richmond would not object to this as it gave the men occupation as well as providing them with a few pennies to spend. He said that as far as he could assess the natural curiosity of the townsfolk had not discovered the true purpose of their watch. This was welcome news for they were approaching Hereford which was uncomfortably close to the Yorkist Ludlow and it would be easy for a hostile party to lie in wait for them in the sparsely populated countryside. The captain was also able to further reassure his lord that the scouting parties which he had sent out daily in sweeping radials from Ledbury had seen no evidence to make him believe that the opposing faction were aware that the Lancastrian heiress and her husband were *en passant* for Wales. It was his opinion that the lateness of the year was almost as much protection as his well-trained troops.

In Hereford itself they encountered the busiest town they had yet visited and Edmund prudently left his captain to see to his men's quartering at Widemarsh while he and Margaret went on alone and on foot to the hospice close to the Cathedral of St. Ethelbert. They had dismounted outside the town by a white cross which they found had been erected in thanksgiving for the end of the Black Death; here they hurriedly crossed themselves and muttered a prayer for the threat of plague was still very real and England was only now recovering from the horror that had decimated the population in the previous century.

Then, happy to be alone, although they knew the captain had misgivings about the decision to part company for a short time, they walked hand in hand into the crowded main street. Jostled and pushed they enjoyed the pleasure of being unnoticed and unwatched. They looked with amusement as a long line of gowned choristers walked demurely under the watchful eyes of a fat monk from their school into the cathedral. The crowded booths of the market beneath their gay striped awnings were well stocked with farm produce and sheepskin goods. Edmund made a mental note to send one of his pages to purchase a fleece-lined cloak for Margaret to wear in the winter ahead of them. From what he had learned from Jasper the stronghold of Pembroke paid for its isolation by receiving, straight from the turbulent ocean, the full force of the southwest gales. This he knew would be in marked contrast with the protected Bletsoe and he did not wish Margaret to suffer unduly.

Extra provisions were purchased in Hereford, for to reach Brecon they had to pass through difficult, unpopulated country once they left Abergavenny. The monasteries at Dore and at Abergavenny had been warned to expect them but it was most unlikely that they would have sufficient food to stock a small army.

The guide they engaged at the monastery at Abergavenny endorsed their wisdom and provided little comfort to Edmund when he told them that the high mountains on either side of the track gave shelter to brigands and wolves alike. Edmund was glad that Margaret was not present to hear this piece of uninviting news and comforted himself with the thought that the little dark man who was to lead them was reputed to be well acquainted with the route.

They left the shelter of the monastery before it was light while the stars still glimmered in a pale morning sky. Margaret huddled the sheepskin cloak around her, grateful already to Edmund for his kindness in providing it for her. She missed her little mare which had been replaced by a pony but realised quickly that its short sturdy legs picked out unerringly the firmest path through the boulders and scattered stones which were sometimes the only passage through cascading rivulets. It was very still and as the way twisted and turned she could hear sometimes the murmur of the Usk as it followed them. With the coming of day the wind died completely and in the cold quietness the old soldiers learned in weather lore exchanged glances and fervent hopes that the guide was as good as he was made out to be. Their anxieties did not diminish as patches of mist seemed to mushroom out of hollows and leaving Crickhowell behind them many of them thought with pleasure of the sure comfort that was to be found within its walls and wished that their captain would see fit to suggest to the Earl that they remained here until the weather cleared. No such fortune was to be theirs and they pushed on at a smart pace behind the dark small guide.

Edmund ordered an early and brief halt for the middle day food because he was beginning to have some doubts of the man's worth as a pilot. There was some arrogance coupled with a slippery quality on which it was difficult to put a finger, that convinced him that the dark Welshman was not all he had been credited with. With the half-formed doubts in his mind the mists were thickening and he could see that unless the wind quickened they would soon be unable to see their way.

He approached the Welsh guide and the man assured him that if the need arose the 'Half-way Inn' would afford them shelter and that it was but an hour's good ride from where they were at the moment. Reassured Edmund joined his wife and realised that she had no sense of fear and was chattering gaily with Betsey and her own groom who were close beside her. He rode back to the van of the troop, speaking with each of the men and soon discovered that at least half of them were in the same mind as he about the wisdom of trusting the guide. He did not communicate his agreement but returned to the front of the long winding cavalcade noting with increasing alarm the thickness of the mist.

When he came up with the Welshman it was to find him slackening his pace and pushing his woollen cap back to scratch his wiry hair.

'What is it?' he enquired brusquely.

'Well, it's like this,' the man said slowly. 'I believe we have passed the old burial mound some way back and by rights it should have lain on our right hand side and — '

'And,' Edmund said in a dangerously quiet voice.

'To the best of my knowledge it was on our left and we are on the road to Cwm-gu.'

'What does that mean exactly?' Edmund said, still in the same quiet voice.

'It means that it will take a little longer to reach the 'Half-way Inn.' I did my best my lord,' he quavered and shrank back as if he expected Edmund to strike him.

'You are lost, in other words,' Edmund said.

'You might say that, my lord, but there is a way out if you will trust me.'

'Trust you!' Edmund exclaimed. 'That is what we have done and you bring us to this disaster. You know full well that it is impossible to turn a troop of horses in a narrow way such as this, let alone when it is made doubly difficult with a heavy mist. We shall have to continue and pray that you are telling the truth and will be able to bring us safely to the shelter of the inn. How much further do you reckon it is if we continue in this way?'

'I should not say it was any longer.'

'Well?' said Edmund.

'It is just that it is somewhat narrow and means we shall have to climb. We should not be delayed so very much.'

Edmund bit back the stinging reproach which he longed to give the man and told him curtly to continue.

He hedged his way to Margaret's side through the way which he realised was already considerably less open than it had been when he went forward to speak with the guide.

Although the troop had not halted, the pace had slowed considerably and when he rejoined Margaret she glanced quickly at him.

'We are lost?' she enquired.

'Yes, sweeting,' Edmund told her. 'I am sorry but it appears we took the wrong fork some way back and we have no other course but to continue on this route which is rather more difficult than the one we intended to take. The guide assures me that it will bring us to the same inn that I was making for when the mists came down.'

'An inn!' Margaret said laughing. 'That will be a change from nunneries and monks' houses.'

'It may be a change for the worse,' Edmund said grimly, 'but it will be better than spending the night in this desolate pass.'

He looked with dismay as huge boulders loomed out of the murk looking for all the world like crouched men waiting to spring. He eased his way through his men, telling the captain the truth of the matter, but only speaking words of encouragement to the men-at-arms. He knew perfectly well that they would guess before long that they were on the wrong road, but the less time they would have to discuss it the better. He hoped that he could trust the Welshman when he said that it was not all that much longer than the lower proper road.

Before long the way had narrowed into a

defile in which it was possible to ride only in single file. He stationed himself directly behind the guide with the captain and sergeant behind and Margaret's groom next to her with Betsey following on her pony's heels. The damp white air was filled with the noise of hooves clattering over loose shale and an occasional, muffled torrent of swearing as a horse slipped and almost unseated its rider. By the slowing pace and the angle of the path he knew that they were already climbing. His horse broke out in a lather and at one point sent a pile of loose stones slipping behind him. He cursed himself for bringing Margaret and his men into this predicament and vowed that he would vet any future guides with considerably more care than he had given to this one. He shouted forward to the man to ask him if he had any idea how much further it was to the top of the pass, knowing that before there could be hope of coming on the alehouse they would have to climb down on the other side. The guide replied that he believed another half an hour would bring them to the summit. It was the longest half an hour that Edmund ever remembered as the path became at each moment steeper and more difficult. To add to his concern he realised by the cessation of the echo which had accompanied them from the start that they were out of the defile and that open hillside was on their left hand. He dreaded to think what the possible drop might be and called back for word to be passed down the column that the party should keep in as much as they could to the right. This was no easy task for the ponies and horses were laden with baggage on both sides but he knew his orders were being obeyed as he heard the clank of metal as lances and cooking pots hit the overhanging rocks on their right hand. He longed to be with Margaret and comfort her but contented himself with the knowledge that she had Betsey and the groom who would give his life for her if the need arose. Although he believed the Welshman when he said there was an inn in front of them he could not even be sure that they would be received in a friendly fashion for these out of the way ale houses were frequently the hideouts of outlaws.

In the midst of this gloomy thought he discovered that they were riding amidst a group of trees, stretching eerily into the now darkening mists. Almost at once his horse stumbled and he shot forward slightly as the way began to fall as abruptly as it had risen.

Margaret had become more and more silent as the tortuous journey progressed. She became conscious of a slight pain that nagged in the small of her back. Much of her energy was taken up with reassuring Betsey that they would not be attacked at each step by the little people that Betsey was sure lived in the cracks and crevices of the overhanging rock. She spurred her servant on with a gaiety she was far from feeling and shared with her some wine from a silver flask that they carried. The pain in her back increased until each step of the pony's jolted her through like a searing knife. She took several deep gulps of the wine but found that although it deadened the pain a little it also made her head swim. Several times she almost cried out as the horse stumbled but somehow managed to control herself for it would never do to let Edmund's men know that their lady was a coward. Coward or not she longed to slide down to the earth and lie there without having to move. The memory of the comfortable guest houses which had been their resting places mocked her with their warm fires and well ordered comfort. She resolved to double her munificence in gratitude for their kindness.

As the path took the downwards turn the pain in her back became a ferocious animal tearing at her flesh and digging it's claws into the vital organs of her body and she clung to the huge pommel of the side-sitting saddle to keep her from falling to the ground in a faint. Several times she lost any knowledge of where she was and only heard the voices and noise about her in a confused blur. At one point she nearly asked Betsey to try and make her way to sit up behind her but her pride would not allow it and she drew on some untapped source of strength to help her continue.

The descent was steeper than the going up and the rocks crowded in on them as before, but quite suddenly Edmund heard the flow of a quick river and when he asked the guide if they had rejoined the main track the man assured him that they had. He continued for a few hundred yards until he was certain that all the party were on the wider path and he then pushed his way, on foot, back to his wife. To his dismay he found her slumped over the pony's neck, but she assured him as he took her ice cold hand in his that she was able to go on.

The guide now struck out with renewed vigour calling out in a loud voice as he recognised familiar landmarks looming out of the dark. Edmund had given orders to his esquire to take his horse while he mounted behind Margaret and cradled her against him. Safe in the surety of his arms she gave way to the pain and lost consciousness.

Almost a mile of straightforward track

brought them up to a roughly constructed log hut where a man, roused by the approaching troop, was standing, holding aloft a burning torch. As the captain and the sergeant dismounted and pushed their way up to him he beckoned into the interior of the hut and an untidy bundle of a woman joined him. Edmund watching saw their faces successively registering dismay, craftiness and greed as they realised the number of the party wishing to take shelter with them.

Any attempt to hold the wayfarers to ransom for this hospitality was short lived as the captain followed by the burly sergeant-at-arms pushed their way unceremoniously into the interior of the hut.

'This will do for the twenty men I have with me,' the captain told the innkeeper, 'but I have two gently reared women with me and they must have separate shelter.'

The man leered at him.

'If they are willing to travel with you they must be ready to share your quarters, we have nothing else but a lean-to where we keep a pig when we have one.'

The captain controlled the urge to hit the man and asked him to show him the stye. The man sniffed and going into the corner of the room pushed open a badly fitting door.

The place was small and the ceiling came

down to the ground at the far end but it was at least private.

'This will do,' the captain said shortly. 'Fill it with clean straw and it will answer well enough.'

'We have no straw,' the man replied.

'Doubtless you have plenty of dried bracken. Fetch that without delay or my men will have pleasure in assisting you.'

Shouting to the sergeant to water the horses the captain reported to Edmund that the place was as evil-looking and smelling as any he had ever encountered but it would protect them from the damp chill of the night. He looked at Margaret and glanced up at Edmund.

'I think she has fainted,' Edmund told him. 'Do you think the place is ready for me to put her down to rest?' He called to one of his esquires to bring blankets and follow him into the inn. He slipped from the horse's back and without disturbing Margaret carried her inside. Betsey, her own aching back forgotten as she saw her mistress's plight, hurried after them bringing a small hand-sack of towels and lotions.

The captain was chivvying the innkeeper as he stumbled in under a load of dried bracken and threw it on to the floor of the stye. The youngest of the esquires spread the blankets and knelt to take Margaret's feet as Edmund tenderly laid his wife down. She stirred as he lifted her head and forced her to drink from his flask. In the light of the guttering crude light he was shocked at the pallor of her face. Betsey gently covered her with the sheepskin cloak as her eyelids fluttered open and she looked up at Edmund.

'Don't leave me,' she whispered, 'don't leave me, ever.'

The men crammed themselves into the hut and threw themselves down making short work of the rest of the day's ration of food. This they washed down with the strong ale which seemed to be the only commodity in good supply in the place. The inkeeper and his wife watched them out of the corners of their eyes while they cooked a greasy stew over a fire which smoked abominably, filling the overcrowded room with fumes. When they had seen Edmund they realised that they were now dealing with the nobility and their manner had changed slightly to one of obsequious cringing which had rapidly faded as they saw that he was quite unaware of them and only interested in the girl in his arms.

As the men settled for sleep one of them opened the door to allow a momentary change of air but it was rudely banged by the innkeeper who brought heavy wooden bars and pushed them into sockets in the wall to bar it.

Edmund stole out of the byre long enough to eat a few pieces of meat and discuss with the captain the advisability of starting out at the earliest light providing the mists had lifted. As he resumed his place at Margaret's side he dreaded to think of the possibility of staying in this den for an hour longer than was necessary. He sat beside her without sleeping through the endless seeming night although his head and eyes ached with weariness. He was distressed to hear her moan at intervals and blamed himself for not having seen sooner that the mists were set in for the day and that a return to Abergavenny was the right course to take.

He was considerably relieved when the captain looked in as it was beginning to get light to say that the sentry reported that the clouds were low but that the fog was cleared.

'Rouse the men immediately and pay the innkeeper his due. We must reach Brecon as quickly as possible.'

Margaret hearing his voice was struggling to sit up and she told him that although she ached still across her lower back, the terrible pain had gone and that she was recovered sufficiently to continue. Betsey shook the woman awake and asked her to rekindle the fire to heat a little water to pour on to some of the dried meat which would make a thin soup for her mistress. Margaret took one or two sips of the mixture and protested that it warmed her stomach and that was all she could manage to swallow. She refused to allow Edmund to take her up into her saddle with blankets.

They reached Brecon before the hour of sext and Edmund told the captain that they would rest here for two days to give all of them and especially the Countess of Richmond, some rest. The man while agreeing that it would be pleasant to enjoy a respite after the ordeal of the previous day, could not help wishing that they could push on, for not until he had safely delivered his important travellers into the castle at Pembroke would he be able to relax completely.

Margaret suffered the kindly ministrations of the nuns with gratitude as they anointed her and rubbed her with oils and applied compresses to her bruised back. The delicious broth they brought her did much to restore her energy and when Edmund visited her she told him that she felt she was a fraud to be lying in blissful comfort, waited on by the good sisters who doubtless denied themselves a fragment of luxury during their lives.

Edmund promised her that they enjoyed looking after the sick and that he was quite sure that if she were called upon to act as a nurse she would be as kind and as willing as they were.

She smiled at him and taking his hand put it to her cheek and fell asleep.

15

Margaret felt a sense of awe as she looked on Pembroke Castle for the first time. She saw it towering over the town as they approached from Carew where they had spent the previous night, and not even Windsor, remembered dimly from her childhood, had seemed as formidable as this towering fortress. In that moment it struck her that while it looked impossible to attack it also gave the impression of a prison and she shuddered and wondered how long she and Edmund would have to remain here.

They had entered in at the east gate of the walled town and made their way through the house-lined street, where every window had a clutch of curious faces, until they came to the main entrance of the castle where they crossed the fosse and came under the barbican gateway. Here the two enormous portcullis were drawn up and the massive doors swung back to reveal Jasper's steward who stood waiting to escort them through the Great Gatehouse. They dismounted under the archway where Edmund presented his wife before entering the lodge and climbing the staircase to the steward's residence. The upper rooms, which were surprisingly large, gave onto a passage which was the communicating link with the tower which Jasper had made over completely to his brother and sister-in-law. The noise of hammering told them that the renovations were not yet complete.

The steward hastened to tell them that the main rooms were quite ready for them and that it was only minor alterations to the rooms being prepared for the retinue they had brought which were not finished.

Margaret's first fears disappeared and she gave a small cry of delight at the beauty of the rooms she had been given. The elegant luxury of the chambers exceeded anything she had seen before and the richness of the hangings outshone the splendour of Collyweston where the Beaufort family in previous years had spared no expense to surround themselves with worldly treasures.

The solar, hung with tapestries was situated on the second floor close to the bedchamber. This room had an enormous tester bed hung with white and gold brocade patterned in fleur-de-lis and marguerites. Both chambers had fireplaces. The steward received their approbation with obvious pride and asked them, when they were rested to sup with him and his wife in their private parlour.

When he finished his tour of inspection with them and had acquainted them with their new home, he left them alone and Margaret turned to Edmund with a beaming smile. He took her in his arms glad to see her enjoyment, for she had been very quiet since they left Brecon and he had been afraid that the unnerving experience in the hills had dampened her spirits.

'Now you can forget the journey, dearling,' he said as he caressed her gently. 'You are safe here and no harm can befall you.'

'Where you are I fear nothing,' she answered huskily. 'When you send despatches to Jasper thank him for all his kindness in making this place so welcoming. I am sure that even the King has nothing as beautiful as this room.'

Edmund laughed at her and drew her over to the narrow window to look out over the rooftops below them.

'Henry wouldn't notice what a room contained or whether it was hot or cold, but I know that when Margaret of Anjou first married him she did her best to rouse some enthusiasm for his surroundings. Her father had always been short of money and she had an eye for luxury and saw her marriage with the King of England as a wonderful opportunity to fulfil her pleasure. One cannot help wondering if things would have turned out differently for her had Henry shared her zest for life and if she would have developed this worship of power. Perhaps if her husband had been a man of Suffolk's mettle she would have put her vast energies to more constructive ends and sent fleets of ships to the distant shores of the world to colonise them for England.'

'Sometimes,' Margaret said dreamily, cradled against his shoulder, 'I wish I were a man, and then I should go to the sea.'

'You horrify me,' Edmund said in mock dismay. 'I can think of nothing worse than that you should have been born a man.'

'I jest,' Margaret replied. 'Only a woman who is lapped in love can afford to dream such outlandish thoughts, for I am truly sorry for the Queen. Jasper told me that since the King's illness she has no interest in anything but keeping the throne for her son and has grown careless in her dress and more shrewish every day. Oh, Edmund, we have so much happiness that sometimes I grow afraid for us.'

He pulled her close to him and kissed her lingeringly.

'There is nothing to be afraid for, my love.

307

I promise you that we shall live here as we did at Colmworth.'

She did not reply but her ready acceptance of his mouth on hers told them both that the exquisite passion which had been theirs was waiting to recapture them when once the formalities of the day had been encompassed and they were alone in the enveloping night.

Betsey, delighted to return to the orderly routine of settled domesticity, had decided that Margaret should wear one of her lavish new gowns for the visit to the steward and she had sent pages scurrying backwards and forwards to the kitchens for ewers of hot water. This occasion called for a bath and she filled a huge copper bowl that the groom begged for her from the washhouse and threw in quantities of rose water. Margaret soaked as best she could in the cramped container and felt the fatigue and stiffness melt away. The feel of clean linen and silk against her skin completely restored her joy in the well-being of her body.

To curb the uprush of longing she felt for Edmund to come in and sweep her there and then into the great bed, she told Betsey that she would wear for the first time, one of the finely pleated coifs she had had made for her bride's clothes.

Betsey handed the mirror to her as she put

it in place, cover her hair and binding it down with crossed ribbons. She made a face at her reflection.

'Now I am truly a matron,' and she sighed dramatically. Betsey, looking at the serene brow and the tenderness of the full, curving mouth thought she had never seen anything less matronly in her life, but she only smiled and handed her mistress a cloak to put round her shoulders in case the parlour was draughty.

The steward's wife, seeing the Countess of Richmond for the first time, found that she could speak only the barest words of greeting for she was amazed at the young girl's poise, coupled as it was with an almost unearthly beauty. She had dreaded the coming of this child-wife, whom she had been convinced would be one of the capricious children of the noble houses who would completely disrupt the household of Pembroke with her whims and fancies. It did not take her long to discover that she could not have been more mistaken in her convictions, for here was a modest young girl, more learned than most of the rough, boisterous men who frequented the castle, deeply in love with her disarmingly handsome husband. She saw too, that the young Earl was cast in a different mould from his exuberant brother and that he had a depth of character which matched his wife's.

Before the evening was over the steward and his wife realised that they were fortunate indeed to have the Richmonds as their guests and that, wrapped in each other as they were, they would have little or no time for causing unheaval in their household. They parted with the lady promising to take Margaret on a tour of the castle the next day.

Betsey, waiting for her in her own apartments, helped her undress and removed the bricks, which she had heated in the fire and wrapped in woollen cloths, from the bed and said 'Good night.'

Margaret lay naked between the warm silk sheets. During the evening the assured manner which had so struck the steward's wife had hidden the delight with which she was anticipating this moment. She heard Edmund come into the room with her heart leaping in an absurd manner and had a brief moment in which to wonder if it would always be like this, or if one day she would come to dread his approach, before he was beside her. The touch of his body and the masterly skill of his hands which transmuted his pleasure swept her to him. She clung to him as if the pent up ardour of the past weeks was waiting for this moment of release. He took her once, then again and again, not remembering in the shared ecstasy one of his former fears for her youth. They loved each other and that in itself was sufficient to put aside any doubt in the world.

At last they slept, the fur covers and silken sheets awry, until feeling the chill he drowsily pulled her close and drew up the bedclothes.

Long before the chill easterly winds countered the sea-laden south-westerlies that blustered through the castle, Margaret was completely at home in Pembroke. She thought sometimes with a pang of dismay that she did not miss the Bletsoe family and would be content to stay here with Edmund for ever. He cut short his frequent visits to Jasper's fellow Marcher Lords to be as much as he could at her side. Although she encouraged him in what she knew was his duty in stirring up, as best he could, the support for their cause, he was not deceived by the brave front she showed him. He realised what she suffered during his absences for he discovered that without her he felt incomplete and he could not put out of his mind the droop of her mouth when he had left her for the first time. He thought ruefully afterwards that the Lancastrian faction would have judged him a poor advocate as his mind had been set, while he harangued and put their case to the poorly educated, ruthless scions of neighbouring castles, on the quickest return possible to Pembroke. The first night he was parted from her he did not once close his eyes and when they were reunited she confessed that she had not slept either, but had spent the long wakeful hours wrapped in the fur covers from the bed, gazing out into the darkness. When she was asleep beside him he had not, even then, been able to sleep. He was troubled more than he had realised by the intensity of their mutual adoring. While her love gave him nothing but absolute happiness it brought with it the tremendous responsibility that had never been far distant since that day long ago in the cell-like room at Windsor when Henry had given her to him in ward. He was glad that she liked the steward's lady and that Simon Hovey had started to send her lessons again. She faithfully carried out the problems and exercises he set her and returned the completed work with the messengers that came fairly frequently between Bletsoe and Pembroke. These visits fell off during the very coldest of the winter, but the Queen, who was caring for the King at Shene, had agreed to release Jasper for the Christmastide period and this had heightened the pleasure of the preparations in the castle. Edmund had privately asked the steward's wife to include

Margaret in the many duties which befell a chatelaine at this time and she had it seemed gladly assisted in the kitchens and still rooms. At last, thinking that he was probably being unnecessarily concerned about his wife's welfare, Edmund slept.

She certainly did not begrudge him his hunting or hawking and one morning, when he had departed early to chase wild boar with a party of neighbouring lords, Margaret was crossing the yard with the steward's wife. She wore a hooded cloak for frost had touched the bare branches of the trees during the night and a chill wind fluttered round the grey stone of the castle. They had been to the stables to inspect a litter of new-whelped puppies. The bitch belonged to the steward and was a long-haired black and white collie which the groom who took them to peep at the corner where she lay huddled in fresh straw with the pink and white offspring nuzzled against her, told them was a master mind in the control of sheep. He promised that when she was working again he would give Margaret a demonstration of her skill.

Margaret asked the lady to come up with her and take a hannap of wine. She was glad of the opportunity to entertain her and she wanted to ask her advice about the placing of a large tapestry that her mother had sent her for a St. Nicholas gift.

'You must be looking forward to having your own house, my lady.'

'Yes,' Margaret agreed, 'but I am very happy here. It is only when a small thing like finding a spare wall to hang this piece of work when it is finished that I realise that this is not quite my own house.'

The steward's wife looked at the enormous piece of barely begun canvas.

'It will certainly be some time before you have completed the work but when you do, would it not be a good idea to open up the small room close to Betsey's which would then do very well indeed for a nursery?'

The woman regretted the words as soon as she had said them, for she did not want the young Countess to think that she was prying. Margaret however showed no sign of emotion as she replied that this thought had not occurred to her but now that the lady had suggested it, it became obvious that the small room would be ideal to exhibit her handiwork.

When she was alone again and she sat in the darkening solar, awaiting Edmund's return, she allowed the full significance of the words to come to the surface of her mind. She realised that since the early days of her marriage, three months before, she had not given much thought to the likelihood of conceiving a child. Edmund filled her life completely and there seemed no need of any further fulfilment. She remembered with almost the same pang of dismay that she did not really crave a baby any more than she missed the family to whom she had always been so devoted. With this realisation came the question of whether Edmund thought it was time she set about the business of producing an heir. She felt fairly certain that he was as content as she was and considered that this blessing would doubtless be added to them in God's good time.

However, when he returned, glowing, from the hunt she looked at him with a slightly quizzical air, wondering if he found her wanting. He showed no signs as he settled down beside her, eager to recount the day's sports, of finding her in any way different from when he had left her in the early morning, and she dismissed the doubts and gave him her full attention. She was surprised in the days that followed that if she wanted or not she could not completely forget that one of the purposes of her marriage was to provide an heir.

Christmas came and went in a flurry of festivities that were a novelty for the sombre Pembroke. The Yule log, burning slowly through the twelve days of the merrymaking, warmed the great hall and spread a cheerful light on the streams of guests that shared in the feasting and dancing.

When a doe-eyed woman was presented to Margaret and she brought with her a small girl, named Ellen who was dark and sturdy it was not difficult to recognise that the child was Jasper's. She had the same grave manner that was her father's when he was concentrating deeply, coupled with a wide-eyed innocence that Margaret found irresistible. She was drawn to the little girl as she had been to her own small brother and sister and spent a morning creating a rag doll for her from her piece bag.

Jasper, throwing off the Queen's burdens entered wholeheartedly into enjoyments that were prepared by his young esquire whom he had appointed Lord of Misrule.

The youth took guests and the menservants to the woods to bring in armfuls of evergreens which were hung around the walls of the hall, and begged extra tapers and lights from the steward to brighten the gloomy place. When he invented outrageous forfeits for Kiss in the Ring and perpetrated his own sophisticated version of Hoodman Blind the guests entered willingly into his games and, protesting, carried out his wishes. When one morning they awoke to find a covering of snow he had the joiners and cofferers making rough sledges on which the party went gaily slipping and sliding down the hills.

During the traditional singing of Carols of Twelfth Night which rounded off the festivities Margaret looked at all the happy faces and heard the full-throated roar of the mingled voices and found it impossible to believe that the country was torn with strife. She knew that even among their carefully selected guests were those who had close relations who professed other loyalties than their own. Jasper had amazed them by bringing the news that the young Duke of Suffolk was betrothed to Elizabeth the second daughter of York. It seemed that unable to further his interests with the Lancastrian succession he was throwing in his lot with the opposing faction. As the brothers talked about the young man Margaret could see clearly the stocky boy talking to her half-brothers about their falcons in the hall at Bletsoe. It all seemed a very long time ago.

Jasper took his leave of them on the next day looking considerably less strained than he had on his arrival. He confessed that he returned to the problem of the Yorkist domination with a lighter heart than before assured by the contacts that he had made with the other Marcher barons that the Queen's cause did not lack supporters and that it was still possible to break the Protector's yoke.

He kissed Margaret on the brow as he said good-bye. Although this salute was common among men and women of even slight acquaintance and gave rise to criticism of the English among the French and Italians, he found it difficult to touch his sister-in-law, for she seemed so wrapped in Edmund that he stood in some fear of causing her embarrassment. At this moment he found her so endearing that he could not resist brushing her lightly with his lips.

To his surprise she smiled warmly at him and took his hand for a brief moment.

'Thank you for sending us here, Jasper' she said 'and for taking so much upon yourself on our behalf. If it were not for you Edmund would be away from me so much. You will take care that you don't get caught up in any of these disturbances that you have been telling us about?'

'I'm too much of an old soldier to do that,' he laughed. 'It is you that must guard against these damp Welsh winds and the demon of boredom.'

'I am never bored,' she said happily. 'Sometimes I am almost frightened that

Edmund and I are so peaceful and quiet when there is such trouble about us.'

'Don't worry about that,' Jasper said. 'You'll have quite enough to think about producing a fine lusty string of offspring for that fortunate brother of mine.'

He was startled by the poignancy of the look she gave him and carried for days the haunting appeal of her lovely face as she stood at Edmund's side and wished him God-speed. Even back in the care-worn Court where he found a distinct improvement in the King's condition, he could not forget her.

Lying in the still darkness of the night after a day spent in discussion with Margaret of Anjou about the possibility of discharging York from his duties now that there was a glimmer of hope that Henry might be able to resume his responsibilities, he found his tired brain returning to the Castle of Pembroke. During all the time that York and Warwick encamped at Westminster with a party three hundred strong to keep all other lords from coming to support the King in his recovery, he could still feel the fineness of her skin as he had touched it and once or twice was sharply called to task by the Queen for allowing his attention to wander at this most vital turning point in their fortunes.

As the days went by and Henry once more escaped from the melancholy that seemed to lie in wait behind his chair, Jasper was pleased that his task in aiding his half-brother and the Queen became progressively more absorbing for he had no time to think at all about any other matter. On February 25th he assembled his own strong escort and went with the King to the Palace of Westminster where York was relieved of his Protectorship for the second time. The Duke accepted this with a show of gratitude for the King's recovery knowing full well that the Bourchiers, who were his tools, were still in power as Chancellor and Treasurer. The Queen and Jasper accepted this situation, biding their time until they had regained sufficient support from the Lords to remove the brothers and substitute loyal Lancastrians.

When the tension of this crisis was relaxed Jasper was relieved to discover that he could think of Margaret of Richmond with more detachment than he had felt since he arrived in Pembroke. Now that the danger had subsided he could face the fact that his brother's wife had more power to move him than any of the passionate beauties who had vied strength for strength with him in his numerous amorous adventures.

Rejoicing at the return to health of the

King but unaware of the turmoil that had been aroused in the breast of the Earl of Pembroke, the household in his castle lived quietly through the winter.

Edmund was absent for three days towards the end of March, looking into a fracas which had broken out between a party of scouts he had despatched and a band of outlaws coming down from their winter quarters. One afternoon while he was gone Margaret had walked on the battlements and revelled in the unexpected warmth of the sun. She took deep breaths of the air which was heavy with spring perfumes and determined that when Edmund returned she would beg of him to take her riding. In his absence he would not allow her to go beyond the walls for he trusted no one but himself to guard her.

Now she leant against a wall which protected her from the wind that was still cool, and soaked up the sunshine. The warmth penetrated her clothing and filled her with a blissful lassitude. Lately, despite her boast to Jasper, she did find that time hung more and more heavily on her hands when Edmund was not with her. Although she applied herself with extra effort to her translations for Simon Hovey, she found it difficult to concentrate for long periods and there was not the same satisfaction in the results. The tapestry, although half completed, palled after three months of stitching at it. She began to dread the times that Edmund had to leave her, not only because she missed him with a physical pain, but because the void it caused was no longer easy to fill. Betsey, conscious of the unrest in her young mistress, tried to distract her by planning a new summer wardrobe but even this usually absorbing topic failed to hold her attention for any length of time. She would look at the long rolls of brilliant silks and sigh and say they were very pretty but she had enough gowns for the time being and perhaps later they would ask the sempstress to make something of them.

During the past three nights that Edmund was away Margaret had been unable to sleep. She had found that she had no difficulty in sinking into the pillows and losing herself but in a very short time was wide awake and from then on would lie tossing and restless until the first light of day. She wished desperately that it was possible for her to accompany Edmund.

He, eager to be home with Margaret of whose disquiet he was aware, had sent word to Gilbert Suoh that as he was passing his estate he would stay to drink a cup of wine. Edmund had received warning from loyal

Lancastrians that there was considerable reason to doubt Gilbert's allegiance to the King. He made the difficult detour to the man's castle only to discover on his arrival that Suoh was not at home. By the smirk on the steward's face Edmund surmised that the lord of the house had had word of his approach and had absented himself rather than be available to hear discussions of the merits of the Lancastrian cause from no less an advocate than the King's half-brother.

This unsatisfactory visit spurred him homewards, fuming at the wasted time. The tempestuous speed at which he rode caused raised eyebrows among his retinue while he spent the hours in the saddle devising means of restoring his wife to her former state of contentment.

In this he was unexpectedly aided by the perverse spring weather that stayed warm and summerlike for his first two days in Pembroke and then without warning clamped down with driving rains and blustering south-westerly gales.

16

They rode out into the countryside during these first sunlit days and the unrestricted exercise and the change of environment did much to dispel her inertia and restore her vitality, although she could not dismiss from her mind the unspoken dread that this was only a temporary lull before Edmund was compelled to leave her again. She chided herself, when she was able, for her possessiveness and tried to comfort herself with the knowledge that he was at least never far from her and that she did not suffer as her mother did with Lord Welles often in Calais for months at a time. Then a voice would whisper that her mother lived all the time and not only when her husband was with her. Lady Welles was self-sufficient whereas she was not. With the coming of dusk she was beset with the melancholies and twice Edmund found her in the small chapel, so deep in prayer that she did not hear him open the door and look in at her. He was troubled for her and was even more gentle and loving to her than usual although he knew very well that this was no lasting cure as it only threw her with more weight into the charmed circle of his care.

On the third morning they awoke to hear rain lashing down from lowering clouds. They rose and dressed leisurely and spent the day quietly within the precincts of the castle. Pages brought dried driftwood and sea coal and built up a good fire which penetrated the damp corners of the chamber. Towards dusk Margaret took up her neglected tapestry and enjoyed once again the soothing rhythm of the needle as she pushed it down and up through the canvas. So absorbed was she that when Edmund kissed her on the back of her neck she started.

He threw himself at her feet and handed her the lute.

'Play for me,' he asked. She put down her work and her hands gliding across the strings plucked out the melody of a Welsh song that she had heard one of the women humming in the kitchens.

The plaintive air, with unexpected harmonies touched his heart and without speaking he took the lute away from her and enfolded her in his arms. He put his head on the bared curve of her breast and she murmured his name. Although he had heard her use the word hundreds of times before, there seemed, to his ear tuned with anxiety for her, that there was something almost desperate in the way she said it. She slid from her stool and knelt facing him, her arms going round his neck and pressing his face to her. He kissed her mouth and felt her body quicken into response. His arms tightened round her and he lifted her to her feet and into the bedchamber where he kicked the door closed behind them. It was not yet their time for retiring but in that moment he did not care what Betsey or any of the other servants thought about their absence.

The rapturous ardour of her passion surprised even him, and when it was spent he bent over her caressing her shoulders and side and telling her of his love for her.

She lay watching and listening to him, nestling in the sweet security of reciprocated desire until sleep came to them both.

It was almost a week before the weather cleared and a pale sunshine broke through the rain. During all this time Edmund and Margaret could hardly bear to be apart, and he found that when he was attending to the daily administration of his troops and reading the despatches that arrived more frequently from the Court and their estates, that his mind was only half on what he was doing. In the middle of composing a letter with the clerk concerning the fee for a piece of land in the manor of Cheshunt he would find himself dwelling on the softness of his wife's flesh or the perfume of her hair and would only be brought back to reality by the polite cough of the man who sat waiting with quill poised for him to finish a sentence.

He could not, however, ignore his scouts who brought in the unwelcome news that from their watching point of Gilbert Suoh's castle that the man was amassing troops. The sergeant in charge said that he had crept close under the walls and had heard the unmistakeable sounds of training and preparation for armed combat. Edmund tore himself, most reluctantly. from the web of enchantment that Margaret wove round him and applied himself to the calling in of the men due to the Lord of Pembroke in times of emergency. Even this he regarded as a token of his adoration of his wife for this was for her protection and this was his first duty.

As he was preparing to meet Gilbert's challenge, word came from Shene that there had been serious disturbances in London between the Mercers and the Italian silk workers who, until the Commons had prohibited it, had carried on a thriving trade in the city. Jasper wrote that he saw this as symptomatic of the unrest against the shaky administration of the recovered King and that his brother should put down vigorously any signs of disaffection in Wales. Coming as it did at this moment it underlined the necessity to prevent Gilbert from launching an attack. His small army was now trained to a complete state of readiness and in the beginning of June he set out.

He had dreaded the parting from Margaret, but it was impossible to keep the preparations from her and to his amazement when he told her that he was leaving on the morrow she accepted his decision with calm. She rose at cockcrow to wish him God-speed and he thought he had never seen her more beautiful as she stood there, smiling serenely and rosy from their bed. She had assisted him into his cumbersome armour and tied her kerchief around the top of his arm, before throwing over the embroidered tunic emblazoned with the royal arms of France and England and bordered in blue. When he kissed her, with difficulty, she did not cling to him with the same desperate urgency as usual and he wondered if it was inborn in woman to accept that men had to fight for them and that she was more ready to let him go when real danger threatened.

It was not until the last stragglers had been herded on to the way and he took up his position in the van of the troop that he had time to wonder if perhaps there was something more in his wife's cooler leave taking. Surely it could not be that Margaret was satiated with loving and secretly a little pleased to be without him! He shuddered and suddenly felt cold. The unpleasant thought haunted him all the day as they made slow progress towards Gilbert Suoh's fortress and did not leave him as they encamped beside a swift-moving stream that gurgled brown over the lichen-covered stones. When the others were asleep he flung his thick cloak around him and strode through the encampment. He spoke for a few moments with each of the watch and returned to the rough tent his esquires had put up for him. One of the young men stirred as he lay down close by, but gratefully went back to sleep when Edmund assured him that nothing was amiss.

Edmund could not sleep and turned on his back. He put his arms behind his head and gazed through the tent's half-open doorway to the starlit sky. The nagging thought of Margaret's farewell returned to torment him and only departed when he reminded himself that it was her desperate dependence that had worried him before and that it was laughable that he should now be concerned because that anxiety had been abated. With this salutary reminder came the remembrance of the last occasion when she had lain in his embrace and had returned ardent kiss for ardent kiss with no sign of diminishing passion. Comforted by this realisation the tension eased and he did not awake until his esquire shook him and handed him a pot of ale and a hunk of coarse bread. He arose fresh and eager to deal with the matter in hand.

On the night of June 6th, they were lying hidden in the bracken close to Suoh's castle. Edmund had sent forward scouts who returned with the information that the men under Gilbert's command were on the point of departure. Edmund told his captain to awaken the men and have them ready to leave at once. He heard in the thin darkness the curses and groans of the soldiers as they stretched cramped limbs and stirred themselves into activity. He stood while his esquires buckled on the leg armour and placed the helm on his head. He closed his eyes and muttered a pray to Our Lady for succour and a safe return to Pembroke. The scouts had told him of a slight incline a few miles distant from Suoh's stronghold which was lightly wooded. This is the captain agreed would afford excellent cover for the Pembroke men. After the last round of inspection had been made they set off.

They took up their positions on the hill as quietly as possible, breaking off extra branches to afford more cover. As it became light the two look-outs reported from the branches of a pine that they could see dust rising from the direction of the castle and that the company must be of a fair size. Talking stopped and the excitement grew as the sergeant went from group to group outlining the plan of attack. He impressed upon them that absolute quiet was essential for the essence of the manœuvre was surprise, and although Suoh would undoubtedly be on his guard for ambush the daring proximity of Richmond's men would be outside his calculations.

At length the sound of hoof beats could be heard by one of the men who lay at full length with his ear pressed to the ground and Edmund gave the order to take up their battle stations. There was muted quiet as the horsemen moved to the rear and the archers fletched their arrows and loaded their cross bows.

Edmund standing a little aloof from the others felt neither alarm or any particular desire to be engaged in combat. He found himself longing, in this his first engagement, for the battle wisdom of the stalwart Jasper. He sprang on to his horse's back as his esquire cupped his hands to give him a leg up.

The look-out dropped his woollen fighting scarf as a signal that Gilbert and his men were within striking distance. Edmund raised his arm and the captain gave the order to begin the attack. A first volley of arrows loosened with deadly precision found their target with no difficulty judging by the howls and screams of pain that came up to the onlookers. A further volley into the confusion was followed up by a charge from the mounted men who rode straight down into the havoc caused by the sudden attack. Edmund riding with them had difficulty in avoiding the fallen men but was so quickly engaged by swordsmen on both sides that he could only see the flash of light on their whirling blades. He stood in the stirrups and lashed out in all directions and was dimly aware that his esquires were close at hand dealing out punishment with lusty disregard of their safety. Beating back their attackers he took advantage of the lull to summon up the foot men who were still waiting in the trees.

Gilbert had meantime rallied his surprised men and had formed them into some kind of order on the ground. The horse men on the flank came forward at his command but were halted in their headlong dash by another flight of arrows that completely disrupted them. Gilbert seeing that his troops were in danger of being routed sought out Edmund, who was now shouting further orders to the bowmen from under his banner, held aloft by a young page who watched the proceedings with enthusiastic enjoyment.

Gilbert reasoned that if he could engage Richmond in single combat and wound or better still, kill him, the men from Pembroke would lose heart and the day could still be Suoh's.

Edmund hearing cries of 'A Suoh. A Suoh' turned just in time to see a large man, whom he recognised must be Suoh by his helm, raise a heavy club in readiness to crash it down on Edmund's head. He dipped out of reach and turning swiftly almost unseated Gilbert with a well aimed smash with the broad blade of his sword. Wheeling again he thrust upwards and as Gilbert faltered, swung his sword arm backwards and chopped at the man's arm. Gilbert dropped the heavy club with a yowl of pain and slumped into his huge, ornate battle saddle. His aides, seeing his predicament rushed into the attack but the Richmond esquires anticipated the blows and drove them off. Edmund saw in a quick look round that Suoh's troops were melting away behind boulders and trees, realising that the day was lost as they saw their leader overcome and lying across his horse. He called to his captain to call off the engagement and look to their own wounded.

The casualties were slight owing to the surprise of the attack and there were only a handful of seriously hurt who had caught the brunt of the first retaliation. These were quickly picked up from the ground and thrown as gently as possible over their companions' horses, while the loose beasts were rounded up and brought into the company. The youngest of Edmund's esquires had a wound behind the knee which was bleeding freely but which he protested was only minor, and bound with a tourniquet, which he suffered in mock indignation, would do well enough until they made camp for the day.

Edmund thought it was advisable to put as much terrain between himself and Suoh's land as possible and as soon as the wounds had been dressed and the sufferers given an opiate concocted from poppy seeds to dull the jolting of the rough tracks they set off. They made a brief halt around Prime for a meal of hard biscuits and pushed on until it was almost dusk when they made camp in the lee of a hill, open enough to be free from a counter attack. Here the cook unslung his great iron pot and prepared a stew from his supply of dried meat. The men ate with good appetite, enjoying food for the first time since they had left Pembroke knowing that the fighting was behind them and that with a bit of luck Suoh would not be in a fit state to rally his men for some time to come.

Edmund during the day had analysed his feelings about the fight and discovered somewhat to his shame that he had almost enjoyed the encounter with Suoh. This ran so contrary to his usual gentle goodwill to his fellow creatures that he found himself praying that Suoh would not die and that he would not have his death on his conscience. He doubted if, without the sudden thrill of combat he would have been able to deal with his opponent. He understood for the first time why some men could spend their lives at war. Now that Jasper had impressed him with the need for keeping the Lancastrian cause boiling since the return of the King's health and the weakening of York's grip he hoped that he would not be called on to put down any further risings. Jasper's last letter had also contained the information that the Queen, now outside York's domination, had gone to her manor at Tutbury where she was busily engaged in drawing about her all the loyal supporters she could muster. Jasper went on that even given a long term of Henry's sanity and a sulky armistice from York, it was doubtful if peace would prevail for the Queen's warlike nature came daily more to the surface and the last Protectorate had determined her resolve not to be subjected to York again. With this and the other disturbances he had reported, Jasper felt he could not be too optimistic about the future and begged Edmund to look to his wife's safety with special attention to underhand abductions.

With the thought of Margaret came the memory of the doubts which had assailed him from time to time, try how he would to quash them, since he had left her at Pembroke. He longed, now that the fight was done with, to hold her in his arms and be assured that nothing had changed between them.

Despite his own desire to be home which was shared by all the Pembroke men who had been called in, he could not in fairness to his wounded, hasten forward too quickly. All but one of the most seriously hurt seemed to be making recovery. When he was informed by the captain that the lad who had suffered a crushing blow from a spike edged club, was restless and unsettling the other men in his distress, Edmund went to look at him for himself. He found him lying on an improvised bed of hastily plucked bracken and was smitten to see that he was little more than a boy. To the astonishment of the captain he motioned him away and said he would remain at the youth's side. He sat beside him unsleeping all the night, while the boy babbled of his mother and the pig they kept at home. Edmund comforted him as best he could and gave him frequent sips of water from his own bottle. He saw in his helpless plight something of the clinging dependence of his young wife and was aware of a guilty responsibility for embroiling him in this engagement in which he was far too young to have any particular interest. He remembered him from the tilt yard when the men had been given their training in the use of arms and had remarked at the time that he seemed over young for military service. The sergeant had replied that he had probably come to take his father's place as one of Pembroke's men and was enjoying the experience.

In the dawn light the lad was quieter and the fever, which dampened the curls round his face, abated a little. Edmund gave orders for a litter to be slung between two of the horses for him and for them all to be under way as quicky as possible.

The day was one of the rare still days of early summer and above them the larks chattered in the sky. It seemed impossible that only yesterday they had been engaged in a fierce sharp fight and that all life was not gentle and peaceful like the clean sheep that cropped against the surrounding hills.

When the sergeant rode up to report that the lad had died Edmund's first reaction was one of incredulous disbelief followed swiftly by a sense of regret for the wasted young life. He told the sergeant to halt the troop and rode back to look at the still figure whose waxen face showed no sign of the pain he had suffered. Edmund was much moved, remembering his watch in the night and the mother that would look no more on her young son. Showing no emotion he gave orders for the boy to be wrapped in his own cloak and buried swiftly. The sergeant took two men and started them digging a trench while others he sent to bring large stones.

When the grey bundle was laid in the narrow strip of earth Edmund said the prayers of committal and helped to build the cairn which would prevent the wild wolves from tearing up the soil to get at the body. Edmund had taken the iron necklet with its thin cross from around the boy's neck and asked the sergeant if he knew where the family lived. The look he surprised on the man's face told him that the sergeant considered the Earl of Richmond was exceeding his responsibilities but the man unhesitatingly volunteered the information that as far as he knew he believed the lad had lived in Carmarthen and that his father was a worker in skins.

Edmund turned on his heel and mounting again, gave the order to proceed. He could not rid himself of the melancholy that had come upon him with the boy's death. The trust that was bestowed upon him as a leader was bound up in some intricate way with that given to him so freely by his wife and he worried again that he was asking too much from her. He resolved that on his return he would make every effort to consider her more and curb his lust for her flesh. The nagging anxiety grew more real and by the time the Castle of Pembroke was in sight he was exhausted with remorse.

Most of the household with the steward had turned out to greet the returning army and shower them with congratulations on the successful outcome of the engagement. A messenger had been sent on ahead to relieve the anxiety of the Lady Richmond and the other women in the castle and now all clamoured for details. When he had seen in the first glance that Margaret was not with the company it was all Edmund could do to answer the questioners civilly and coherently.

'Where is my lady?' he asked.

'She is waiting for you in the solar with the messengers who have lately come from Shene with papers from the Earl of Pembroke.'

Edmund extracted himself from the well-wishers who crowded round and hurried up to the solar. Margaret was seated at the window as he burst in, and despite the men in the room, ran to him with arms outstretched. He was so glad to realise her happiness at seeing him that relief flooded through him in a hot tide, and it was all he could do to prevent himself from shouting to those present to get out and leave them alone. He kissed her on the brow taking in, in a brief look the shadows beneath her eyes and a certain pinched look about her cheeks, but she was presenting Jasper's esquires to him and calling for wine and he thought perhaps it might be a trick of the light and that he must look deeper when they were alone.

Edmund went to the garde robe to be relieved of his leather jerkin and put on a fine linen shirt and soft doublet. When he returned he fell gratefully into the most comfortable chair while Margaret sat on a stool beside him. He longed to stroke the curve of her arm and feel her cool hands about his neck, but took the rolled parchment that the esquire proffered and broke the seal.

Jasper wrote that the situation was as fraught with danger as it had ever been, for although the Queen was making every effort to awaken interest in the Lancastrian cause, she was meeting with much apathy. The Great Council which had just been held had been attended by only a handful of Lancastrian Lords, all the others, pleading pressing business. To add to this navies had been sighted heading for Calais and Giennes and had roused the suspicion of laying siege to the places. The peace which had been bought by buying of the burghers with about £50,000 had put another feather in the cap of the young Earl of Warwick, who was fast becoming a power with which to reckon. Jasper urged his brother not to relax his efforts in consolidating the support of the Welsh. Edmund pulled a rueful face at this advice coming as it did so soon on the skirmish from which he had just returned.

The letter finished with felicitations to them both and a special message for Margaret hoping that all was well with her and that Henry and Margaret of Anjou would be able to spare him to pay them a fleeting visit during the summer months.

Edmund thanked the esquires for bringing the message and the other documents that he would give his attention to on the morrow and commended them to a few days rest in Pembroke before setting out on their return journey. They bowed themselves out and Edmund went to the window calling Margaret to come with him. She came to him and he held her at arms length, the light from the casement falling full on her face. He studied her with a searching look, his head on one side.

'As Jasper asked, is all well with thee, my love?' he said at last.

'It is very well,' she replied, her eyes shining. 'It is very well indeed, Edmund, for I am with child!'

17

He stared at her as if she had just told him
that she had seen the fairy folk that were
Betsey's nightmare, then he clasped her to
him, smothering her face with kisses and
stammering incoherent sentences.

'You are not ill?' he demanded as the
horrible thought struck him.

'No,' she laughed. 'A little sick in the
mornings and I have a certain distaste for
fatty dishes. Otherwise I have never felt
better. Is it not wonderful?'

While she had been at Pembroke without
him after he left for Gilbert Suoh's territory
she had found that she was not suffering as
she had on previous occasions and had spent
her days in a peaceful contentment. She had
confided to Betsey some time before that she
thought she had conceived but had made the
girl promise to say nothing. When Edmund
left she had had her first bout of nausea and
in the last week had been sure that her belief
was correct. She experienced a tremendous
sense of well-being that she carried within her
a token of Edmund's and her loving. That this
token would, in the future, be a tangible

entity she had hardly yet realised. Betsey had brought her pieces of silk to embroider and she had started with enthusiasm to sew the small garments but soon discovered that she would put the work down after a few stitches. She was much happier dreaming about what she had to tell to Edmund and watching the clouds drifting by.

'We must send the news back to Jasper when the couriers leave and to your mother, too! Perhaps you would like to have her with you now, or perhaps Margery?'

She shook her head smiling at his generosity, for she knew very well that he would not really want to share their happiness and would prefer to have her to himself.

'Nearer my time perhaps it would be pleasant to have Margery here. But everything is very well just now. It is a good time to carry a child because the heat of the summer will be over before I become too large.'

'How do you know all this?' he laughed.

'You must not forget that my mother is not yet past bearing children and I have first hand knowledge from her. I wonder what she will think of me making her a grandmother again?'

'She will doubtless take it in her stride and be sending you — and me — quantities of good advice. You must ask her to tell Simon

Hovey that I consider you have enough to do without making translations for him and that we hope he will make special intercession for you and the babe.'

As she smiled at his concern for her he was struck by a sudden thought.

'When is the baby likely to be born?'

'In mid January, as far as Betsey and I can make the reckoning. It will be an honour to bear the child so near the date of Our Lord's birth.'

'Oh, Margaret, you will take the very greatest care of yourself, won't you?'

'Of course, I shall,' she whispered and sat down in the window seat. He knelt in front of her almost afraid to touch her, but she pulled his head on to the fullness of her breast and ran her finger through his hair in the soothing gesture he had craved. Suddenly he was reminded of the dead youth and his problems of yesterday and he was gripped with fear for her, but he said nothing and caught her to him in a convulsive gesture. At least, he told himself, there was no real reason for any coolness he had suspected, and he was sure now that his concern had been self-inflicted and Margaret loved him as much as ever.

At least in Wales the summer passed quietly enough if rumour of conflict came from all over the rest of the kingdom. Gilbert Suoh, slow to recover from his wound in the arm, made no more attacks on Lancastrian troops and the nearest outbreak of violence was in the West Country where the Earl of Devon clashed with Lord Bonville. The Queen, with York following her every move, went into Cheshire rallying loyal supporters for the crown and Jasper wrote of his increasing fear that the matter could not be resolved without a show of arms again. He sent his congratulations to his sister-in-law and begged her to keep the happy news to herself for the heir to the mighty Beauforts would be an added target to Yorkist discontents. Henry professed himself delighted at the good news and begged them to have the same care for the new heir when it arrived. He counselled them that the Queen went in constant danger of the abduction of the young Prince Edward and he was constantly guarded night and day. Jasper told them that he would have to delay his hoped-for visit to them as the Royal Family could not spare him at this time.

Lady Welles sent messages of her great content at the news of the forthcoming baby and with pages of good advice, sent bolts of soft woollens and costly damasks for the child's use. She sent private word to Margaret on the need to send for the midwife in good time and simple precautions to ensure a plentiful supply of breast milk, for she did not subscribe to the fashionable practice of wet nurses.

Margaret, to whom all this seemed a long way off, lived through the summer in a haze of contentment. The worries of the Queen's party seemed part of another life and she was hardly interested when Edmund told her that a Great Council had been called to meet in Coventry in October and that the Bourchiers had finally been removed from power and the Treasuryship given to Shrewsbury and the Great Seal to William of Wayneflete.

Edmund, on the other hand, worried more than before for he had caught the truth from Jasper that forthcoming conflict was inevitable. He felt deeply sorry for Henry to whom he owed so much and redoubled his efforts to keep the Lancastrian support at full strength. He undertook the training of Welsh men and despatched them to secret hiding places on Jasper's estates. He sent urgent word to the stewards at Collyweston, Ware and Cheshunt for their full quota of armed men to be in constant readiness.

In his private world his love for his wife was enriched by her pregnancy. It was obvious that she was created to be the mother of many children, as her mother was, for her loveliness bloomed as her time went by. The filling out of her bosom and waist suited her and she suffered little discomfort and was good tempered and patient. When she felt the first faint flutterings of the child against her ribs she experinced the only anxious moments she had known and was soon put at rest by Betsey who told her that this was the quickening and much to be desired.

Her love for Edmund deepened as their love-making decreased, which a few short months ago would have seemed impossible. They would lie, close and naked in the great bed, whispering of their joy in each other glad of the lengthening nights which gave them added time together.

Betsey, who could not write, sent verbal messages to the Lady Welles that she was not to fret over her daughter who was better than she remembered during her short life. She did not tell Lady Welles, but she prayed that the Earl of Richmond would not be required to fight at his half-brother's side until after the birth of the baby, for she thought this would be the only cause for alarm for the young mother. She knew, more than any one else, that Margaret's life was inextricably bound up in her husband's and that she suffered when they were parted.

Edmund had sent to Jasper to purchase from the jewellers in Cheapside, a sapphire ring to give Margaret on the feast of St. Michaelmas, and going to the velvet lined box where he kept odd buckles and pins on the morning of the feast he saw with a pang of shame the iron necklace and small cross which he had promised to return to the youth's mother in Carmarthen. He took out the ring and promised himself that when he made his next rallying tour he would include this town in the itinerary.

He put the ring on Margaret's finger and was surprised to see tears in her eyes. His own throat tightened and he remembered again the poignancy of the lad's suffering. Was it to be that the memory of that sadness was always to be connected with his wife?

If anything should happen to this adored wife of his, through what, at that moment, seemed his selfish passion, he would die with her. His responsibility for the death of the young soldier would be as nothing compared with killing her who was his whole life and who had given herself to him without counting the cost. Sweat started at his forehead and he looked away.

'What ails thee?' she said as laughter replaced the tears. 'Thank you so much for this beautiful ring. You did not think that I was displeased with it, did you?' she queried, a note of anxiety creeping into her voice.

'No of course not,' he replied. 'I need some air. Take me for a walk on the battlements. It is time I made my inspections.'

Betsey brought her a velvet cloak and arm in arm they walked to the Westgate and Monkton Towers and through the inner ward past the Great Keep to the rose garden. The bushes were rich with the red gold leaves and the few remaining blooms were touched with autumnal brown. Margaret chose the deepest red survivor and breaking the soft stem with difficulty gave it to Edmund, threading it through the chain of Lancaster about his neck.

'My heart,' she said simply.

Her words did not dispel his depression which gathered force all the morning. In the afternoon he took a groom and went riding, choosing easy moorland tracks where he could give the horse his head. The exuberant dash through the air which bore unmistakeable signs of the chill of autumn revived his spirits and he rode back into the castle in a more cheerful frame of mind.

He found Margaret sitting at the solar fireplace with a minute piece of white sewing in her lap. She looked so wholesome and serene that the depression fell away from him and he gave a great shout for the pure joy of living and snatching her from the chair, whirled her round the room and collapsed in a laughing heap in front of the recently kindled fire. Safe in her arms with her hair against his cheek he was happy again.

In October Jasper sent word that there was a large movement of troops around the Ludlow area and he advised Edmund to look into the matter. He reported that at the gathering for the Great Council at Coventry the young Duke of Somerset, who was Margaret's cousin, had been involved in a fight with the town watch in which two or three men had been killed. The alarm bell had been sounded and if the Duke of Buckingham had not come to the rescue of the young Somerset he would have met with the same fate. This unfortunate incident had not enchanced the Lancastrian cause and with the King expected in the Midlands for the next month or so, it was necessary to keep a check on any military massing that might be under way.

Edmund knew that he must obey this summons with all speed and made preparation to depart in mid October. To his dismay, just as he was about to set out Margaret caught a chill. Although she would not hear of his staying with her he, nevertheless, postponed his departure for two days, until she was up and quite recovered.

Seeing that she was well again he could delay no longer and on a morning in late October he came to take his leave of her. She held him close, taking his hand and cradling it against her cheek in the old familiar gesture. She kissed the palm of his hand and clenched his fist.

'My dearest Edmund,' she whispered.

'I wish that I had not to leave you, but I cannot fail Henry and Jasper at this moment.'

'Of course not. I should be selfish indeed to want to keep you just at this moment. Anyway, a matron as I am with a child great inside her, must be brave.'

'I do not plan to be absent very long. We shall ride as quickly as possible to the point that Jasper considers is the meeting place for the Yorkist armies and having sent reports to him at Kenilworth where he expects to be with Henry, of the size of preparations I shall return to you to await his orders. I should not be away for more than a week at most. You will always be in my thoughts. God bless you, my love.'

He bent and kissed her tenderly and turned swiftly away. She watched him out of sight, biting at her lower lip to stop it quivering. When she could no longer see him she gave way to the tears that had been lying close to the surface and sobbed inconsolably.

Although she had professed bravery, it had cost her an immense amount for she felt very much the reverse. She put her melancholies down to the fever from which she had only just recovered and went to the solar fire, holding out her hands which were cold and damp.

Betsey who had been hovering in the background, bustled in with a cup of wine and kicked the fire into a blaze. She busied herself with the fire irons while Margaret gulped down the drink, hoping that the mild opiate which she had distilled in the wine would not take too long in acting. The apothecary had assured her that it was only a herbal concoction and that it would not harm her mistress but would assure her of a dreamless sleep.

A page brought in a bowl of bread and milk, which Margaret only pecked at, feeling of a sudden strangely sleepy. She made no protest as Betsey suggested that a doze might be a sensible idea and allowed her to help her undress and get into her bed. In a very short time she was asleep.

Betsey, delighted to see her strategy working so well, tiptoed out to send the pages for a truckle bed to put up within earshot of her mistress's door. With my Lord of Richmond away it was her clear duty to guard

Margaret night and day, and it was just such a chill and upset over parting that might bring on a premature birth.

Betsey's devotion to her young mistress had increased as her dependance on her grew. She had not told Margaret but she had received word from Richard Stukeley that, as he had not heard from her when she was likely to return to Bletsoe he had considered that she no longer wished to wed with him and that he was taking the step of marrying Maggie, one of the maids from the dairy. She had grieved silently over this piece of unwelcome news for several days after she received it, but then found that she no longer cared anyway. She was too busy taking care of the Countess and there was a stream of handsome men in the service of Pembroke who were only too willing to flirt with her and restore her pride. She pushed her own affairs out of her mind and set herself to the task of providing occupation for Margaret while her husband was absent.

She found Margaret willing to be diverted. She still did not take to sewing but was quite prepared to sing at her lute and teach Betsey some of the more simple card games. The steward's lady came several times, bringing some delicacy she had prepared and imparting the daily news of the castle.

Margaret was happiest however, when she was walking on the battlements. Here she would stand, with the wind whipping at her hood, gazing inland to where she thought Edmund might be or else looking down the haven towards the sea.

'Do you think,' she said one evening as they stood watching the sunset, 'that there really is another continent beyond Ireland and that it is possible to reach the Indies in that direction?'

'I am sure I don't know, my lady, but I am certain that if you stay out here now the sun has gone you will catch another chill.'

'There must be something that inspires men to risk their lives and their fortunes in the search,' Margaret said as they went down the narrow, winding stair to the solar. 'I wonder if my son will want to travel and find out for himself.'

It was first time that she had thought consciously of the child, leaping strongly within her, as a person and she spent the evening dreamily imagining a youth with Edmund's characteristic charm telling them of his hopes and ambitions. She found the thought a little heady and she made a note to tell Edmund of her conceit in their son's future. Now that the subject had presented itself to her she wondered what the future would hold in store for him and realised with a pang that, whether boy or girl, the child would be born within a vortex of dissention. Now that the Queen had an heir the child's position would be less precarious, but if it were a boy, he could be second in Lancastrian succession to the throne. With this extraordinary realisation came the wish that Edmund were here to discuss it with her and she spent a restless night, mulling over the thought in her mind.

When he had been gone for five days she started counting the hours to his return, looking every moment for the messenger that he was thoughtful enough to send on ahead of his more cumbersome troop, to announce his coming.

On the sixth day of his absence she felt strangely low spirited and could not hide her feelings from Betsey, who assured her that it was only in keeping with her condition and that it was quite natural to have fits of depression at this time. The girl, however, warned the steward's lady to send word to the midwife to present herself at the castle where she would be lodged in the steward's quarters for the moment.

Margaret kept the fire well stoked during this day so that when Edmund returned there would be a cheerful greeting for him. She tried to read but found her eyes were tired and she could not concentrate, so she sat gazing into the fire, her Book of Hours unopened on her knee with her ears strained for the faintest sound of the winding of a horn. Betsey stayed close beside her and when they both realised that there was little chance of Edmund's return that day, she urged Margaret to go to bed.

Margaret sank gratefully into the warmed sheets and fell asleep almost at once. In less than an hour she was wide awake, shivering with the cold. She heard the watch making their rounds of the castle and sat up, panic gripping her by the throat. Her heart beat quicker and quicker, drumming the blood into her ears until she stumbled from the bed, dragging her robe around her. She thought back to a similar occasion at Bletsoe and was reassured when she recalled that the sensation had passed quickly and the fear had spent itself. She fought the panic until to her relief, she grew calmer, and the urge of throbbing pulses subsided. She wrapped the bed gown tightly round herself and pulled the covers over her head. Exhausted, she slept, but with a nagging disquiet that there had been some unpleasant happening at Bletsoe which had caused the previous state of alarm. Think as she would she could not bring to mind what it was.

Betsey, looking in early the next morning, was glad to see that she was still sleeping and went out closing the door gently behind her. As she did the youngest of the pages, knuckling sleep from his eyes, came up to her to tell her that one of my lord's esquires was in the solar and wished to speak with Lady Richmond at once.

'What does he want?' Betsey asked sharply as fear quickened her tongue. A hundred distracted thoughts chased round in her brain as she followed the page. 'I'll come to him myself, for my lady is sleeping.'

She stopped on the threshold of the solar, her hand to her mouth as she saw the white-faced young man, who stood disconsolately turning his feathered hat in his hand.

'What is wrong?' she said quickly without further courtesies.

'The Lord Edmund has been taken ill in Carmarthen and — '

'God's mercy,' Betsey wailed, 'how shall we keep this from her?'

'Keep what from me?' Margaret asked, standing in the doorway. Startled at her unexpected appearance neither of them replied. 'Keep what from me?' she repeated.

Betsey looked hopelessly at Edmund's

esquire, who meeting her eye, fell on his knees before Margaret. Betsey, seeing that there was no other way out, moved unobtrusively to Margaret's side.

'You bring news of my lord? There is something amiss with him? Don't keep me in suspense — tell me!' her voice rose.

'I bring word that my lord has been taken ill at Carmarthen, my lady, and is asking for you.'

The colour drained from Margaret's face and she swayed a little. The young man and Betsey made quick movements to help her but she shook her head and supported herself by clinging on to the back of a chair.

'Tell my groom to have a horse saddled in the hour, and to you, sir, find the captain of the guard and ask him to muster a band to leave with me for Carmarthen.'

'But, my lady,' Betsey protested, 'you cannot ride all those miles so near your time. My lord is probably suffering from a chill such as you have had and will be better by the time you reach him.'

'Pray to God that he will,' Margaret said.

'Think of the child,' Betsey wailed, unheeding.

'He is asking for me and I must go to him. Our Lady will take care of the child and of me. Make haste, sir!' she pleaded with the esquire who stood, hesitating, in the doorway. 'Betsey come and help me dress and put our things into a bag.'

'My lord will not forgive me if I let any harm befall you,' Betsey said close to tears.

'There is no greater harm can befall me than that my lord should want me and I should not be there,' Margaret replied in a harsh tone that Betsey had never heard before. 'Page go to the kitchen and bring us something to eat and ask them to prepare food for our journey.'

Betsey saw that it was hopeless to argue and hurried into the garde robe to fetch out Margaret's warmest dress and most voluminous cloak. Margaret stood while she fastened her gown, unaware of what was going on. She could think of nothing but that Edmund was ill and needed her.

She forced herself to eat a few mouthfuls of the food the frightened page brought for her and listened politely while the steward's wife added her pleas for her to remain at Pembroke. She brought out the heavily loaded argument of it not being safe for Margaret to set forth, but realised that she might just as well hold her peace for the Lady Richmond was quite adamant that she was going to Carmarthen and there the matter ended. From then on the steward's wife gave her all the assistance she could in making a quick departure and brought her a pomander she had made and a flask of wine to carry on the saddle. Margaret thanked her with words that seemed to come from some distant place and rose at once as the esquire came in to tell her that all was ready and that the captain awaited her below.

'Where is my lord lodged?' she asked as they went down to the yard.

'In the inn where he was staying for the night. The keeper and his wife had been most kind.'

'What was he doing in Carmarthen?'

'He went to visit the mother of the boy who was killed in the attack on Gilbert Suoh's castle, my lady.'

She remembered hearing about the boy's death and even in her deep anxiety had time to think of Edmund's typical kindness in making this human gesture.

The esquire took his leave of her after she had refused his offer to accompany her.

'You have ridden all night, sir,' she said gravely. 'You must have your rest and then if you will, come up with us the day after tomorrow.'

She was hoisted into the saddle with difficulty and was glad that they had chosen a broad-backed, short-legged pony for her. The effort of mounting had made her head swim but she held on to the pommel and nodded that she was ready to start. She was glad of the tempering experience she had suffered in the Brecon hills last year for it gave her courage now. She sat erect, bracing her body and was pleased to find she could manage quite well.

It was some time before she looked round at her escort and was surprised at the strength of it. She saw the undeniable wisdom of this for a pregnant Lancastrian heiress was a highly desirable target for a man of York and sheer weight of arms could well be the deciding factor in case of an argument.

She passed the day torn with the thought of Edmund suffering and of not being at hand to comfort him while she fretted at the slow speed which they made towards him. She did her best to curb her impatience when they halted to water the horses and to eat some food. She walked back and forth with Betsey beside her to keep the blood flowing in her legs, for the pressure of the babe threatened to turn them to logs of wood. The captain, in sympathy for her anxiety, hastened his men through their meal and called for them to mount.

Although the wind was cold there was no rain and the roads were dry and easy to pass.

Betsey rode behind her mistress, but Margaret did not turn her head or speak with her. She sat with a set face, her eyes straining into the distance before them. At last, as the early dusk fell about them, she was rewarded by the sight of smoke rising from many fires and the subdued glimmer of lanterns from the town.

Leaving the main party behind, the captain and Margaret, with the sergeant and two soldiers dismounted and made their way through the narrow streets, where the open drains smelled vilely, to the inn where Edmund was lodging. Margaret had almost fainted when she put her feet to the ground and had clutched at the saddle until the nausea went over. Holding her skirts in her hand she set off at a good pace.

Coming into the yard of the inn she raced forward to the door and knocked, seeing without taking it in, the red cross scrawled upon it.

There was no reply and she knocked again more loudly, bruising her knuckles. Still nothing happened and the sergeant stepped forward pounding the door with the handle of his axe. Shuffling footsteps could be heard from the other side, and the door was opened a small crack.

'It is my Lady of Richmond come to visit

her husband,' the captain shouted. 'Let us in so that we may come to him.'

'Can you not see the cross upon the door?' a voice quavered from deep within the house. 'My Lord of Richmond has the plague and the monks have taken him away.'

The plague! Margaret's heart stopped beating at the dreaded word and she felt the earth tilt beneath her. The others arrested by the full significance of what they had just heard, stood perfectly still.

Fear drove Margaret on.

'Where is the Lord Richmond?' she shouted, while noiseless screams forced themselves in her throat.

'The Grey Friars have taken him.'

The door banged shut. No one spoke but the captain moved to Margaret and she gratefully leaned on his arm.

'Find quarters for the men outside the town, sir,' she said dully. 'Take Betsey with you, while I go to the Greyfriars House.'

'The sergeant will see to the men and Mistress Betsey, but I shall come with you.'

Margaret said nothing, unable to see for a mist that shuttered her eyes and unable to feel for the horror that had overtaken her.

The captain stopped at another alehouse further down the road where Margaret was amazed to see warm lights and hear the sound of laughter. How could this be, she thought, when I have just heard the world has come to an end?

They followed the directions given to them at the inn, but they were unnecessary as they approached the hospice for the grey November night was lit with the yellow smoke from several sulphur fires which burned around the precincts.

The old monk who admitted them looked with compassion at the stricken girl who asked to be taken to her husband. He rang the bell to summon one of the lay brothers and watched her as the darkness swallowed her while she was led away to one of the small cells where the friars nursed the plague-stricken. He fell on his knees and motioned the captain to do the same. They could only pray.

18

Margaret followed the monk who walked in front of her with his arms folded and his head bent. There was much that she wanted to ask him but she could not form the words. The walk to the cell felt as if it took her hours and she doubted if she would have been able to find her way out again unaided, as they made many turns and came out several times into the open air.

At last she saw, silhouetted against the yellow smoke, a low stone building where the monk motioned her to follow him. She caught her breath as the air redolent with fever hit her, but she did not falter. The monk put his torch in the sconce in the wall and in the dim light she could make out a straw bed covered with blankets. On this she could see Edmund.

She ran to him and fell on her knees beside the crude bed. As he heard her he moved his head with great difficulty and she saw the ghost of a smile. Tears poured down her cheeks as she saw the ravages that the fever had scored on his face. His eyes were brilliant and sunken in his head and purple blotches burned beneath the sockets. A bowl of water stood on the floor and she dipped her kerchief in it and wiped his forehead. He moaned slightly and she saw the hand which was plucking at the blankets try to reach hers. She took it in hers, cradling it against her bosom, murmuring his name.

The monk, who had been praying by the door, came to her and begged her to come away with him.

'No, Father,' she shook off his hands that would have helped her up.

The friar saw her determination and went out to find some food for her. He had nursed the young Earl throughout the night and this day and he knew that death would come within a few hours. He knew too, that the young Countess, who he realised was also very near her time, was putting herself and her baby in danger of contracting the plague, but he understood from the haunted look on her distraught face that nothing was going to move her from her husband's side while he still breathed and there was the slightest chance that he might recover.

When he returned with a wooden bowl filled with steaming broth she was sitting in the same position in which he had left her. She looked up at him with unseeing eyes as he handed her the soup, but she took it from him, thanking him quietly and began, in a mechanical fashion to sip it. The friar withdrew to the corner of the sparse chamber and leaning his back against the wall, closed his eyes. He would not leave them but he could not bear to see the agony of suffering in the girl's eyes.

Margaret did not ask him if there was anything further which could be done for Edmund for she knew the answer. She understood that the friars had spent hours trying to abate the fever and that they would have brought leeches and applied poultices and plasters. That they knew and that she now realised that all this was hopeless was a foregone conclusion, for it was plain to see that the plague had a complete hold of him. She tried not to think of the details she had heard about plague sickness and applied herself to making him as comfortable as possible. Her young mind could not encompass the knowledge that she was about to lose the mainspring of her life. In an age when death was a common companion she could not envisage it hand in hand with the adored young man for whom she lived.

She held his hand tightly in hers, although from time to time he moved restlessly and his whole body writhed. As the night wore on she found herself slipping out of reality and sitting afar off regarding them both from a dispassionate distance. She heard a long way away the bell calling the friars to matins and another summoning them to lauds. She was dimly aware when the friar was replaced by another and saw the Abbot who came briefly with a covered vessel and was as quickly gone.

She was brought back into complete wakefulness as Edmund was shaken with violent rigours while his face contorted in unearthly grimaces. Her unchecked cry of terror brought the watching monk hurrying to her side and he did not stop her when she lifted Edmund's head and cradled it against her shoulder.

As she did so she caught the faintest whisper of her name coupled with the one word. Love. Holding him tightly to her she felt his body slacken. She held him away for a long moment then, realising that it was ended she gathered him to her again with a pitiful moaning wail and slipped into a merciful unconsciousness.

The monk disengaged her entwining arms and laid Edmund gently on to the straw mattress, where he lay at peace, with the suffering of the past two days wiped away. The monk folded his hands on his breast and picking Margaret up, went to find the lay brothers who would attend to the laying out and the quick burial of the Earl.

In an isolated cell, an old woman, hastily summoned from the town, removed Margaret's clothes and burnt them in one of the fires before washing her face and dressing her in a spare cassock from the friar's wardrobes. Margaret had recovered sufficiently to help the woman but she did not speak. Her head felt empty of all thought and an icy hand held her heart squeezed in a frozen grip.

The captain coming from the gatehouse, at the Abbot's bidding, to escort his mistress to her home, was appalled by the stricken look on her face. She moved as in a dream, going with him as he led her away without so much as a backward glance or a word to the friars. They shook their heads as she disappeared through the gatehouse, grieving for the youth that had been wrenched away from her with this most tragic blow. They went sadly to the chantry and began the Masses for the departed.

Margaret remembered nothing about the journey back to Pembroke in a hastily improvised litter. Betsey had wept uncontrollably as the captain brought her mistress back to her; she had not needed to ask about the Earl for Margaret's look had told her everything. Betsey had found blankets and cushions and made the litter as comfortable as possible. She wished that she had some of the apothecary's opiate to give Margaret, for the girl lay quite still, without speaking, gazing in an unblinking stare to the sky. Betsey had seen the same bewildered look on the face of a dog who had had its leg broken in the jaws of a rabbit trap and she was afraid for the moment when feeling came back.

At the castle the hushed corridors echoed the shuffling footsteps of the returning party as they made their silent way through the horrified inmates to the Countess' own apartments. In the solar a great fire was burning and a table had been set with wine and a cold chicken. Margaret shook her head as Betsey offered them to her and she walked to her chamber door, closing the door behind her.

The steward's wife, who had come up with them, stopped Betsey as she went to follow her mistress.

'Leave her,' she said quietly. 'She will sleep and that will be the kindest thing of all. You sit here with me and drink this wine.'

Betsey sank into the chair before the fire and gratefully took the cup the lady held out to her. She was exhausted with the two long rides and the strain of the day and was glad to have someone to share her responsibilities in the frightful prospect that confronted them all.

'I cannot believe it,' she said at last. 'I don't know what we shall do with her. If only her mother were here and we could ask her. It might be a good idea to send for Miss Margery if she could make the journey at this time of the year. Oh, what shall we do for her?' she wailed as the full significance of the disaster came to her.

'We must send word at once to Lord Jasper,' the steward's wife said. 'He will tell us what to do and will come himself as likely as not. It will be a somewhat different Christmas from last year,' she said sadly as she remembered Jasper's last visit and the castle ringing with laughter. 'Do you go to bed Betsey now and I shall sit and watch for you. There are plenty of women to help me, who are only too willing to be of use at a time like this. We must pray that the shock does not bring on the baby, for then we should certainly have three deaths and not one on our hands. I think if she can sleep now it will be the biggest healing power we can hope for.'

Betsey dragged the truckle bed to the door of Margaret's room and fell into it fully dressed and was immediately asleep. The steward's wife crept into the bed chamber and found Margaret lying, uncovered as she had thrown herself down, on the bed. She quietly fetched blankets and put them over the girl and leaving the door ajar, took up her place beside the solar fire and began her vigil.

Margaret slept without waking through the rest of the night and all through the next day and the following night. When she awoke at last she opened her eyes and looked up into the circle of anxious faces peering down at her. She took a mug of heated milk which Betsey had ready for her and said quietly.

'Please ask Sir Priest to come to me and go with me to the chapel.'

One of the women hurried out to send a page to fetch the chaplain while she went to spread the news that the Countess was awake.

When she returned from the chapel she found Edmund's esquires waiting for her in the solar. They fell on their knees as she entered and she came up to them and touched them slightly on their shoulders.

'What would you have us do, my lady? We have sent messengers to Lord Pembroke.'

'That is well,' she said in a flat voice.

'If you wish it we would prefer to remain with you, at least as long as you have need of us,' the elder of the two went on, finding it difficult to express his feelings or his sympathy in the face of her stony detachment.

'Please remain,' she said.

'The Grey Friars have sent a man with a letter for you.'

'Where is it?'

'Here, my lady.'

'Read it to me then,' and she closed her eyes and leant her head wearily against the high back of the chair.

The young man hesitated to tell her the contents of the parchment as he read them and sensing his reluctance she opened her eyes.

'Go on,' she said quietly, 'there is no worse news in the world than that which I already know.'

'It says, my lady, that the Lord Edmund — ' he broke off and winced as he said the name, 'was buried yesterday in the coffin which had been kept for the Abbot and that hourly Masses are being said for his soul. The Grey Friars wish the writer to convey their deepest sympathy to you and tell you that they are praying constantly for you and your unborn child.'

'That is kind of them,' she said without a flicker of expression on her set features. 'Be good enough to send the messenger back with a letter containing my sincere gratitude for all they did for us and ask the man to hand over a bag of gold, which you will give him, to the Abbot as the first token of our appreciation, in the hope that the friars will use it for future succour of the sick.' She closed her eyes again and rested her head on the chair back. The young men saw that the interview was closed and bowed themselves out.

In the days that followed the kindly women who hovered round her found it was impossible to invoke any further response from her. Even Betsey could not coax her to talk or to eat more than a few mouthfuls a day. They tried reasoning with her but they soon gave it up as hopeless, afraid to hurt her more with their importunings.

No preparations were made to celebrate Christmas. The steward, taking precautions against the possibility of the Yorkists staging an attack when the news of the death of the Earl of Richmond became widely known, doubled the strength of the army at Pembroke and hoped fervently that the Lord Jasper would be able to spare time to give him a lead on his future conduct of the stronghold's affairs.

In early January news came from Bletsoe and Kenilworth that Margery and Jasper were setting out together to visit the stricken castle. Margaret read her mother's letter, taking it to the window to catch the dim light of the winter's day, but she refused to break the seal on Jasper's and put it unopened into the small wooden chest that had been Edmund's gift to her.

As the month wore on she was taken with a restlessness of body and spirit and insisted on walking twice a day on the battlements. The cold, fresh air restored some of the colour to her waxen face and a little of the lethargy left her. Nothing it seemed would restore her interest in life, for she lived from one day to the next as if she were performing a rite that had been inflicted upon her by some demon.

The watching women had thankfully seen her approach the full term of her pregnancy, glad in the knowledge that as each week progressed both she and the baby stood a better chance of survival.

The sad mantle in which the company was wrapped lifted in the last week of January when Jasper and Margery arrived at the castle. The steward, his wife, the esquires, Betsey and all the entourage met them with gratitude and poured out the pent up anxiety of the past two months. So that when they met Margaret in the solar they were prepared for the wraithlike girl that rose politely to meet them.

Margery, fighting shocked grief, longed to

take the dignified still figure in her arms and engulf her in sympathy, but checked herself in time, and kissed her half-sister's cold cheek, murmuring gentle condolences. Jasper felt his heart contract as he unwillingly looked at Margaret. It was almost more than he could endure that the lovely girl he had last seen in the full flower of beauty should be reduced to this pathetic waif. Her eyes beneath the simple coif were startlingly large and bright, and her hands, folded in front of her showed white and thin. She carried the child without effort, the clothes she wore helping to conceal the swollen stomach. She did not proffer her face for his kiss and he picked up her hand and raised it to his lips. As he straightened himself he found her gazing at him, all colour drained from her. For what seemed an eternity she did not move her eyes from him until quite suddenly she closed them and sat in the chair behind her.

'Jasper, oh Jasper. You are very welcome here!' and the tears which had refused to give her relief since she had last held Edmund in her arms trickled in great drops down her cheeks and she wept unrestrainedly. Jasper, unable to see for the tears in his own eyes, knowing better than to touch her in this moment of renewed feeling stepped back and it was Margery that comforted her, rocking her backwards and forwards and crooning comfort as a mother with a sick child.

As the pent up suffering of the last weeks gushed out in a flood of weeping, Margaret felt a sudden stab of pain in the small of her back. Unable to help herself she jerked upright. Margery whispered in her ear, 'Are you in pain?'

'Yes,' Margaret answered.

'Do not be afraid. We shall go to your room in a moment and Betsey will know what to do for you.'

Margaret released herself and sat up. She took out a kerchief and dried her eyes.

'You must be tired after your journey,' she said to Jasper. 'When you are refreshed and have eaten, come back to talk with me again.'

Betsey, meeting him in the doorway curtsied and looked past him to where Margaret sat, her hand to her side, by the fireplace. She took in the swollen eyes and the relaxed figure in the same instant that Margery came up to her, and in a quiet voice asked her to bring the midwife to see Margaret.

The woman came and gave her opinion that the babe would not be born that night and strongly advised the Lady Richmond to go to bed and sleep as much as she could to gather her strength for the next day's ordeal.

'Please tell Jasper I am sorry not to see him again tonight but that I look forward to the morrow,' Margaret said as she went into her chamber with her sister. Much to the surprise of all the other women, Margery came out a short while afterwards to say that Margaret slept and she thought it would be a good idea for all of them to get as much rest as possible. Later she and Betsey took it in turns to sit up listening for any possible noise from Margaret's room.

Betsey looking out at cockcrow saw that snow had fallen silently in the night and that the castle was blanketed in white. As she stood, enjoying the peaceful quiet, she heard Margaret cry out and rushed into her. Margaret was sitting on the side of the bed doubled over as she tried to ease the grinding pain which threatened to extinguish her.

Margery came running as Betsey called her and sent a page to rouse the midwife from the small chamber across the passage. The woman came quickly, and the other women followed close behind her with towels and ewers of hot water. Margery went into Margaret's room with Betsey and the midwife and shut the door firmly on the bevy of others who wished to crowd into the place.

The midwife made a quick examination and said over her shoulder to Margery that it would not be long.

'How long have you been in pain?' she asked Margaret.

'A little for some hours I think, but it was only a short time ago that the pains became strong.'

She gripped hold of Margery's hand as a fresh dagger of pain caused her to arch her back and writhe in a torment. Betsey fell on her knees and rolled Margaret on to her side and gently rubbed the lower part of her back. Margaret relaxed for a moment as the pain subsided and was then caught up in another onslaught more violent than the last.

Over her contorted stomach the midwife and Betsey exchanged glances.

'There, there, dearie,' the woman comforted her. 'It'll soon be over now.'

Margaret pushed her thumb into her mouth and closed her teeth hard to stifle the screams that were bubbling up in her throat.

'You cry, my lady,' Betsey said. 'It doesn't do any good to bottle it all up.'

Suddenly all in one moment of what seemed to Margaret a tearing apart of her whole being and a tremendous rush of ease the child was born.

Dimly through a haze of weariness she

heard the thin plaintive cry of the newborn.

'It's a son, my lady!' she heard Betsey cry. 'A fine lusty son!'

For the first time since Edmund had died in her arms a faint smile lit up her wan face.

'That is good,' she said and fell into a grateful doze.

Some hours later Margery brought Jasper to see his newborn nephew. He stood at the end of Margaret's bed, not looking at the wrinkled baby who was lying, wrapped in his swaddling clothes, at his mother's side, but at the girl his brother had so loved.

As he watched she opened her eyes and she smiled at him, slowly as if she were learning something half-forgotten.

'Edmund's and my son,' she said in a voice only slightly louder than a whisper. 'Will you take care of us, now?'

'With my life, if need be,' Jasper replied and came and knelt at the bedhead. 'Will you call him for my brother?' he asked.

'No,' she replied without hesitation. 'There was only one Edmund and he lives always in my heart. I shall call my son Henry for he owes his being to the King; without him I should not have been Edmund's wife.'

She closed her eyes, tired with the effort of talking and drifted into sleep again.

Jasper watched as she turned her head

towards her baby in the time-old protective gesture of mothers and looked down at them with great compassion. The young widow and the fatherless boy that one far distant day he would help to become the King of England.

THE END

We do hope that you have enjoyed reading this large print book.

Did you know that all of our titles are available for purchase?

We publish a wide range of high quality large print books including:
Romances, Mysteries, Classics
General Fiction
Non Fiction and Westerns

Special interest titles available in large print are:
The Little Oxford Dictionary
Music Book
Song Book
Hymn Book
Service Book

Also available from us courtesy of Oxford University Press:
Young Readers' Dictionary
(large print edition)
Young Readers' Thesaurus
(large print edition)

For further information or a free brochure, please contact us at:
Ulverscroft Large Print Books Ltd.,
The Green, Bradgate Road, Anstey,
Leicester, LE7 7FU, England.
Tel: (00 44) 0116 236 4325
Fax: (00 44) 0116 234 0205

PLAIN DEALER

William Ardin

Antique dealing has its own equivalent to 'insider trading', as Charles Ramsay finds out to his cost. Offered the purchase of a lifetime, he sees all his ambitions realised in an antique jade cup, known as the 'Loot'. But as soon as the deal is irrevocably struck he finds himself stuck with it like an albatross around his neck — unable to export it without a licence, unable to sell it at home, and in a paralysing no man's land where nobody has sufficient capital to take it off his hands . . .